The C

Ben Yallop

Part One of *The Complex Throne*

Dear Lance,

"One can never have enough socks, said Dumbledore. "Another Christmas has come and gone and I didn't get a single pair. People will insist on giving me books."

Happy reading!

Ben Yallop

Copyright © 2014 by Ben Yallop

ISBN-10:1501027190

ISBN-13: 978-1501027192

Cover design by Kate Hennessy
www.katehennessyphotography.com

For Elodie

"We shall not cease from exploration, and the end of all our exploring will be to arrive where we started and know the place for the first time"

T. S. Eliot

PREFACE

The Circle Line lies at the heart of the London Underground, the longest and oldest underground railway in the world. The first London Underground trains, then wooden open-roofed carriages pulled by steam engines, began to operate once the first line had opened in 1863. Although it was not until 1949 that the Circle Line began to appear on the famous 'Tube map' as its own separate route, the track existed long before that and the line, in its current form, is notable as sharing almost its entire 17 mile length with other lines. Between 1900 and 1918 the track was electrified and has been updated and improved since but, in the 1990s, those who ran the Underground network were forced to review service on the Circle Line.

Somewhere between Edgware Road and Baker Street trains were frequently breaking down and losing power, sometimes losing lighting and leaving passengers in darkness. Following increasing numbers of complaints it was realised that there was a serious fault on the line but, on investigation, engineers were unable to identify the problem. Trains continued to fail and the cause could not be found. The London Underground management took the unusual step of consulting passengers on the breakdowns in the hope of getting some clues, such as sightings of smoke or sparks, but the response was even more unusual. Many passengers were only too willing to talk about the strange things they had seen, but these had little to do with the train.

It was said, by regular users of the railway, that people were being strangely affected by the area through which the train was passing. Passengers had been observed feinting, having panic attacks and becoming unwell on that section of the line. Such episodes had become increasingly common since the electrical problems had started. One passenger revealed that, during a particularly lengthy breakdown, with the carriage in darkness, he and other commuters had seen groups of people standing silently outside their carriage, next to the tracks. Other letters seemed to describe the same thing.

Shocked by the results of their consultation the London Underground management looked back though its comprehensive records, going all the way back to 1863. As large parts of the network passed through historically significant areas many finds had been carefully catalogued. It became apparent that large numbers of teeth and fragments of bone had been found on the section of track in question. Old official reports referred to the area as the 'Plague Pit' and the British Museum was able to confirm that the site was the suspected location of a very large medieval plague pit, containing the remains of as many as 20,000 people.

The discovery of such pits had been a problem throughout the history of the Underground. No-one knew how many pits had been dug or where they were located and, as the line expanded, many pits were discovered without any warning. In the 1960s a tunnel boring machine punched into a pit at Green Park spilling bones and skulls. Between Knightsbridge and South Kensington the track curves dramatically, apparently to move around 'a pit so dense with human remains that it could not be tunnelled through'. Aldgate Station, on the Circle Line, is built on top of a large pit.

Eventually, after a blessing, the electrical faults on the Circle Line disappeared and the strange incidents and sightings of otherworldly visitors on the Underground network ceased.

Until now...

.

PROLOGUE

On a dark and otherwise deserted country road a solitary figure appeared from a patch of swirling fog and, after taking a quick look around, hurried to a hiding place behind the spiky gorse that grew at the side of the tarmac by the dry stone wall. He sat facing away from the road, his back against a tree, as he stared into the shadowy fields beyond. The low moon fell between several trees leaving stripes of black, darker than the rest of the night. In between the shadows the weak light caught the thin mists that clung to the long damp grass making it seem as though pale spirits rose from the earth, marching away in long insubstantial lines. But no mist touched the man as he sat waiting. It flowed around him, seemingly reluctant to catch him in its ghostly caress. The figure smiled to himself beneath the shadow of his dark hooded cloak and a short laugh caught in his throat as he thought of what lay ahead.

As he caught sight of the car that toiled slowly up a slight hill in the distance his breathing quickened with excitement, the fog of his breath seeming to add to the grey opaque host around him. The twin rectangular headlights drew nearer throwing beams of yellow light onto the low stone walls that separated the winding road from the black fields. The man eased himself into a better position, pushing his cloak away from his pale meaty arms. *He should have thought of doing this ages ago.* Since the boy was proving to be such a nuisance why not come directly to the source? It had taken a lot of work to find the path that led him here, and the distraction at the tavern had taken some organisation, but it would soon be worth it. He had got here at exactly the right time. His captive had been most useful in providing such information. He readied himself for what was about to happen.

Then, from within the mists, near to where he had arrived, he heard a low voice and realised that others had arrived. He instinctively drew back into the shadowy cover of the bushes, not fearful, but curious as to who else had sought out this solitary country lane so soon after him. Peering out, he could see at least two figures standing in the middle of the road, indistinct in the dark, damp fog. For a moment he considered simply killing them on the spot, whoever they were, but then he realised that the car was very close now and moving more quickly. He saw that he had no choice but to act. It was almost upon his hiding place and might hit those standing in the road anyway. He threw his hands towards the car and there was a brief, almost imperceptible, flash. The car immediately lurched sideways and quickly began to skid, its wheels clipping a large rock at the side of the road. The figure jerked his pale hands upwards as if pulling on a fine wire. The car flipped, spinning a barrel roll in the air to smash into and through the stone wall opposite him, the sudden sounds of grinding metal and breaking glass filling the air as white and yellow sparks flew along the road. The car rolled several times hitting loose rocks with sickening force before slamming into the side of a large tree. One of the sparks, struck from the slide of metal across stone, seemed to freeze in the air and then glow brighter as it dropped towards a puddle of petrol, leaking from the stricken car. The tiny light fell and for a moment nothing happened but then, as the man pulled back his hands into the sleeves of his cloak, a flicker of flame twisted itself towards the petrol tank.

More sounds reached the man then, crouched painfully amongst the sharp twigs of the bush, but for a moment he ignored the distraction, intent on the small fire. The others who had appeared were moving quickly, and although he knew he had nothing to fear from anyone else he did not want to be discovered. It would be easier in the future if this was thought to be an accident. A movement caught his eye and he looked back in the direction from which the car had come. Another set of headlights was approaching in the distance. As he watched he saw a blue light wink on above the headlights and begin to flash. He turned and watched the flames a brief moment longer, the bright light reflecting in his dark eyes. The car was mangled and twisted. It had been a horrifically violent crash. No-one would have survived, and the flames reaching for the leaking fuel would make it certain. The man smiled. It was done then. He turned away from the road and hurried out of the bush into the darkness of the fields, his smile growing as he heard the explosion behind him. The light of the sudden fire threw his shadow out ahead of him as he listened to the screams of despair and fear that pierced the night. The field ahead of him was dark but the future was going to be bright.

CHAPTER ONE

Seventeen years later

Police Constable Reg Green coiled a grubby white telephone cord around his index finger and tried his best to stifle a yawn. The effort made his eyes water and he used a thumb and forefinger to wipe away the tears. He realised that he had not been listening but, as he tuned back in, the voice on the other end of the phone did not seem to have noticed and continued to grumble.

Eventually, he was able to end the call with reassurances that the matter would be dealt with and he put the receiver back onto its cradle. He gave in to the yawn as he looked out of the window. It had been dark for some hours and it was near the end of his shift. Had the call come just a little later he could have left it for someone else. The message had come from the night warden at Stonehenge ten miles away. Apparently, a small group of people had broken into the famous site and were up to no good inside the ancient stone circle. They had lit a fire and were seemingly settling in for the night.

Security staff were on their way but the warden wanted a police presence in case there was any trouble in dealing with them. Mrs Reg would have to put dinner back in the oven.

'Hippies' muttered Reg to the empty room as he gave another yawn.

He pulled on his thick coat and thought again. It was too mild for the extra layer. The news had said that it could be the warmest October on record and the weather had meant record numbers of tourists were still visiting the county to see the mysterious stones. Leaving the quiet, dimly lit police station he crossed the car park, started his car and headed out of Salisbury towards the light of the moon.

He navigated the country road with the certainty of one utterly familiar with the unique twists and turns. As he took the car up a hill his mind wandered, as it always did on this particular road, to the events that had happened the night he had found the baby. That had been a strange night and, now he thought of it, must have been around this same time of year. He shivered at the thought of it. He had been following the road when he had seen flames in the distance, at the top of this hill. He had arrived to find a single car almost completely destroyed by a horrific accident. The ensuing fire had been so intense that it had melted the tarmac. No-one could have survived it and indeed the bodies of a young couple had been found in the front seats. But as he had got out of his car a small cry had caught his attention and there, lying by the side of the road, wrapped in a blanket, had been the boy. How he had survived Reg could not fathom but it was certainly nothing short of a miracle. No-one had been able to solve the mystery of how that baby had come to be alive when the other occupants of the car had been killed. Indeed, no-one had ever been able to ascertain the cause of the crash either. Some of the more superstitious observers had claimed that this road was haunted and said that a ghostly apparition had somehow intervened either causing the crash or plucking the innocent child from the burning wreckage. Nearby residents told stories of the appearance of a ghost on this stretch of road, who would stand at the sight of the crash. One of the dead it was presumed.

Lost in his reverie Reg almost didn't see the figure that suddenly appeared by the road. As he crested the hill he suddenly saw a flash of movement from the corner of his eye. He stepped on the brakes and stared into his rear-view mirror all at once. As the car screeched to a sudden juddering halt he saw someone dart away, out of the narrow rectangular space that the mirror allowed. A tiny blue flash caught his attention. Instantly, Reg was out of the car jogging back to the same spot where the accident had occurred so many years ago. But the road was deserted. He looked everywhere, even peering over the low stone wall and behind the nearby trees but there was no-one there. Reg could not help but think of the stories that said that this hill was haunted. A shiver ran up his spine and he felt the hairs rise on the back of his neck as if static electricity crackled in the air. But, he thought, it could not have been a ghost. The spirits of the dead did not leave flowers and he stood and stared at the fresh bouquet of unfamiliar blooms that lay at the foot of a tree.

Despite the delay, as Reg neared the ancient site of Stonehenge, he could see that the security man who he had spoken to was yet to arrive. The faint glow of firelight was visible from the road; the trespassers evidently still content to enjoy their party amongst the stones. Reg pulled into the car park and cut the engine. He was tempted to wait for security to arrive. He was still feeling somewhat unnerved by the appearance of the ghostly figure on the road and something about the ring of rock behind him always made him feel nervous. He had often wondered at the mystery of the place, that such massive stones had been transported over such a distance to this remote plain, moved by a people who should not have been able to do so. Whenever he visited he could feel the charge in the air. The place had a certain aura, thought Reg shaking his head. It was no wonder that the site attracted so many visitors, and often unusual ones at that.

However, he gave a sigh and turned on the swirling blue lights on top of the car to announce his presence. He pocketed the keys and began to walk towards the firelight. As he crested the short hill the revellers came into focus and their noise became clearer. About ten people were there, seated around a small fire. One played a guitar and male and female voices sang along to a faintly familiar tune. Definitely hippies, thought Reg, as the faint smell of smoke reached him on the night breeze.

Then, all of a sudden, he felt something cold strike his hand. The temperature and force of the thing was shocking against the comparative damp warmth of the night and he jumped. Looking down in surprise he was relieved to see it was only a raindrop and he turned his face upwards to look for the clouds which he had not noticed before. Another raindrop hit his face, then another, then before he could blink a drop hit him just by the eye causing him to flinch and turn his face towards the ground.

Suddenly, there was an incredible blue-white flash and a huge crash of thunder. The heavens opened and cold rain, almost hail, lanced down, stinging Reg's exposed skin and quickly soaking him. There was another flash and a massive bang that rolled around the sky above him.

Reg held his hand against his forehead to shield his eyes and looked towards the trespassers who were now on their feet hurriedly gathering their belongings. At least that was one less problem to deal with, Reg thought to himself, sorely regretting leaving his coat at the station. But, as he watched, a bolt of lightning suddenly struck the top of one of the Sarsen stones with an almighty crack. Screams rang out from those within the circle. Reg instinctively rushed forwards through the blinding rain.

He had not made much progress when he saw something curious was beginning to happen. An eerie blue glow, as if lightning still lingered, was shining from within the stone circle. The stones themselves seemed to shine in the darkness, the campfire having been already doused by the heavy rain. The glow continued to brighten and now Reg could hear a faint humming sound, at the very edge of his hearing. He turned his head as he moved, trying to locate the source, but it seemed to come from everywhere at once. Panic was setting into the party-goers but now that Reg looked again it was almost as though the figures were blurred and insubstantial. He stared in surprise as they misted and paled before his eyes and then, as the force of the hum quickly increased to a crescendo, another bolt struck Stonehenge. It seemed to hit every stone at once bringing the glow to a dazzling intensity. Reg was forced to shut his eyes and he stumbled on the rough ground and fell to his knees. There was a new scream ahead of him which was abruptly cut short.

Instantly, silence descended at Stonehenge. Reg opened his eyes to a world of clear skies. The rain had completely stopped and there were no clouds to even hint at the severity of the storm. He pulled himself to his feet and staggered the last metres to the stones. The circle was empty. The only evidence that there had been anyone there a faintly smouldering campfire and a single tent peg, which glowed a dull red in the dark damp grass. Reg looked wildly about him. He was utterly alone. Why did people keep disappearing?

Eighty miles away and one hundred and fifty feet below the ground Aleksy Nowak whistled to himself as he carried his bag of tools through the tunnels of the London Underground. He was glad to be here, as warm as he was in his overalls, high visibility clothing and hard hat. He enjoyed manual work and the unsociable hours meant he was able to bring in good money. The dark echoing tunnels of the Circle Line did not bother him as they did some of the other men. He laughed at the ghost stories that were told about these tunnels. Grown men afraid of the dark? It was ridiculous. They said that men disappeared down here but no-one ever seemed to know of anyone who had actually vanished.

The light on the front of Aleksy's hat bobbed up and down as the yellow plastic helmet slid over his closely shaven head, the torch flashing against the train lines next to him as he walked. Up ahead, and around a corner, he could just make out the faint glow from the powerful lights that marked the area where he would be working on cleaning the line of the dust and hair that collected in the corners, blown along by the warm winds that pushed around the tunnels and platforms. Despite the lights ahead the darkness of the tunnels pressed around him.

Suddenly, Aleksy caught sight of a small bright blue flash out of the corner of his eye, a tiny burst of silent static lightning. He stopped abruptly and quickly turned his head, realising that he was passing a narrow passageway into an adjoining tunnel. He blinked, the shape of the blue light echoing on his retina. A movement drew his headtorch and his gaze to the floor where a sizeable rat sat washing its face, its beady eyes catching the glare of his light. Smiling to himself, and pursing his lips to resume his whistle, Aleksy made to continue walking when another movement caught his attention. The dark archway before him had seemed to darken momentarily, if it was possible for something as dark as the inky blackness of the space beyond to dim still further. Aleksy had the sense that someone, or something, had just passed by. Looking back towards the rat Aleksy could see it now lay dead. As he moved closer he saw that it had fallen completely still, its glassy eyes staring into nothingness, its body partly crushed as it something had just fallen upon it. He suddenly felt nervous and his skin prickled as he neared the brick wall. He leant through the archway and swept his torch across the darkness beyond.

The first thing that was evident was that this tunnel was dramatically colder and Aleksy's breath fogged in front of his face, caught in the light of his torch. The tunnel was evidently disused, the tracks were buckled and warped and the floor was thick with a deep white dust which lay across rubble and other detritus. Seeing nothing out of the ordinary Aleksy set down his tools and slipped into the adjoining tunnel, his feet crunching strangely on the white powder. A low hum seemed to emanate from somewhere in the darkness. He turned his head trying to seek the source of the noise. He was sure that there would be no trains running at this time of the night. He walked to an arched alcove, pausing in front of it. His torch beam did not seem to reach the back wall as it should have done. Indeed it barely seemed to penetrate the void. Looking down he saw that more of the white dust seemed to be swirling into the tunnel he was in, already covering the dead rat behind him. He bent down and scooped a little of the dust up onto his fingers. It was freezing cold and, as he watched, it melted on the warmth of his fingers. The impossible realisation dawned on him. He was holding snow. But how? He looked around at the thin layer of white and noticed a set of footprints which seemed to begin at the alcove ahead of him. A sudden chill crept over him as he realised that the prints pointed towards him, and past him. Someone else was here. A sudden metallic bang from his tools caused him to jump as something shifted in the bag back in the other tunnel. Startled, he looked again towards the archway and suddenly felt a presence behind him. A shiver of fear ran down his spine. He tried to turn and move away but found he was unable to move. It was as if he had been paralysed and fixed to the spot. Then a pressure seemed to press against his entire body at once. The light from his headtorch flickered and died as the pitch of the hum increased. With a shout forming on his lips Aleksy felt himself begin to lose consciousness and then the darkness consumed him and he fell into oblivion.

Sam snapped awake, already holding his breath, listening for the sound he knew had woken him. He felt his heart hammering in his chest and he quickly pressed his eyes tightly closed but his ears rang in the silence as if the very air hummed around him. Not even the sounds of his grandfather's friend, Valerie, sleeping in the adjacent room reached him. He tried to replay his thoughts to remember the sound. Had the stairs outside his door creaked? Had he heard a whispered voice from behind his bedroom door? Was there someone there? A presence? His slim body shivered involuntarily at the thought.

His imagination began to betray him and he quickly tried to suppress the thoughts coming into his head. He woke like this fairly regularly, sure each time that some sudden sound, a sigh or footfall, had entered his subconscious but never waking quick enough to hear it again. The problem now was getting back to sleep. The silence scared him as much as the dark and he dared not open his eyes for fear of what he might see. So, he lay perfectly still, unsure what was worse, turning his back on the door or facing it to see what came through it, straining his ears for the slightest sign that there was some other human habitation in the world, someone other than him, alone in his bed with the ghosts.

Eventually, he heard a solitary car approach on the road outside and he hurried to fall asleep while the reassuring sound was still audible but the thrum of the engine soon changed pitch as it passed the house and moved away. Silence reigned again, returning the faint hum to his ears. Then, again, there was a noise, a soft thump from the other side of the door. Sam squeezed his eyes still tighter so that shapes danced across the inside of his eyelids, as he waited for the nightmare to end. He tried to tell himself that no-one had ever been hurt by a ghost. They just glided around didn't they? Grey and indistinct shadows. The thought was no comfort and his heart continued to pound in his chest, the noise of his heartbeats a train moving over tracks, *duh-duh duh-duh*.

But no other sounds reached him until much later, when the soft buzz of Valerie's faint snores began to filter through from the other end of the hall. The spell of silence was broken and he fell back into the uneasy and troubled world of sleep.

CHAPTER TWO

When he next opened his eyes the curtains glowed dimly with the light of day. Sam pulled them open to let the morning light fall into the room. There was not much. The sky outside was slate grey and, raising himself on an elbow, he could see that the garden was hazy through mist, the yellows and browns of the fallen leaves blurry on the green lawn. Raindrops speckled the window.

His eye moved to the framed photo standing on the sill. It was his favourite photo of his grandfather, taken years ago, before the old man's mind had begun to wander. The man in the photo looked back at Sam, his eyes twinkling behind black-framed glasses, the wind catching his straight grey hair and lifting it slightly.

Falling back into the bed Sam sighed, trying not to think about what lay ahead today. But that only allowed his mind to return to the sounds he had heard in the night. It had been months since he had woken like that. Perhaps the noises had been the ghost of his grandfather, here to say goodbye before they buried him in the cold damp earth. More likely it was the impending funeral that had shaped his dreams. Sam ran a hand through his tousled brown hair and pressed his eyes closed again. It seemed stupid now, to think of ghosts. He wished he could be braver but he had never felt comfortable in the house and especially at night when he felt, so often, as though someone was watching him.

It would not be any easier now that his grandfather had gone. Adam Hain had been Sam's entire family and he missed him like he had never missed anything. The feeling was a hollowness in his chest and he kept thinking what it must have been like at the moment that his grandfather had departed this world. Had he woken? Tried to cry out when he realised that it was to be his last breath? Had he been scared? Sam couldn't imagine Adam Hain being scared of anything and he comforted himself by imagining his grandfather making peace with the past and then deciding to pass on. Sam wasn't sure whether the suddenness of it all was a good thing or not. Life had been difficult for some time. His grandfather had been becoming increasingly agitated and paranoid before the end and Sam had often had to put a brave face on his own sadness. It had been awful to see a once strong and proud man become so confused, rambling about people and places that didn't make sense. And now, Sam was alone.

Downstairs, dressed in a black suit, black tie and white shirt Sam ate a silent breakfast with Valerie. She had moved into the house a week ago, the same day that Sam had found his grandfather lying stiff and cold in his bed. She had been a friend of sorts to Adam but Sam knew that his grandfather had only truly cared for him, the only surviving member of his family. Indeed that care had come with a dedication that had sometimes bordered on zealous over-protectiveness. Valerie looked at Sam and gave him a sad smile as she nervously stroked her grey bob, her hand shaking slightly.

'How are you feeling, dear?'

'I'm okay.' he said, although he could not disguise the waver in his voice.

'We need to leave at ten.' said Valerie, 'It'll be better to arrive before anyone else. Have you got your reading?'

Sam stared into the depths of his cereal and tapped his breast pocket.

'Good boy.'

Sam wanted to point out that he was not a boy. He was an adult. But Valerie had been kind in keeping him company in the otherwise empty house and, as well as not wanting to upset her, he did not have the energy to disagree. Besides, sometimes he did feel like a child and that made him feel angry at himself. Today he felt more childish than ever after his disturbed sleep. The great hollowness in his chest seemed to become a heavy weight that pressed against his stomach and he began to feel queasy. He mumbled an apology to Valerie, pushed away the half uneaten breakfast and crept away into the house leaving Valerie to sit back in her chair, tears pricking her eyes.

Sam took himself into the front room, which overlooked the narrow road and the woods beyond. A fine drizzle was still falling, coating the window in a thousand tiny droplets. Sam knelt on the sofa, his arms propped on the windowsill, his nose and forehead flattened and cold against the glass as he stared into the trees. Refocusing his eyes he looked at the reflection of the room behind him. He could see the doorway into the hall. Unnerved, he left the room and ran up the stairs into his bedroom.

Sam had always felt uncomfortable in the hallway and on the stairs. That part of the house felt somehow oppressive and was prone to strange changes in temperature, often growing cold quite suddenly. Sam often thought he could hear a hum, like electricity cables running nearby. He found the hair would rise on his neck sometimes.

The only thing that Sam liked about the hallway was the painting of the girl. His grandfather had painted it before Sam was born and it had hung in its space at the top of the stairs for as long as Sam could remember. The girl was, thought Sam, the most beautiful person that he had ever seen. Her portrait looked slightly to the right of the frame, her green eyes focussed on the middle distance. Long dark hair framed the smooth tanned skin of her face, a scattering of freckles dusted her nose and cheeks. Each time Sam ran up the stairs he would fix on her face, trying to ignore the creepiness at his back. Sam had once asked his grandfather who the girl was but Adam's face had clouded over and he had made it very clear that he did not want to discuss the girl. Sam had never broached the subject again and now her identity would forever be a mystery to him.

But as much as he disliked the hallway it was the cellar which Sam disliked the most and he rarely ventured down into it. The house was clearly quite old and there were hatches in the cellar where coal would once have been poured down into it. Now it had white walls and a strip of fluorescent lighting which, at least, made it considerably brighter than it once would have been. But it was still a place that Sam seldom ventured. The dark hole in one wall made him particularly nervous. The hole had been made by the removal of a section of brickwork, big enough for a man to crawl into, or out of. The black space beyond ran under the hallway. The house had been abandoned when Adam Hain had come across it in his youth and he said that the hole had been there then. Local legend said that the disappearance of the former tenant had been something of a mystery.

Adam had filled the hole with his store of large pieces of wood. There had always been wood around. He had been a keen amateur carpenter as well as a decent painter and had carved various fantastic figures, squat men and strange animals, which now sat around the house on shelves and windowsills. Sam even vaguely recalled that his grandfather had partially rebuilt the house himself. But, the cellar had always been Adam Hain's favourite room and had never seemed to make him feel nervous. He had used it as a workshop and kept his various tools down there with firewood and odds and ends in different stages of repair. On one wall, above a battered dartboard, there even hung an old sword, spotted with rust.

Just before they were due to leave for the funeral Sam crept out of his bedroom. He could hear Valerie singing softly to herself downstairs. Sam had known her all his life. She lived half a dozen houses away, nearer the centre of the little village. When he was little Sam used to go to her house to choose a toy from a vast store which she kept in a spare room. Valerie's house was almost as strange as his own but for entirely different reasons. She made a living from painting illustrations for reference books on plants and insects and she always had leaves, twigs and flowers in pots dotted around the house. She had once given Sam a number of swallow-tail caterpillars. His grandfather had found him an old glass fish tank and together they had watched them eat, build their cocoons and hatch, a miracle of natural transformation as their pale yellow and black wings flapped as they dried. In his naive youthfulness Sam had wished he could change himself so easily, that he could undergo some magic transformation, that he could grow wings and fly.

Sam forced himself to walk down the stairs, even

though he felt a need to run. The feeling of unease was almost familiar so often did he feel it. Valerie was in the kitchen. She turned to greet him and Sam could see that she had been crying again. In his misery he had all but forgotten that there would be other people just as sorry to be attending Adam Hain's funeral today. His grandfather had not had many friends but, having lived in Pluckton for most of his life, he had got to know many of the others living in the village well enough. Crossing the kitchen, Sam awkwardly gave Valerie a brief hug and she hooked her arm in his and gave him a smile as they left the house.

Arm in arm they left the house and turned towards the village church where the service was to be held. Sam saw that the family next door already had their carved Halloween pumpkin in the window, its triangular eyes fixed on the woods opposite, its jagged teeth curving upwards in a half smile. Sam's eyes slid back to his own house and he felt his heart skip and his stomach lurch. There at the upstairs window, looking out towards the woods, just as the pumpkin had been, was an indistinct face. Sam gasped. It was clearly there, although he could not make out the features from this distance. He looked to Valerie to see if she had seen it too but her gaze was fixed on the church spire ahead of them. He released her arm and turned back to look at the house but the face, if it had been there, had gone. All he could see was condensation. Patterns on the glass. Unsettled he quickened his pace.

Pluckton Church was the oldest building in the small village which lay in a natural fold in the land, surrounded by fields and woods. The church was small, plain on the outside but pretty inside, with stained glass windows along one side and rows of golden brown wooden pews set between pale grey stone columns. Sam still felt unnerved as they passed underneath the huge horse-chestnut tree that towered over the lopsided graves and the cracked and worn paving stones. Valerie pushed open the large wooden door and they stepped inside. The vicar, Reverend Allsopp came over to greet them. Sam and his grandfather had rarely gone to church. Adam Hain had not been a religious man, but very occasionally Valerie had coaxed them into walking through the dark to midnight mass on Christmas Eve. In a way it was odd that Adam had elected to be buried in the traditional way rather than be cremated. The vicar knew them anyway. The village was small enough that he probably knew everyone.

'Good morning, Samuel.' said Allsopp, patting Sam gently on the shoulder, 'A sad day' he added as he straightened his thick glasses, which never seemed to stay high enough on his nose. He gave a glum smile to Sam's unhappy nod and then strode away between the pews, humming softly, his white and black gown billowing after him.

Despite its small size Sam had never known the church to be crowded. Today was no exception. There were not many mourners at the funeral. Adam Hain had kept to himself for the most part and with no surviving family, other than Sam, there were few people to fill the wooden pews. Only a handful of people huddled together in the first few rows. Most of them were fairly elderly. Adam's few friends had been of a similar age and so staff provided by the undertakers carried the coffin down the aisle towards its place on the trestles at the front. Sam watched as it drew near. It was made of a light coloured wood, with intricate carvings on each of the sides. The front showed a bird with outstretched wings rising from a bed of flame and as the box passed Sam could see that the sides depicted strange scenes with large temples and small houses behind odd creatures and misshapen figures. With a start Sam realised that his grandfather had made the coffin himself. The tableau was typical of his unusual work and the characters seemed to be similar to those small wooden carvings that still lay around the house. Turning as the coffin passed him and reached the front Sam realised that Revered Allsopp was not particularly impressed by the designs etched into the wood, a slight frown creased his brow and Sam quickly stopped his intent study of them, anxious not to offend.

It was hard to believe that there was actually a body in there, thought Sam, although the coffin certainly looked heavy enough. The weight was evident in the way the pallbearers moved and grunted as they set it down. But, all the same, it just did not seem real that his grandfather was within that wooden box. Sam could feel the eyes of those who had come to mourn on his back as the coffin was set in its place at the front of the church and the pallbearers retreated.

Reverend Allsopp startled Sam out of his thoughts with up-stretched arms and sudden proclamation of God's love, followed by a particularly booming 'Amen.' He led the sermon, even managing to slip in a reference to heathen imagery, before all but shouting the hymns. It was just as well that he was loud for there was little other sound in the church. He gave little pause save for Sam to give his short reading, a passage apparently chosen by his grandfather.

Then they shuffled outside where a plot had been found for Adam next to Sam's parents. It was cold standing out on the damp grass, amongst the trees and gravestones. Breath fogged in the air and the whole place smelled of dampness. Orange-brown leaves stuck to the front of Sam's black shoes. He absent-mindedly wiped them away with the heel of the other shoe. He had been particularly dreading this part of the proceedings. Tears welled in his eyes and he rubbed them away. To see his grandfather's, his mother's and his father's graves all next to each other was almost more than he could bear. He felt sick. He rubbed at the scar on his forearm, hidden under the white shirt and black jacket. A faint pink puckered line ran like a fleshy snake from his third finger, twisting around his arm to his elbow, a souvenir of the car accident which must have nearly killed him and had certainly killed his parents. No-one had ever managed to work out how Sam had survived it and come to be lying, almost entirely unhurt, on a tuft of grass by the side of the road.

Suddenly feeling as though someone was watching him he looked up and thought he saw a figure slip behind a tree but although he watched for a few minutes no-one reappeared.

After it was over Sam said his thanks to those that had come before sending Valerie back to the house without him. He took himself back into the church and took a seat at the end of one of the long wooden pews. He needed a moment alone. Adam had become more and more frail but still it was all so sudden. Not long ago Sam and his grandfather had been laughing and joking. Then he had begun acting so strangely. Jumping at shadows, talking about places and people that didn't exist, the bizarre ramblings of an old man, who had always been strange and prone to bouts of oddness, suddenly and inexplicably struck by apparently complete senility. Now he was gone. Sam lowered his head into his hands and rubbed his eyes, salty tears under his fingertips leaving cold patches on his cheeks.

He took a deep breath and sat up again to face the

front of the church, and started. A man was standing there, staring at him, a strange grin on a smug face, his hands clasped behind his back. He wore a dark pinstripe suit, a black shirt and a bright pink tie which seemed completely at odds with the sombre outfits that the other mourners had been wearing. His black hair was plastered across his head, wet and shiny.

The man held Sam's gaze a moment longer, his fixed grin immobile under his pale pointed nose. Then he strode towards Sam, a single hand extended. Sam looked at the hand, unsure. The man gave a small nod of encouragement and Sam reluctantly put out his own hand and they shook a limp clammy handshake.

'Fiddler.' said the man. Still the grin did not move. Sam was confused for a moment until a business card appeared in his hand almost magically. It read 'Adrian Fiddler & Co. Solicitors' and gave an address in central London.

'Oh, er, Hain.' said Sam.

'Yes, I know.' said Mr Fiddler, his smile slipping momentarily. 'I'm here to execute your grandfather's will.' He brought his other hand from behind his back and held out a package wrapped in thick brown paper. Sam's name was written on the paper in black felt tip. It looked like his grandfather's handwriting. Sam held it for a moment, running a finger over the lettering. The package had the feel of a medium-sized hardback book.

'Well, aren't you going to open it?' said Mr Fiddler, a thin line appearing on his forehead. He was practically drooling with anticipation, leaning over Sam on the tips of his toes.

'Um, not just yet.' said Sam, unzipping the rucksack he had brought and placing the package into a hidden inside pocket. He did not want to open it now. His feelings were just too raw, and he certainly didn't want to open it in front of this irritating, grinning man. Sam just wanted to be alone.

'It's been in our possession for some time now.' said Mr Fiddler. 'It came to us in quite, uh, unusual circumstances.' He was clearly frustrated that he was not going to get to see the contents.

'Oh right.' said Sam 'Well, thanks very much.' He zipped his bag closed and slipped one arm through a strap. If he was not going to get to be alone here then he would find somewhere else.

Mr Fiddler twisted his hands and looked sideways at the floor as if he was trying to think of something else he could say to prolong the conversation, but Sam got up and began to walk away, towards the door, leaving the man to stare at his back, his grin gone and frustration etched upon his features.

'Wait.' called Mr Fiddler, 'I almost forgot.' He scurried towards Sam, pulling a sheaf of pages from an inside pocket. 'You need to sign these papers, young man. You are now the sole owner of your grandfather's home and his possessions. He left it all to you.'

'What?' asked Sam, dumbfounded. He had not thought about what would happen to all the things that his grandfather had owned.

'Yes,' said Mr Fiddler, 'Quite the surprise, eh? Just sign here and here' he said, directing Sam to the appropriate places on the paperwork.' You know we would be happy to continue acting for your family' he added 'We've been solicitors to your grandfather for some time.'

Ferus crept from his hiding place at the edge of the woods to peer at the house. He was pretty sure that this was the right place. He would have to check. It seemed deserted. There were no lights on and no sign to suggest that the boy was there. He pushed the hood of his black robe back from his face with his huge hands. He crossed the empty road and ducked into the alleyway which led to the back garden. A tall wooden gate blocked his way. Looking behind himself to make sure he was not in view he ran and, pointing his outstretched hands to the floor, effortlessly leapt the gate in a single jump, his cloak billowing behind him as he moved. Despite his massive size, he landed soundlessly in the paved yard. He looked around but could still see no sign that anyone was home. He walked to the back door and examined the lock carefully. He closed his eyes for a moment, his hand outstretched and the lock clicked. Turning the handle he entered the house.

CHAPTER THREE

Sam walked home slowly, his eyes on the grey stone beneath his feet. He reached the house and stole a quick look at the window where he thought he had seen the face before. The window was empty except for a little condensation on the bottom half, trickles of water running through it. That must have been all it was. Sam turned his key in the front door and stepped into the hallway. Immediately the house felt wrong. He crept towards the stairs, holding his breath, listening. A faint noise came from a room ahead of him and Sam's heart skipped a beat. A floorboard creaked under his foot and he immediately snatched his foot up, leaving it hanging in the air. A silent moment stretched out.

Valerie stepped into the hallway. 'Hello, dear' she said. She looked at Sam standing on one leg, the door open behind him and she raised an eyebrow. 'Are you alright?'

Sam lowered his leg sheepishly.

'Come on,' said Valerie, 'Shut the door, it's getting chilly out there. Did you know we left the back door unlocked?' She turned and went back the way she had come, leaving Sam to close the door and follow her.

Having changed into jeans and a thick hooded jumper Sam called to Valerie that he was going out as he stuffed a scarf, gloves and hat into his rucksack. He crossed the empty road and ducked between some bent and rusted railings into the thick woods opposite his house. The morning mists had mostly cleared but the air remained grey and damp. Sam threaded his way through the trees, green and yellow leaves still clinging to skeletal branches above a carpet of brown. He followed a faint path to arrive on an old tarmac road, long since disused. The undergrowth was slowly reclaiming it from the sides and weeds poked through cracks and bubbles in the surface. He vaulted one of the square-pyramid shaped concrete blocks, with its rusted red-brown metal hooks set on top. These blocks were, Sam knew, designed to stop any vehicles from passing down this road, not that any would or could now. The road led nowhere. It started at some rusted gates and led through the woods to a disused tumbledown building, more a pile of stacked bricks than a structure. The army owned the land but had not used it for many years, allowing it to become overgrown. It had had some importance in the last war but now it was forgotten. A patchwork of deep woods, cratered and tussocky fields and even deep brick-lined trenches, the woods were full of places to explore and hide. There were even a number of small, single room concrete and brick bomb shelters, but the most striking feature was the tunnel. It was called Seven Floors by all the local kids. The entrance lay in an unassuming building, deep in the heart of the woods and it drew children from all over the area. Not that many went in. It was rumoured to be haunted. Sam had been as far as the entrance inside the building to look down the long slope that led into darkness. Older and braver people had told him that that tunnel sloped down and down for miles, with rooms off each side holding old army equipment from the Second World War. Everything not bolted down had been stolen, old radio equipment here, a helmet there. Sam had been told that the tunnels could be used to get to secret places all over the county, perhaps even as far as the very edge of the London Underground. He wasn't sure he believed that but they certainly ran under his house. But Sam wasn't brave enough to go down. He preferred to climb the trees at the edge of the nearby field. He had a particular favourite. It was tough to climb, and he almost fallen from it more than once. But in its centre were a number of boards and planks, nailed in place by someone years ago. Up there you could see anyone coming into the woods. The cracked road was in plain sight, as well as the yellow grasses of the open field and the rope swing in the distance, the only really open parts of the area. Sam felt pretty safe whenever he was up there, hidden behind branches thicker than his chest.

He went there now and stretched his legs out ahead of him across the planks, his back against the smooth thick grey-brown trunk, relieved to be alone at last. He could feel the cold of the damp wood underneath him along the backs of his legs. He pulled his scarf around his neck and let his mind wander. Perhaps here he could get some peace away from other people. He felt as though no-one really understood how he felt, although a small part of him worried that that was just the usual youthful perception of the world.

As he sat there, on the edge of being too cold, he thought about his future. He had just inherited a house. The thought of the house made him wrinkle his nose. He really didn't know what to think about inheriting that place. He had always found it a strange building, sure there were restless spirits walking its hallways and stairs. He wasn't sure that he would be able to spend time there without the warmth of his grandfather's personality to push back the darkness into the corners. And knowing that his grandfather had died there. Sam shivered. He could sell it, he supposed, and buy somewhere else, but that felt like a betrayal of Adam Hain. His grandfather had always lived there, as far as Sam knew. Where Sam had felt nervous about the spookiness his grandfather had seemed to revel in it, often praising the location and delighting in its quirkiness. Sam remembered broaching the issue of ghosts but his grandfather had given him a strange look and waved away his fears. 'Sam,' he had said, 'There are no such things as ghosts. One day you'll realise.' He seemed to want to say more but Sam had ended the conversation. The only time he ever felt uncomfortable around his grandfather was when Adam got serious like that. Sometimes Adam Hain's mind seemed to wander during these sorts of conversations and he would tell Sam stories of other places and strange creatures and dangerous men in dark cloaks. As a child Sam had listened intently to these tales of other worlds, caught up in the enchantment of it all and often both thrilled a little scared, but as he had got older Sam had found it difficult to hear his grandfather speak so earnestly about things which were so clearly nonsense. He was too old for such stupid stories although, he had to admit, that these stories were perhaps no stranger that believing in ghosts. Belief. Was that what it was? He had once, when he was quite young, awoken in the night needing badly to go to the bathroom. He had crept from his bedroom and onto the stairs. As he had looked down into the hallway downstairs he had had a momentary vision of a small figure turning the corner and disappearing. He had known instantly that the person had not been real. Terrified he had dashed back into his room and, much to his shame, had had to relieve himself in a bottle that he had found. The next day he had smuggled it out of his room and flushed the contents down the toilet. The whole thing had seemed like a dream but Sam was sure of what he had seen.

Adam Hain had had his own strange beliefs, of magic and paranormal phenomena and people who had presence, whatever that meant. All Sam knew was that the house, 'The End of the Line' his grandfather had named it, was haunted. He had done some research into ghosts and hauntings on days when the summer sun shone through the windows and the terrors of the night seemed far away. He had read that some thought that certain places contained an undefined energy which affected the human perception at some undiscovered level. He had read that the buzz of electricity coursing through overhead cables could cause the human ear to do strange things and hear things which were not there. But at night when darkness fell upon the house and the lights struggled to push it back, such scientific theories did not hold much comfort for Sam. Other things had happened which could not be explained in such a way, physical things. Sudden changes in temperature and the movement of objects around the house. Such events were rare but they had happened. And Sam wasn't the only one to feel the weirdness of the place. What few friends he had didn't like to venture inside. He had once been getting on quite well with one of the girls in his class. After she had visited the house once she had refused to go back and, unable to meet at her house because of her strict parents, they had drifted apart and the relationship had ended before it had really started. So, Sam had mixed views and divided loyalties about the house. He'd think about it another time, but the thought of Valerie leaving and returning to her own house filled him with dread.

As Sam sat in his tree a faint noise reached him from the road away to his right. He drew his legs up so as to be better hidden by the branches around him. Other kids occasionally visited the woods, challenging each other to enter the tunnels or to hang on the rope swing across the field, and more than once Sam had been bullied into handing over what little money he had been carrying. He generally avoided others when he was here, preferring solitude. He peered from his hiding place to look at the buckled tarmac beneath him. A man stepped into distant view. This was unusual enough in itself. Adults rarely came into the woods, with the exception of Mr Edwards who used to exercise his soppy cocker spaniel in the field. But this man was strange and, Sam saw, very large. He stopped in the road, only just visible from Sam's hiding place. He was wearing a long black coat which stretched almost to his feet, a hood pulled up against the damp air. But there was something weird about the man, not just his apparent massive size. Having stopped he made no sound but turned his head slowly this way and that almost as though he were sniffing the air. Suddenly fearful Sam drew back again so there was no chance that the stranger might see him. He was glad that he had been sitting silently and motionless when this figure had appeared. He chanced another look and was amazed to see that the man was looking at a large black bird which stood directly at his feet. The bird looked much like a large crow but there was something odd about it. It looked mangy, almost scaly; its wings more leathery than feathered. The bird bobbed its head and then bounced away. The man quickly jerked his head upright as if he had heard a noise and Sam again drew back behind the branches, holding his breath. After a minute of listening to his heart hammer in his chest, sure that it would give him away, Sam looked back. The man had gone. This was much worse. Now Sam had no idea where the stranger might be. He waited as long as he could bear then carefully and quietly swung himself down from the tree. He ducked behind a holly bush and listened but could hear no-one. He wound his way through the trees back towards the gap in the railings. A crow above him cawed loudly, bending its body down to peer at him through a beady eye, before hopping sideways along the branch and taking flight. It landed in front of him and bounced along a few times, keeping an eye fixed on him before giving another caw and flapping away. Sam hurried on until the trees were behind him.

Behind Sam, but unseen by him, a small pair of eyes seemed to appear within the shadow of a small oak tree and blinked up at the treehouse which Sam had just left. The eyes belonged to a small figure who was very good at remaining hidden to all but the most watchful and patient observer and the boy had not seen him. The figure rose and remaining in the shadows cast a glance at where the robed figure had appeared on the road before hurrying after Sam towards the house.

Still unsettled by the stranger in the woods Sam crept quietly into the house. *His* house, he remembered. He could hear a low voice coming from the room ahead and he tiptoed down the corridor to hear who was speaking. Valerie was on the telephone, speaking quietly, a sad tone in her voice. Something about the way she was talking caught Sam's attention and as he moved closer he heard her say his name. He hung back, curious to hear what she was saying, immediately feeling guilty about spying on her. She sat side on to him, her grey hair hiding her face.

'Such a dear boy,' said Valerie 'but jumps at his own shadow. He could do with some more friends, a girlfriend too. He's handsome enough, anything to get him over Adam's death and the strange nonsense he was coming up with.'

Sam heard the indistinct mumble of a voice on the other end of the line before Valerie spoke again.

'Yes, it was so sad wasn't it? It affects so many. It scared me. I mean, did he even know that he was going senile, bless him? He was always...hmmm, exactly, but all that talk of another world. I think he saw the end.'

Sam tensed. How dare she talk about his grandfather going mad on the very day they had laid him in the cold earth? He felt a flash of anger shoot through him and a bang came from the other room. He heard Valerie jump. And say,

'Oh nothing, sorry, a picture just blew over in a draft', Then more loudly 'Is that you Sam?'

He took a deep breath with his eyes closed to calm the anger that bubbled inside him.

'Yeah.' he called and moved down the hall and up the stairs, running up them, his eyes fixed on the painting of the dark-haired girl, as the hairs rose on the back of his neck as they always did.

Later Sam was laying the table in the kitchen for their evening meal. Valerie had spent the afternoon baking and had made a large steak and mushroom pie with mounds of buttery mashed potatoes. Sam's mouth was watering at the smells. He set out knives, forks and spoons. There was a fruit crumble of some sort browning in the oven. He looked at Valerie and smiled. As angry as he had felt earlier he really was grateful for her company and she had gone to a lot of effort in this meal.

Sam had just finished placing the cutlery when there was a sudden loud bang from the front of the house, like a firework going off. Sam and Valerie looked at one other and together walked towards the front door. Sam suddenly felt very nervous. Something wasn't right. As they walked down the corridor Sam could have sworn he heard a cackle. Then the letterbox moved slightly. A creak echoing in the still hallway. Then the flat piece of metal swung inwards with a sudden loud snap. Sam and Valerie both jumped, Valerie screamed as a noise came from the kitchen behind them. Sam turned his head and looked behind them but could see nothing there. Turning back towards the door he saw with a start that two glowing red eyes were peering at him through the rectangular gap. Valerie screamed again and grabbed Sam's arm. The red eyes moved upwards out of sight and a grotesque mouth appeared in its place. A fixed and hideous grin of misshapen teeth. Sam held his breath; Valerie's nails digging into his arm.

'Trick or treat!' said a childish voice on the other side of the door followed by the giggle of a small girl.

Sam let out the breath he had been holding and Valerie began to laugh as she walked forwards and opened the door. A small figure stood on the step, a devilish mask on top of a black witch's cloak.

'Who is that in there?' Valerie said to the mask.

A small girl pulled the mask over her head and grinned, showing several missing teeth. 'It's me!' she said delighted.

'Well, hello Sophie' said Valerie. 'And hello Steve' she said looking over to a man, standing on the pavement, his arms folded and a faint smile on his face.

Hi, Valerie' he said with a wave, 'Happy Halloween.'

Sophie thrust a basket in the air above her head, it was already half full of chocolate and sweets.

'Okay' laughed Valerie 'Let me see what I've got.' She turned and walked towards the kitchen.

'Do you like my costume?' asked Sophie turning to

Sam, suddenly serious and scowling. 'Look, I've even got extra toes.' pointing Sam towards a pair of latex slippers which covered her own feet. 'Daddy says I'm an ab-om-in-ation.' she added, struggling with the word.

Sam steadied himself against the wall; his heart was still hammering in his chest. He had forgotten it was Halloween. He was so on edge at the moment. It was ridiculous. He was just about to relax and answer Sophie when a scream came from behind him and he heard Valerie exclaim. He rushed into the kitchen. She stood with one hand curled against her chest, her other hand outstretched, her index finger pointing towards the table. It took Sam a moment to realise what she was looking at. He looked at the kitchen table, at the cutlery he had put out a moment ago. With a gasp he realised that it had all moved, every fork, knife and spoon had shifted and now all pointed in the same direction as if drawn by some giant magnet. Looking again, he saw that every drawer and cabinet had opened. Someone, or something, had been here.

Sam lay in bed. It was still early, and he was not sleepy, despite an emotional and tiring day, but Valerie had wanted to turn in, unnerved by the events in the kitchen. *What was happening?* thought Sam. There had always been odd things in the house, but he thought it was only really him that had noticed them before, and certainly nothing had ever moved in the way that the cutlery had moved this evening. That was poltergeist activity, Sam thought with a shudder. Valerie had certainly been quite scared by it and had been unable to stay in the kitchen to eat the meal she had prepared. Sam had had to make her two cups of strong sweet tea to settle her nerves and she had only picked at the pie as they ate in the lounge in front of the television and a reassuringly banal sitcom. At first she had found the evening news even too much, stories about a gas explosion in a pub and a worker who had become lost in the London Underground.

In the faint moonlight coming through the curtains Sam looked around the room, noting the shapes of his possessions, most of them gifts from his grandfather. He reached for the glass of water next to him and knocked his wallet onto the floor. Stretching he picked it up and opened it to see the photo of him and his grandfather, taken in happier times. He switched on the torch he kept nearby and looked at it. He didn't look much like Adam Hain. Sam's hair was brown; his grandfather's was blonde before it went grey. He tossed the wallet into his open rucksack and lay back down facing the wall. Eventually he drifted off to sleep.

Sam's breathing was shallow and he slept soundly until a faint noise began. It was partly a chime, partly a hum, the noise of a small coin spinning in the air waiting for someone to call heads or tails. Sam stirred, still asleep. Thin wisps of fog began to escape his nostrils as the temperature dropped in his room, twin Chinese dragons of mist rising above his head. He stirred again drawing the covers closer under his chin, a small shiver causing his body to shake slightly. On a shelf above his head stood a Galileo thermometer, one of the many presents from his grandfather. It was a glass cylinder, filled with a clear fluid in which were suspended five round glass bubbles each of a different size. Depending on which vials floated or sank one could read the temperature. As Sam slept the bubbles all slid soundlessly to the bottom of the thermometer.

But then the hum slowly faded away with the cold air and the glass bubbles rose back up the tube. Sam slept on.

In the darkness of a cellar a mouse seemed to hang in the air, almost impossibly still, although alive. The skin at the nape of its neck pinched where it was held, four feet above the floor. A patch of light fell upon the mouse from a cigarette lighter above it. *Clunk, chink, clunk, chink.* The lighter opened and closed, the light of the flame flashing on and off. A pale hand moved forward from the darkness, dimly visible in the faint light, meaty fingers pointed towards the ground in mimicry of the mouse's legs and tail. The hand made a twisting movement and the mouse, still hanging in mid-air, began to twist lazily. A voice spoke in the darkness.

'What is your report? Are you certain he is there now?'

'Master Ferus,' came the reply 'the space between continues to thin although the doors are not predictable. It is Halloween. The boy is asleep. But,' the voice hesitated, 'I do not understand why we need to be so secretive. If this boy is the subject of the prophecy then....'. The voice trailed off with a choking noise.

'Do not ever question me again. Now is the time to act, but I do not want to reveal our interest in him less someone intervene before his death. If he is the one then this must seem like an accident. He senses our presence and that cursed dwarf has already been sniffing around.'

The hand hovering above the mouse suddenly clenched into a fist and the small grey furry body crumpled with a series of small but still sickening cracking sounds. The hand opened and withdrew into a dark sleeve. The mouse's misshapen body fell to the floor sending a small puff of dust swirling and twinkling in the dim light of the flame.

CHAPTER FOUR

Aleksy Nowak awoke with a start, utterly disorientated. He was lying on a rough stone floor, cold and damp. He sat up and looked around wildly, feeling slightly dizzy as he did so. There was not much light to see by but ahead of him and above and to the sides he could see only grey stone walls. He felt a draft behind him and slowly turned his head and then his body, still sitting on the cold floor. The last wall was not a wall as such. Thick iron bars stretched from ceiling to floor.

Aleksy climbed slowly to his feet wincing as he did so and moved over to the bars. Where on earth was he? He ran his hands over the smooth metal. He could see little beyond the bars, a dark passageway stretched away to either side. He was in a cell. How had he got here? He fought the rising panic and tried to calm himself. He cast his mind back. He had been walking along the Circle Line section of the Underground. He was still wearing his high-visibility jacket and work trousers. And then there had been another tunnel, and a hum, and a... he frowned... and a force that had pushed him towards a doorway. He ran a hand over his closely shaved head, he could remember nothing else. Had he been abducted by aliens?

A sound shook him from his thoughts. The scream of hinges on a distant door perhaps, then a clang which echoed through the darkness. Aleksy backed away from the bars suddenly certain that whatever was coming wasn't going to be good. It was as he reached the rear wall and put his back to it that he realised what the cell was missing. He turned franticly, studying each of the bars, the walls, floor and ceiling in desperate panic. He was locked in a cell that had no door. Then as footsteps approached he began to feel something change. His mind felt as though it was being driven out of his head. Another mind seemed to be quietly slipping inside his brain and before its terrible power his own mind became increasingly opaque. As a figure wearing a black cloak arrived in front of the bars Aleksy felt the last of his own coherent thoughts disappear like birds flying silently over a distant horizon. A tiny and far away part of him faintly registered surprise as the bars at the end of the cell parted as though the cloaked man had simply opened a curtain and then even that thought winked out of existence and he was transfixed.

Ferus lifted his meaty hands and drew the hood of the black cloak away from his face exposing his pale face to the dark night, his black hair accentuating the pallor of his skin as he stood silently in the garden. A grin briefly shaped his square jaw and he closed his eyes and put his hands out before him and toward the house, fingers splayed like a blind man feeling an unfamiliar shape. But Ferus was far from sightless. He moved his hands gently to and fro and then after a few moments his hands stopped their search and another grin flashed briefly in the shadows. His fingers wiggled slightly.

Opening his eyes Ferus saw that within the house a faint orange glow had appeared at one corner of the quiet building, just visible through one of the windows. Ferus allowed one arm to fall to his side but kept the other outstretched as though studying his fingernails. He turned his wrist. Quickly a flicker of flame was reflected in a window as a flame curved and snaked hungrily as it tried to find its way through the building. It came across a small breath of air where a window had been left open slightly and sucked in oxygen. Buoyed by fresh air the flames twisted towards some heavy curtains and began to eat them. They were soon alight, a sheet of orange and yellow hanging and then falling, dropping to the floor. Dark smoke coursed upwards travelling across the ceiling, boiling and churning, desperate to move up and out of the room to choke the life from the living above. The fire crept along the floor, eating and melting the carpet it found there, searching for fuel to feed its hunger. It came across a sofa and shrieked in delight as it engulfed it in its molten embrace. Suddenly, a shrill and piercing alarm rang out above the crackle of burning wood and fabric. The fire seemed to roar in answer and continued its infernal spread as quickly as it could, devouring everything in its path.

In the garden Ferus raised his hands to the black cowl and drew it back over his head making it seem as though he had vanished into the shadows, the only clue that he was still there was the orange flicker in his eyes as he watched the fire. Then after a few moments even that tiny sign disappeared and he was gone.

Sam was dreaming of cloaked men and crows, standing amongst gravestones, when a piercing shriek entered his visions. Groggily Sam turned over and reached for his alarm clock but as he began to wake he realised that was wrong. *Smoke*, some primal part of his brain told him. *Fire, smoke, wake, move.* Sam was awake then, falling sideways from his bed, already grabbing for clothes. He could smell it clearly now and hear it too, the unmistakeable noise of a substantial fire. The crash and pop of it. He dragged on jeans and a t-shirt as quickly as he could, feeling conscious that Valerie should not see him naked despite the obvious danger. He caught sight of his rucksack and grabbed it, stuffing a discarded jumper into it as he leapt over the books and dirty clothes that covered his floor. He pulled his arms through the straps of the rucksack and shouted Valerie's name as he opened the door.

The wall of heat and light hit him like a punch and he felt his hair move and lift as the hot wind rushed past him. The hall ahead of him was ablaze on one wall, the fire seemingly desperate to cross it, licking at the ceiling, searching for a hold. Sam put his head down and ran down the corridor towards Valerie's room, feeling the heat strike the side of his face and thump at the soles of his bare feet. He crashed through the door into the dark bedroom, which immediately felt cool after the infernal hallway behind him. The bed was empty. He shouted for Valerie again, but there was no answer. Desperately he looked under the bed and in the wardrobe, the only two places she could have possibly been. Belatedly he realised that he shouldn't have rushed into the room as he did. He remembered seeing a film in which even experienced firemen had been blasted off their feet by fires hiding behind doors which exploded with the sudden inrush of oxygen. He had to be more sensible.

He turned back towards the corridor. Despite having been in the room for only a matter of seconds the fire had intensified and had moved across the hall. Both walls and the ceiling were alight, smoke rolling and fighting to get into the room with him. Looking into that hallway was like looking into the entrance to some hell. The other end was black, a void in the maelstrom of orange and yellow daggers that ringed the passageway. Looking around him in increasing panic Sam saw a pair of pink, fleecy, rubber-soled slippers lying next to the door and he hastily pulled his feet into them before taking a deep breath. He ran.

The fire snatched at his clothes and hair as he sprinted down the hall. The heat was immense and he felt as though his skin was screaming in protest. As he reached the end of the hall he saw that the painting of the beautiful girl that had fixed his attention for so many years had caught alight. In a moment the fire had eaten through her face, holes appearing in her perfect cheeks. Her hair caught and the painting curled as she disappeared forever.

Sam turned and stopped at the sight from the top of the stairs. The fire here was even hotter, fiercer. A fountain of flame thrust up through several collapsed stairs about halfway down. Sam couldn't see what was on the other side. He briefly considered turning back but then, without having really thought about it, he was moving down the stairs as quickly as he could, as he reached the missing stairs he closed his eyes and leapt blindly.

He landed awkwardly on the bottom stairs and spilled forwards, scraping his forearms along the floor and banging his head on the wall to the side of him. A white flash filled his vision as his forehead connected with the skirting board. Heat pressed onto him from all sides and for a moment he felt as though he was pinned to the floor, pressure seemingly holding down every part of his body. Panicking he got his hands underneath him and pushed backwards, managing to rise to his knees. He had been lucky, he had landed in a patch of floor that was not yet ablaze but fire raged ahead of him and as he watched part of the ceiling ahead of him collapsed. The way to the front door was blocked.

He forced his way from his knees to his feet, slightly dizzy from the effort and the blow he had taken. He threw himself into the room to the side of him. The fire raged here too and the smoke was thicker. He began to cough uncontrollably and the dizziness intensified. There was nothing for it but to fight his way to the back door. He plunged through smoke and flame, one arm above his head. He felt something strike him between the shoulder blades but the rucksack took the brunt and, although he staggered, he kept his feet. He was almost there when the fire let out an unearthly scream as though it sensed that he might make his escape. It rose up before him like some hellish beast. Sam dodged sideways and saw that a window had broken. Without thinking he dived for it and threw himself through it. It was like plunging into a cold bath and he managed to take half a breath before the ground rushed up and hit him, knocking the smoky air from his lungs. With a tremendous effort Sam again scrambled to his feet and dashed down the garden. He reached the back wall and turned to look at the house as the fire shrieked again. He wheezed and coughed, his throat raw.

The entire building was ablaze, part of the roof had collapsed, flames surged from the windows curling around the painted brickwork leaving it blackened and burnt. As Sam watched the chimney tottered and fell through the roof sending a new gout of flame billowing upwards to chase a million sparks that danced above the inferno. Sam wiped a sooty hand across his forehead, smearing a trickle of blood across his face. Everything he owned. Everything his grandfather had given him. Gone, in a matter of minutes.

He again thought of Valerie. She might have made it out. She would be at the front of the house. With no way to pass the burning building Sam climbed gingerly over the back wall, landing on the path that ran behind it. He jogged slowly along it, turning twice to reach the road at the front of the house. He could see Valerie there looking up at the fire and the massive column of thick smoke that piled into the air as if a hole had opened in the ground and the very centre of the Earth was fighting its way out.

Sam was about to call out to Valerie, her attention fixed on the sight in front of her but then he noticed something that made him stop and flatten back against the corner of the wall. Valerie was there, standing alone and staring at the house, her hands to her face in horror as she shouted at the house, barely audible over the roar of the flames. But behind her and in the shadow of the trees, where she could not see them, stood three cloaked men. From the position of their bodies Sam saw they were not staring at the building, but at Valerie's back. Instantly Sam felt a sense of unease as he saw them. As he stood there a moment, the feeling increased. Suddenly, Valerie seemed to make a decision and she took a few purposeful steps towards the burning building. But as she did Sam saw a flash of movement. Suddenly, Valerie was falling to the ground as if she had been stuck

Then Sam saw flashing blue lights appear back in the village. If there was a siren it was not audible over the roar of the fire. The men saw it too and as a trio suddenly turned and walked into the woods behind them. In a moment they were gone. Sam sprinted to Valerie and skidded to a stop beside her on his knees.

'Are you okay? Are you hurt?' gasped Sam

'No, not really' she said, struggling to stand 'I'm a tough old bird. What happened? I thought you were still in there, and then... and then...I think something must have hit me on the head'. She raised her hand to the back of her skull.

Sam felt anger flash through him. He looked to the gap in the railings where the men had vanished, and he looked ahead to the blue lights. He made a decision. Those men had done something. Patting Valerie's hand, he gave her a smile then turned and ran. He threw himself towards the woods, anger and adrenaline driving him forward. He dived through the gap in the railings and felt the cold darkness of the woods envelop him, shutting out the crash as part of the house collapsed behind him and Valerie called out his name in fear and despair.

Sam blinked furiously, trying to see amongst the black trees. The image of the fire still danced across his vision and he felt even angrier as he wasted valuable seconds waiting for his eyes to adjust to the gloom. The coolness and damp of the leaves around him was welcome though and it wasn't long before he dashed forwards towards the broken road, ears and eyes straining for any sign of the men who, he was sure, had taken everything from him. He felt, before he saw, the buckled tarmac under his feet and he pressed forwards, turning his head from side to side, his throat still raw from the smoke. It felt like he was trying to swallow razor blades. He thought that he could see someone moving up ahead and he quickened his pace.

All of a sudden a heavy weight hit him around the waist and he was thrown into the bushes to one side. He landed heavily, face down, mud and leaves bitter in his mouth. The weight rolled with him and he wrestled with it, trying to throw it off, until he realised that it was moving. Someone was holding him down. He had been caught.

CHAPTER FIVE

A voice hissed in Sam's ear.

'Stop struggling you bloody fool. You'll get us both killed.'

Sam squirmed and wrestled himself onto his back. Immediately a slim but strong arm pressed itself across his neck and Sam felt a horrible pressure on his windpipe. He couldn't even swallow. He stopped his struggle and gave up finally looking up at the man sitting astride him, his face pressed close to his own. Sam couldn't see much. It was still dark and they were under trees and bushes where little moonlight penetrated.

'That's better.' whispered the voice, 'What in Rivenrok did you think you were going to be able to do?' The pressure on his neck eased slightly and Sam took a gasping breath.

'Geroff me.' he managed, the effect of the smoke and the assault making his throat feel like it was lined with sandpaper and filled with golf-balls.

The figure astride him leant back, taking his forearm off Sam's neck completely. For the first time Sam was able to get a good look at him as the man leant back into a patch of moonlight. His attacker was younger than he had presumed, perhaps only a couple of years older than Sam himself. His blonde hair fell across his eyes in a way that Sam had never managed with his own. He was lean and strong, toned muscles evident under a close fitting shirt. Sam had a brief flash of *deja vu*. This person was familiar in some way that he couldn't place. As he tried to grab at the thought it moved away like smoke in the wind.

The young man was watching the shadows, his attention elsewhere. He seemed to have forgotten Sam entirely. Then without warning he swung a leg over Sam's chest, almost catching him in the face. Sam flinched knocking the back of his head on the hard floor. The young man stood up, and moved stealthily into the shadow of a tree where he peered into the darkness in the direction that Sam had been running.

Sam rubbed at his throat. 'Who are you?' he croaked. He had been intending to continue his pursuit but this new figure had taken the wind from his sails and although he felt irritated by the newcomer his desire to catch three dangerous men and take them on single-handedly was being quickly overtaken by common-sense.

The figure didn't even turn to acknowledge Sam's question.

'I said, who are you?' asked Sam more crossly.

'Keep the noise down.' the youth whispered, finally looking around but only for a moment. 'Name's Hadan.'

'Why did you stop me?' Sam allowed the anger to remain in his voice.

'I stopped you because you were about to get yourself killed. The Riven want you dead. But I don't think you want to die just yet, do you Sam?'

'How did you know my name is Sam, and ... wait a minute, someone, someone wants me dead? What's going on?'

'You're lucky to be alive', said Hadan, 'I should have
realised that you were in danger tonight. I could have got
you out sooner. I'll tell you more, but you have to come
with me. Weewalk will want to meet you and its not safe
here. We should have come back for you earlier, after
Ferus followed you into the woods.'

'Who?' Sam shook his head. 'Look, it doesn't matter. I
should go back and check on Valerie. Thanks to you I'll
never catch those men. I'll need to go and talk to the
police.' He wanted to get away. This Hadan person was
clearly odd and probably dangerous.

'I wouldn't recommend going back.' said Hadan,
finally turning to give Sam his full attention, 'As soon as
they realise you survived that fire they'll be back to finish
you off and next time they might not bother trying to
make it look like an accident. You want to make sure no-
one else gets hurt, you'd better stay away from them.
Everything changes tonight. We've got places to go, you
and me.' Hadan smirked 'Nice shoes by the way!'

Sam looked at the pink fluffy slippers that he was still
wearing and then to the column of smoke above the trees,
lit orange by the fire underneath. Blue lights flashed in
the darkness, just visible between the trees, and there
were faint calls and shouts from those who battled the
flames.

'What are you talking about? Who are *they?*' said Sam
feeling cross again. He had been so full off rage and had
been determined to catch the men who had struck Valerie
but this person had completely pulled the rug from under
his feet and Sam felt disorientated and frustrated and not
a little frightened. But what could he have done? He
couldn't fight one boy roughly his own age, let alone
three men. He shook his head; his mind was unable to
process everything that had happened. He clambered to

his feet, feeling a little shaky.

'Come with me' said Hadan and he began to cross the road towards the woods, looking carefully towards the way where the figures in black had gone. 'It's important.'

Sam stood for a moment, stunned by everything that had just happened. Everything he owned was gone.

'I can't just follow you. I can't just leave the scene of a fire.' Sam turned back towards the fire, which was just visible in the darkness and began to jog back towards the remains of his house.

Hadan swore and called after him 'Sam, come back. I need to tell you why you're in danger.' but Sam continued through the trees. He looked back once but by then the road behind him was empty. If the strange young man had ever been there, he had completely vanished.

Sam opened his eyes and winced as he swallowed. His throat was still raw. The paramedics had said that he would be feeling the effects of the smoke for some time. If it hadn't been for the pain in his neck and the way his entire body, and especially his head, ached then he might have thought it had all been some terrible nightmare. But here he was in Valerie's house. He had never reached his own home, or what was left of it. He had run across a policeman as he was jogging back through the trees and he had been ushered into an ambulance that was waiting well away from where the firemen were losing the battle to bring the flames under control. After the cut on his head had been cleaned and the ambulance staff had reassured themselves that a trip to hospital wasn't needed, they had let him go into Valerie's house where the policeman had questioned him at length about the night's events. Sam had told him everything, even about the strange young man Hadan, although he wasn't entirely sure that his conversation with the youth had actually taken place.

Eventually, satisfied that he wasn't going to do anything stupid, Sam had been ushered up to bed by Valerie. He had only slept for a few hours but now it all seemed distant, like the fire had taken place in some other reality.

Sam sat on the bed in Valerie's spare room for a few minutes, checking his various injuries. He had some particularly impressive scratches along one arm to add to the scabbed cut above his eye. Then he pulled on the dressing gown that had been given to him last night and he walked gingerly down the stairs. At the bottom Valerie appeared and threw her arms around him.

'Oh Sam, I was so worried about you.'

Sam returned the embrace a little awkwardly.

'I'm just glad that you weren't hurt too badly by those men I saw behind you.' he said. 'Who were they?'

'I have no idea. Perhaps they're people that your grandfather was involved with in some way. Perhaps he owed them money or something. The police said to keep an eye out and that we should report anything suspicious.'

Sam looked at the floor. 'I need to go and see the house.'

'There's no point, Sam. There's nothing left. Nothing to see. I'm so sorry.' Valerie began to cry.

'Even so, I need to look for myself.'

'Sam, I can't stop you but please don't try to go too close. It's not safe. I've washed and dried your clothes as best I could whilst you were asleep. We'll have to buy more. I think there are some old trainers by the back door which might fit you.'

Once he was dressed Sam stepped out onto the street. It was colder today and a steady rain was falling, a hundred thousand concentric circles at his feet. He pulled a scarf from his rucksack. The contents of that bag were the only things he had managed to save from the fire. Everything else was gone. He took a deep breath. The faint smell of smoke still seemed to hang in the air. He started walking along the pavement, parallel to the woods when he heard a noise. It sounded as though someone had opened a bottle of fizzy drink. He looked around trying to see where it had come from. The noise came again. *Hissss.* Looking to the woods Sam saw a face looking at him from within some undergrowth. As soon as he looked the face disappeared.

Curious, he stepped off the pavement and towards the woods. As he neared the thick bushes he heard a low voice.

'Don't go back. It's not safe.'

'Who's there?' Sam asked, trying to peer into the bushes. 'Who are you?'

'Come with me. Quick. Quick. They're coming!'

The bushes rustled and moved but still Sam could not see the source of the agitated voice but such was the urgency in the voice that he squeezed through a gap and entered the woods. He just had time to see someone moving away from him through the thick leaves.

'Hey!' called Sam 'Come back!' and he hurried to catch up. He saw snatches of someone here and there, someone short he thought, wearing yellow but he could see no more. Then, as Sam crashed through some branches, he almost fell into a small clearing and finally, there, he saw who he had been chasing.

For the first time Sam was able to get a good look at the man, if he could properly be called a man. Large round eyes peered out from a hairy face, a bushy reddish-brown beard covered most of the features below straight and sleek brown hair. A bulbous nose protruded above the bushy moustache. But the thing that took Sam most by surprise was the man's size. He was tiny, less than four feet tall, but stocky, slightly hunched and with large hands. He wore an extremely odd assortment of clothes, the most noteworthy of which was a yellow, tattered and dirty child-sized dress which showed knobbly knees briefly before they disappeared into large, creased and rather muddy and battered leather boots.

'Who are you?' Sam said trying not to stare too hard. He had always been taught not to embarrass people who were different, his grandfather had been very clear about that. And now Sam looked more closely this person looked similar to his grandfather's carvings. Very similar. There was a carving in the centre of the mantelpiece in the lounge that looked very much like this small man. That piece of wood would now be nothing more than ashes. Sam felt a sadness crash over him. The small man smiled a large and friendly grin showing white teeth.

'Keep the noise down.' he whispered looking around. 'Name's Weewalk.' He bowed. 'Weewalk Pukwudgie at your service. I believe you met my friend Hadan here last night?'

Sam remained silent.

'Look, we need to get you away from here. The fire last night was no accident. Hadan and I can protect you. We *need* to protect you.'

The little man looked at Sam carefully. Underneath his bushy beard his mouth twitched and he opened it to say something else. Then he closed it again and chewed his lip briefly before giving a huge sigh.

'Please,' he said 'I need to get you away from here. At least come with me so that I can show you something. Please, follow me.' and he stumped between the trees opposite, deeper into the woods. Sam hesitated for a moment and then followed, visions of his grandfather's craftsmanship echoing in his mind's eye.

They passed beneath the dark wet trees, Weewalk easily moving between the dripping limbs and branches that poked Sam as he tried to keep up. Weewalk seemed to whisper to himself as he moved, occasionally looking back and fixing Sam with a stare from those big eyes. Sam had never seen such a strange person. He had met someone with dwarfism before. His grandfather had had a friend who was less than four feet tall. She had even appeared in films because of her height. But Weewalk was something else entirely. He was less in proportion somehow. And why on earth was he wearing a grubby and tattered yellow spotted dress? Sam was burning with questions but he kept his distance from Weewalk and moved cautiously, ready to bolt back the way he had come if he sensed danger. As they walked Sam realised that they were heading towards the haunted tunnels which he was usually so keen to avoid. Suddenly doubtful he whispered urgently at Weewalk's small but broad back.

'Hey, where are we going?'

Weewalk looked over his shoulder. 'Dragsholm eventually. We have a hidden safe house there.' he said. 'We're best away from here.'

None the wiser, Sam continued to follow at what he judged was a safe distance.

They arrived at the building that housed the entrance to the tunnels and Weewalk ducked through a hole in the brickwork.

Sam hesitated. 'I don't think we should go in there.' he called.

Weewalk stuck his head back through the hole 'Why not?'

'It's sealed off for a reason. They don't lead anywhere.'

'Oh, don't they? You seem pretty sure of that. You can get all the way to the London Underground if you know the way. They were connected during a huge war.'

Sam sighed, 'I have a friend who went in and he said that he heard things, further down. Strange noises. Bangs and thumps from places where there shouldn't have been any noises. And he saw, he thought he saw a ghost.'

'And do you believe him? Do you believe in ghosts?'

'Sort of.' said Sam carefully 'It's complicated. I mean I'm not sure but my house was pretty strange at times. Bumps and noises at night, cold patches, that sort of thing. I'm not saying it was ghosts, perhaps there's a more scientific explanation but there is, was, definitely something odd about it. These tunnels must run pretty close underneath it.'

'Well.' said Weewalk with a laugh 'I promise you have nothing to fear in here. And perhaps I can shed some light on your hauntings.'

Sam had to squeeze through on his stomach. The cold empty room beyond was pitch black but a match sparked into life before him and he saw Weewalk had produced a candle which he lit quickly and raised above his head.

'This way.' he said, and walked through a doorway, over pale grey dust and rubble into another room. This room was just as bare as the first. There were no windows and only one other doorway. The one opposite that which they had just entered led to a passageway and then down a slope and into even greater darkness. The light of the candle could not penetrate it.

'Sit here a minute.' said Weewalk 'I think we need to discuss a few things before we go any further. It's going to get a little... strange down there.'

'It's already pretty bloody strange up here.' said Sam ruefully. 'Who are you? Why did you bring me here?'

'Please sit.' said the little man.

They sat with their backs against one wall. Sam was horribly aware of the gaping mouth of the tunnels to the side of him. Deathly cold air seemed to leak from the doorway like the breath of some malevolent phantom and he pulled his scarf more closely around his neck. Every now and then a sound seemed to echo up from the depths, indistinct clunks and ticks. Once Sam thought he heard a sad moan escape the maw of the open doorway, but it could have been his imagination. He strained his hearing but did not hear the sound again, although he felt no less comfortable to be near the door for all that.

Weewalk dripped a little wax from the candle into the well of a crumbling red housebrick and set the rest of the candle into it, placing the brick on the floor where the candle guttered and spat in the cold wind.

'So, Sam.' he said 'Where shall we start? What do you know?'

'I don't know anything other than three men tried to kill me by burning down my house.'

'Not men.' said Weewalk 'They're no more men that I am, although the heavy looking one, Ferus, might have been one once. The other two were yeren. So, you have no idea why they wanted to kill you?' He scratched his beard. 'You said that you believe in ghosts?'

'What's that got to do with anything? Why me? What do these people want? I haven't done anything wrong!'

'Tell me. Ever sense anything strange? Been on your own at night and felt like there's been someone else there? A presence? Ever seen a misty figure walk through a wall? Glowing orbs passed your face but when you focus there's nothing there? Things moving on their own? Heard funny sounds in the darkness?'

'I can hear them now.' said Sam shooting a look at the entrance to the tunnels.

'Can you?' said Weewalk with a small smile, also looking at the doorway 'Very interesting. And what do you think it is? Making those noises?'

'Ghosts.' said Sam softly 'Spirits of the dead. Echoes of those who have died.'

He felt strangely keen to talk about this now. Having lived his entire life in a house which he was sure was possessed he wanted to know more, however scary it was. His grandfather had always dismissed his questions and he hadn't felt comfortable discussing it with anyone else. This Weewalk, whoever he was, seemed to know something. Right now Sam just wanted some kind of theory that he was not completely mental. That thought stuck him suddenly. Was he even awake? It had been the most bizarre night. He had heard of grief affecting people in funny ways. Was he still in his bed at home? He surreptitiously pinched his arm not sure whether the ensuing pain was good or not.

Weewalk must have noticed for he said 'Don't worry, you're awake. You can pinch me if you like.' His face softened then 'This must all seem very strange. Okay, I'll tell you some things, but I can't guarantee that this is going to make your life any more straightforward. Perhaps I should show you something first. Something very very few people have ever seen.'

He produced a long stemmed pipe from a pocket somewhere under the grubby yellow dress.

Sam laughed and Weewalk raised an eyebrow.

'Just wait.' The small man lit the pipe and took a couple of deep puffs until there was a small cloud of smoke above his head. 'Now, watch.'

Weewalk closed his eyes and seemed to go into some kind of trance. In the flickering candlelight Sam was astonished to see the smoke move in a way that was unnatural. Where the grey blue smoke should be dissipating it had become immobile and then as Sam watched, his mouth open, it began to take shape until an insubstantial figure, a ghostly torso, hovered above their heads. Sam pushed himself to his feet and began to back away, terrified, his eyes fixed on the thing before him. Weewalk opened one eye and looked at Sam from under a bushy eyebrow then he gave his head a quick shake and the smoke seemed to revert to normal as it disappeared into the cold dark air.

'Sam, come back and sit down. You have nothing to fear.' said Weewalk as he tapped out his pipe and put it away.

Sam stumbled and put one hand on the wall, still open-mouthed and staring at the air where the figure had disappeared. 'What, what was that?'

'An illusion of sorts, nothing more. Nothing that can harm you. There are places Sam, where we don't want men to go. So, we scare them off. Here, come sit down and I'll explain.'

Sam took a deep breath and wobbled back to Weewalk and sat down again, his knees drawn up to his chest. Once his heart rate had returned to something approaching normal he gave a weak nod and the little man began to talk.

'Your world, this place in which you live, is not the only world. There is another and it lies alongside your own. Our worlds, yours and mine, rub against each other, causing friction. This causes strange things to happen, things which people in your world do not understand and have tried, over the years, to explain without success. Ever walked into a place and it felt odd? A sudden change in temperature? A charge in the air that causes the hairs on the back of your neck to rise? That's where the worlds are close and are pressed against each other, rubbing, causing the friction. Electricity. Static. It can even cause metallic objects to move or shift.'

Sam looked up 'All the cutlery on the table moved the other day when no-one was there!'

Weewalk nodded. 'Occasionally, but only rarely, the worlds are pressed so tightly together that it is possible to cross between them. These doorways, lines we call them, are dotted around the place. Sometimes when we need to use them we have to scare men away from them so we can come and go. Because these places already feel cold and strange to many of your people it takes little effort from us, a noise here, some smoke there, to chase you off.'

Weewalk turned to face Sam and fixed him with a hard stare, 'Sam, it is not ghosts you must fear. They are but a trick. It is those who shape the ghosts and cross the paths where the barrier between worlds is thin that you must beware. There are many lands in my world and many different peoples but one group, people from the land of Rivenrok, are coming to kill you and your kind. People have been disappearing. The Riven have been taking some and killing others. They seem to be very keen to get to you.'

Suddenly they heard a noise from the direction of the woods, where they had entered the building. The '*kerlok*' noise of a rock moving under foot. Weewalk stiffened and held his breath. Sam, seeing the fear in the little man's face, did the same. They both heard a quiet voice, coming closer, but could not hear what it said. As it neared a sense of dread settled into Sam's stomach and deepened. Weewalk put his lips to Sam's ear.

'Come with me. These people will kill you or worse.'

Sam nodded, suddenly fearful. Everything that the little man had said had been utterly incredible but what Sam did feel sure of was that the fire had been no accident and now he could feel a palpable sense of malevolence coming from the direction of that voice. He stood as quietly as he could and snapped the candle from his makeshift stand, spilling warm wax down his fist. It began to gutter more wildly as he lifted it. He stood in the middle of the room. He looked at Weewalk and the sloping tunnel behind him. He swallowed a lump in his throat and then followed Weewalk down into the darkness.

CHAPTER SIX

The tunnel sloped steadily down, a concrete and brick shaft into the cold earth. Blackness had enveloped them almost as soon as they had entered, pressing in around them. The flickering candle seemed to have little effect. They had been walking for several minutes before the oppressiveness of the room behind them seemed to ebb away. After a short while doorways began to appear to either side but the candlelight did not penetrate far. Sam stopped to look in one, feeling braver in the darkness than he expected thanks to Weewalk's presence. The room was almost entirely empty except for a very old looking machine in one corner and a bundle of faded newspapers and battered cardboard boxes in another. Weewalk did not wait for Sam to look and so he had to hurry to catch him up again. The little man seemed perfectly able to navigate without the light of the guttering candle that Sam carried.

As they walked into the depths of the earth, Sam became aware of a hum ahead of them. It was a sound that he couldn't quite focus upon. Unsure of the source

Sam turned his head but couldn't locate it. He had a friend who lived well outside the village near one of the giant electrical pylons which towered over the surrounding fields. The noise was something like that made by the current in the cables but with a slight ring to it, like distant bells. A thousand questions flooded Sam's mind. He wasn't sure what to believe. Here in the darkness, by candlelight, walking behind this strange little man with noises swirling up from the depths of the inky blackness, Sam could almost believe the story he had been told. That there was another world. There was no doubting that the last twenty-four hours had been bizarre. He risked a whisper.

'Where are we going?'

Weewalk whispered back over his shoulder 'There is a line down here, one of the passageways I mentioned to another place, Dragsholm, far from here. We'll be safer then.'

'Are you from the other world?' Sam asked

'Yes,' said Weewalk 'I am a kobold.'

'A what?'

'A kobold.' repeated Weewalk. 'A mine kobold to be exact. My people used to work in the depths of the ground in Mu harvesting valuable minerals. Some of us have travelled to your world before, in the past. There are entrances to our world to be found deep underground and sometimes your people would hear us mining and knocking at the rock. I think we gave rise to your myths about goblins, dwarves and something called tommyknockers. As well as mine kobold there are house and water kobold. Each tribe prefers to live in different places. I'm more of an underground kind of person.'

They continued in silence for a long time as Sam tried to decide the best question to ask next. More than once he considered running back. What on earth was he doing here? Eventually the tunnel no longer sloped down but continued straight ahead.

'Nearly there.' said Weewalk, making Sam jump at the sudden sound. Weewalk pulled out what looked like an old compass and studied it. Peering over his shoulder Sam could see that the needle was swinging wildly. They turned a corner and entered a room. A large metal door stood in front of them, slate grey paint peeling away from deep red rust. In the centre was a large lever. Reaching above him Weewalk pulled the lever sideways. The squeak of metal friction filled the air and echoed back up the tunnel making them both wince. Weewalk tugged and the door swung towards them with another squeal. They stepped through into another room. There was more machinery here. It looked to Sam like the equipment that appeared in submarines in the old war films his grandfather had sometimes watched. Weewalk moved on into a side room. The hum was more distinct here, not louder necessarily, but more noticeable. It still remained maddeningly elusive and made Sam want to rub his ears like a dog bothered by a high pitched sound. At the same time Sam felt cold breath flow onto him and the hairs on the back of his neck rose.

'Here we are.' said Weewalk studying the compass again and with a swing of his arm he indicated a patch of shadow in a corner that was perhaps even darker than the rest of the room. Sam held up the candle but no light entered that area. Indeed, it seemed to suck at the candlelight, drawing it in hungrily.

'This is a door?' asked Sam

'Precisely,' said Weewalk 'Unfocus your eyes, what do you see?'

Sam allowed his vision to blur, and jumped as something pale floated past his nose. He looked around him, but there was nothing there. Blurring his eyes again

Sam realised he could see several small orbs floating around the space where Weewalk had indicated, like dust motes catching the light. They seemed to be drawn to a particular patch of wall, and floated in and through it.

'Now,' said Weewalk 'you see it, right?'

'Yes, I think so.' said Sam.

Weewalk began to move his hands. 'Then step back a moment.' he said turning to the area with the orbs.

Sam took several cautious steps backwards to lean against a dusty wall, and then he thought of spiders and stepped forwards again, his hand anxiously brushing his hair, trying to look relaxed.

Weewalk tensed. His arms ahead of him, palms outstretched. He looked as though he were lifting a great weight. His arms began to shake with the effort and his shoulders hunched though Sam could see no visible sign that he was holding anything. A sudden breeze entered the room buffeting Sam's face. He felt the hair stand up on the back of his neck again. The candle guttered and died, plunging the room into darkness. Sam immediately had the impression that someone or something else was with them and he struggled to hold his nerve. He might have run if he could have been able to see anything but the darkness was absolute. Then there was a tiny blue flash and Sam had a sudden strobe-light split-second vision of the room. Weewalk stood before a round and black hole in the wall. The lightning had seemed to flash on his fingers. He was still hunched over with the effort. Then the room was black again.

Weewalk gave a heavy breath. 'Right,' he said, 'It's open. Ready to take your first line? Move towards my voice.'

Sam slid his feet forward, arms outstretched until he felt his fingertips touch something.

'Good, that's me.' came Weewalk's voice. 'Now, on

you go. This is going to feel weird, but don't worry you're safe and I'll be right behind you.'

Sam felt Weewalk's hands on his arm and allowed himself to be guided forwards. 'Wait, I'm not sure about this.' he said. Then the hand was at his back, then it was gone and Sam, arms outstretched, shuffled forwards feeling the air suddenly grow cold again. He stepped to where he thought the wall must be and then the world seemed to implode upon him.

He was deaf and blind he thought. It felt like his ears had disappeared completely and he couldn't tell whether his eyes were open or closed. One moment he felt as though he was falling, not to the floor but away from it, then the next he felt as though he was flying. He was disembodied, not part of the world, then he suddenly found gravity beginning to exert itself on him again and, without feeling any kind of impact, there was ground under his feet. He staggered forward a step unsteadily. His vision quickly returned and he found himself standing under a large tree near a wild and remote shore. The whole thing had taken moments or years. It was impossible to tell which. He stumbled against Weewalk who had appeared behind him.

'Where are we? What happened?' he shouted in panic.

'It's okay, don't worry.' said Weewalk. 'You're safe. There's nothing to worry about'.

Sam felt his body, slapping at it like he was trying to find something in a pocket, reassuring himself that his body was still there.

'Really. It's okay. Don't worry.' said Weewalk again.

'But, but...' Sam didn't know what else to say. He looked around feeling panicky. How would he ever get back again? He felt his legs shaking and he sat down heavily.

'It's alright. You're safe.' said Weewalk standing over him. 'Everyone finds it strange the first few times. But I'll look after you. Come on, let's get you indoors.' He set off, his big boots leaving darker green footprints in the dewy grass. Sam hauled himself to his feet, still feeling shaky, his heart hammering in his chest, but he followed.

Weewalk headed towards a rough shack ahead of them. As they walked Sam had the time to look around him and absorb his surroundings. They had arrived on a section of deserted coastline. A few stunted trees and the shack were all that broke that horizon. The smell of salt filled the air. It was cold, the wind cut through Sam's clothes and he shivered. The light suggested that the dawn had not long arrived. The sky was overcast, a flat light grey. The crash of waves hitting the long narrow yellow sand of the beach dominated the air.

Sam took a deep breath. Despite the coldness of the air it was good to have the freshness of the salty breeze around him.

'Hadan is waiting for us in the shack ahead' said Weewalk, above the rhythmic roar of the waves.

'Is he from your world too?' asked Sam.

'Yes, but it's probably best not to ask him about it. He doesn't have particularly fond memories of Mu and Rivenrok and he can be a little prickly about it. Don't mind him though. It's just his way. He's one of the good guys.'

'Like you, you mean?' said Sam.

'Yes,' Weewalk laughed 'Like me. Don't worry, Sam. You're safe with us.'

As they reached the shack Sam saw it was bigger than he had first thought. The absence of anything with which to compare it in the flat featureless landscape had made size difficult to judge. It was made of rough wooden planks, a stone chimney at one end billowed smoke.

Weewalk thumped on the door and a voice came from within.

'Who's there?'

'Me', said Weewalk and glanced at Sam as he shivered next to him, 'With our friend.'

There was the sound of a bolt drawing back before the door opened to reveal Hadan. He glared at Sam.

'Decided to listen to us now have you?'

'Why'd you bolt the door?' asked Weewalk quickly.

'Thought I heard a ropen on the roof.' said Hadan 'Turned out to be a gull, but doesn't hurt to be too careful.'

Weewalk laughed 'It's not like you to be so careful.'

Hadan simply huffed and turned away into the shack so that they could enter.

Ferus sat back in the chair watching the two slaves fight. They had started slowly at first, each man unwilling to hurt or be hurt but the incentives that had been added to the pit had soon overcome their wariness as well as their weariness. Ferus turned to the man next to him and laughed.

'See, now they're fighting! It's amazing what men will do when their life depends upon it.'

The man next to him merely raised an eyebrow a little higher above his hooked nose and continued to watch the bloodied men, expressionless.

A messenger jogged into the room and whispered into the man's ear before hurrying away.

'What is it?' said Ferus irritably.

The man looked uncomfortable. 'Master Ferus. I'm afraid I have some, ah, some bad news. I am sorry, but the boy escaped the fire.'

Ferus gave an angry snarl and the light in the room seemed to darken momentarily causing others to cower.

'How did he get away? This is an embarrassment. Nobody ever lives. People will begin to think that he is the one from the prophecy. The King must not hear of this. Do you know where the boy is?'

'Yes, master. He travels with one of the kobold. One who has some lesser presence.'

'See if you can find him and then send one of your garoul to keep them busy, and make sure that the job gets done. I think it is time for me to collect some secrets. I need to know more about this boy.'

Ferus looked at the back of the man before him with disdain. The other patrons of the inn shifted nervously, desperate to leave but anxious not to move and draw attention to themselves. The room was silent and no-one stirred. Even the innkeeper had frozen, halfway through cleaning a tankard with a grubby cloth.

'The mighty Tarak Everune.' Ferus sneered as he approached the man on the stool, slumped at the bar. 'Secret keeper and hero. Now fat, cowardly and drunk. I remember when not even the greatest of us could have tracked you down or lured you out and now here you are.'

'Whatd'ya want Cinders?' coughed the man, not turning to look at him 'Use that fire magic of yours to light me a pipe or leave me be.'

The room seemed to darken and grow cold as Ferus balled his fists. Everyone else seemed to take this as a cue to leave and they all moved at once, tripping over and knocking chairs in their haste to leave. The innkeeper simply dropped to the floor and rolled under the bar. Ferus walked the last three steps to the man on the stool. Grabbing a handful of long, lank greying hair he pulled the man's head back and smashed his face into the puddle of spilled ale on the counter. The man's head bounced off the wood and he flew backwards. He landed in a heap on the floor, blinking up into Ferus' face.

Ferus wiped his hand on his black robe before bending down and cracking the man a vicious blow across the face. It was satisfying to be able to use open violence rather than the creeping around he had had to do with the boy. Here he didn't care that his arrival would be talked about.

The inside of the inn made him feel sick. It was places like these where men would plot against the Riven, to discuss rebellion. He felt dirtied by it. He struck the man again.

'Presence is all very well, but sometimes it's just more satisfying to use more conventional violence, don't you think Tarak? When did you lose your presence? Was it when your wife died? Or have you killed it with drink?'

Tarak just lay on his back, blood running from his nose, in a line over his cheek.

Ferus turned away and began to walk to the door. 'I've finally come for the secret you keep. You're coming with me' he said over his shoulder and Tarak's body stiffened before sliding along the floor after Ferus as though pulled by an invisible rope.

After they had left the innkeeper crept from behind the bar and shook his head at the empty room.

How had it come to this? he thought to himself. The one person that they had thought might be able to save them all, now nothing more than an overweight drunk. But it was worse than that. They had hoped that Ferus and the Riven King wouldn't think the secret keeper worth their attention once Tarak had turned to drink, but in a way it was inevitable that they would come for him. That man held many secrets. Why wouldn't the Riven King want them? The only surprise was that it had taken this long. The innkeeper shook his head again and let out a breath. Still, at least Ferus had left the inn standing. He supposed he should feel lucky.

It was then that the first ball of fire smashed through the window, then another and another. The fourth hit the innkeeper in the chest, taking him off his feet and smashing him into a wall. Within moments the place was in ruins but the innkeeper was not conscious when the burning roof collapsed upon him.

A fire was crackling in the grate. A pot above it emitted a warm and delicious smell and Sam felt his stomach grumble and his mouth begin to water.

'I'd clean up first', said Weewalk, following Sam's gaze. He gestured towards a large wooden bowl before a mirror. Sam walked over to it, slipped his rucksack from his shoulders and pulled off his jumper. The bowl was full of water. Looking in the mirror he saw that dusty smudges covered his face and there were cobwebs on his clothes from the escape through the tunnels. He thought back to the feeling of malevolence he had felt in that dark room and a shiver ran up his spine.

He dipped his hands into the water and scrubbed at his face, feeling it tingle and realising the water was salty, the tang of it on his lips. He rubbed at the scab on his forehead more gingerly, feeling the lump there too. He winced as the salt water stung the wound. The water before him turned dirty and he looked again at his reflection. Rinsing his hands and shaking them dry as best he could he went and sat at a table to one side, pulling at the wet ring of his t-shirt at his neck before pulling his jumper back on and pulling back his sleeves.

Weewalk set a wooden bowl of what looked and smelled like apple porridge before him, with a cup of cool fresh water. Sam nodded his thanks, his mouth already full of porridge.

Hadan busied himself with what possessions lay

around the shack putting them into two packs which lay open on a bed.

'How are you feeling?' asked Weewalk.

'Better.' said Sam 'Thank you for looking after me. I don't know what to do now. Everything is different. I've never felt anything like what we felt back in those tunnels. Such... evil.'

Weewalk clambered up onto a chair opposite Sam. 'Ferus is one of the worst you'll ever come across. With some luck it will be a while before it is realised that you survived the fire.'

Hadan came over too and sat to one side of the table, studying Sam with a hard gaze.

'I've got a question Weewalk,' he said, 'What are we going to do with him? We can't keep trying to hide people from Ferus. If he's as important as the Riven believe then they'll come looking for him.'

Weewalk sighed.

'Why did you help me? Why come to get me away?' asked Sam.

'Well, we're looking for someone. And we try to save people who are threatened by the Riven.' said Weewalk. 'I don't think it's safe for you to go back. No-one will believe whatever you have to say and your police certainly won't be too impressed by a story about an arsonist who can move between worlds.'

'Where are all the other people who you've saved?' asked Sam.

'Ummm, we haven't actually managed to save anyone yet. We nearly did. Once. But, anyway. you're here now. The longer you evade the Riven the more interesting you'll become to them. They'll think you're special. We'll have to find somewhere safe for you to stay while we work out what to do. We don't live here.' He gestured to the shack. 'We don't really live anywhere, although we have stayed here on occasion. We tend to move from place to place making a nuisance of ourselves as much as we can. At the moment we're just trying to find a way back to our world. The lines between worlds have always been very rare and usually fixed in position. But recently we have noticed that they are becoming more numerous, perhaps as our worlds rub more closely against one another. Strange things have been happening and the paths, the lines, have been shifting.'

Weewalk looked at Hadan who glanced up from where he was carving a series of numbers in the wood of the table with the point of a knife.

'We're concerned about what it means for the future. At the moment we can't find the right line.' Hadan said.

'At some point I'll tell you a little more about the history of our world, Mu.' said Weewalk 'and then you'll understand. We are the resistance. There are a few others, here and there, but there's not many of us left. Staying with us is far from safe. Over the last few hundred years a dark power has grown in our world and its actions threaten us all. The Riven. They're cruel and powerful and getting stronger. The Riven King has gone to great lengths to destroy rebels like us. He came once to my home. He killed my family, my friends. He led a band of Riven who all but wiped out the kobolds that day. I've made it my mission to protect others, where I can, to stop them going through what I went through. Only I haven't been doing very well so far.' He turned to Hadan with a sigh. 'I wonder whether we should consult someone else, like Tarak perhaps?'

'That old drunk.' snorted Hadan. 'He's useless.' He slammed his knife into the table making Sam's bowl jump 'Tarak Everune is a drunk and a traitor. He's lost his presence. He's finished.'

'The Riven King, is that Ferus?' asked Sam.

'No,' said Weewalk. 'The Riven King is much more powerful than Ferus, though Ferus is powerful enough. The King hasn't left the Rivenrok Complex, his palace, in many years. Ferus is one of his most important deputies, sent out to do his master's dirty work. That work is mainly hunting down and killing those who have any power that might threaten the King.'

'But why come to get me?' said Sam.

Weewalk now looked at Hadan. 'He could sense a presence.' he said, gesturing towards Sam. 'Ferus was quite keen to kill him.'

Hadan looked stern 'You're saying he has some ability?'

'It's possible. The signs are there. He could even be the one.' said Weewalk laughing.

'What do you mean?' asked Sam, 'What ability?'

Weewalk looked at Sam carefully for a moment.

'What do you believe is possible Sam? Do you believe that people can move things with their minds?' He stretched his fingers towards the table and Sam jumped backwards, almost falling off his chair, as his porridge spoon rose out of the bowl before him and hung in mid-air. Then it dropped back with a thunk.

'Telekinesis, in your language. But we call it presence.' said Weewalk

'How?' said Sam 'But that's magic.'

Hadan snorted 'There's no such thing as magic. Only children believe in magic tricks. Magic is simply a word to describe events which haven't been properly described by your science yet. Your people used to think fire was magic. This is no different.'

'I think you have some of this power within you.' said Weewalk 'Often it's awakened when someone who has the potential for it goes through some massive trauma like when their life is in danger or sometimes it occurs when somebody goes through some great emotion, such as when a loved one dies.' Weewalk gave Sam a hard look. 'Ever heard of women who are suddenly able to lift great weights after an accident to save a trapped child? They could never do that in an ordinary situation. It's like a beacon when the presence gets released. Drawing the Riven in.'

Sam rubbed at his arm as he often did when he was nervous. He remembered only too well when he had found his grandfather's body. Weewalk noticed the puckered line that ran along Sam's finger.

'Nice scar.' he said 'Where'd you get it?'

'Oh, I got it when I was a baby.' said Sam looking sad, 'My parents and I were in a car accident. They died, but somehow I survived. The police couldn't work out how I lived. They couldn't even work out what caused the crash. It's a mystery. I must have been thrown from the wreckage because the entire car went up in flames. They said there was nothing left. I was found lying by the side of the road. They didn't even see me at first. The only injury I had was this burn. He held up his arm and pulled the sleeve of his jumper further up for them to see the scarlet third finger and the pink snake that wound up his forearm.

Sam looked down to see Weewalk staring at his arm curiously.

'What?' he asked 'It's not that bad!'

'Oh,' Weewalk said 'Sorry, it's just...'

'Weewalk, you look like you've seen a ghost.' said Sam.

Weewalk seemed to recover himself and smiled 'I'm sorry, it's nothing. It's just, well you say its a mystery but we've found that few things happen without reason. But, please forget it. Here I'll show you some of my scars. I got this one from a fight with a huge garoul, almost ripped me in half!' he said, and began to pull up the hem of his spotted dress.

'Urgh!' said Sam 'Please, it's fine. I don't need to see that.'

At that moment there was a clatter on the roof and they all looked up. Hadan dashed to the door, opened it a crack and looked out.

'Time to go', he cried and slammed and bolted the door and then began throwing the remaining things into bags.

'Sam, grab your things' urged Weewalk and they all dashed to pick up their belongings.

Just then something hit the door with enormous force. The bolt flew into the room as the wood around it splintered. They all stopped. There was a moment of pure silence. They looked at each other, frozen. Then there was an almighty crash and the door was smashed into pieces. Something terrible threw itself into the shack and roared.

CHAPTER SEVEN

Kya sprinted across the open plain, getting ever more distant from the Rivenrok Complex, her feet a blur above the short yellow grass. But she knew she could not run forever, the pounding of heavy feet behind her was getting closer and she could clearly hear ragged breath. She would have to turn and fight.

Despite the pounding of blood in her ears she could hear the line not far away, hear its hum. But, she wouldn't reach it in time. She skidded to a stop, her boots kicking up dust as she span and faced the giant. It lunged immediately, desperate to reach her, its eyes wild, its teeth bared. Kya twisted and placed a foot into the thing's groin, moving onto her back and rolling underneath it so that its own momentum carried it over her. It staggered forward but it quickly turned back to her as Kya pulled her knife from her belt.

She did not have to fight the Sitecah very often. But this one had caught her scent and would not give up. She knew that the giants patrolled this piece of land mercilessly. It was the main reason why the line nearby was used so rarely. But she had been told to come this way. She didn't know whether this Sitecah had simply come across her trail, or whether it had been sent. Someone might have seen her leave. The beast stopped for a second, sizing her up. It was big, easily twelve feet tall. Shaggy red hair covered much of its body. Its small eyes narrowed as it tightened its grip on the large club in its hand.

Kya used her presence and pushed, so that she leapt up, away from the ground and towards the giant, twisting as she did so, spinning inside its flailing arms and slashing with her knife. The monster bellowed in rage and fell back as blood glistened on the red hair covering its chest. But it was barely injured, and certainly not beaten. It threw its head back and roared so loudly that Kya could feel the air move around her.

An answering howl came from behind it and Kya saw what she had been dreading. Three more shapes thundered towards her. She threw her knife into the air ahead of her and, with a movement of her arms, the blade flew towards the face of the nearest Sitecah. She didn't wait to see it land. She turned and ran again, her long dark hair streaming behind her.

She could feel that she was getting closer to the portal she needed to escape. Up ahead she saw an old, squat building appear over the crest of the grassy hill and she turned towards it. That was it! As she neared the building, her legs began to tire and she turned her hands to the ground and used presence to push off the ground so that she moved in huge leaps. She reached what appeared to be an abandoned farmhouse and scrambled onto the porch. Offering a silent prayer she moved a hand across the door, her eyes closed. It was a presence lock, she realised with relief and in a moment there was an audible click. She turned the handle and opened the heavy door. It swung open and she dashed inside, the giants close on her heels. She turned and slammed the door shut, bringing down a large iron bar to seal it. The first Sitecah smashed into the door with a howl of rage, but the door held and Kya scampered away from it and slumped, her back against a wall, grateful that someone had had the sense to build a very, very strong door.

The interior of the house seemed to consist of a single room. Broken furniture lay scattered about. There was no way out visible other than the door through which she had come. Thankfully, she could sense the line was here. Its unique hum emanated from a space inside the fireplace. Although lines were rare, where they did exist it was common for lines to be within houses, and especially fireplaces, in this way. When people found entrances to lines they often built a house around it, keen to keep access for themselves.

She stood, looking around before she used the ethereal door thinking there might be something of use. But there wasn't much to see in the gloom. The windows were heavily shuttered and barred and they allowed little light into the dusty room. Whoever had been brave or mad enough to live within the shadow of the gaze of the Riven King and at the heart of the land of the Sitecah had clearly had the sense to build a strong home. Looking again she could see that much of the interior structure of the building was crafted from metal. This was less a home, more a fortress. On one wall she found several racks which looked as though they had held weapons long ago. They were empty now. Next to the racks she found a cracked mirror hanging from a single nail and she took a moment to study her reflection, pushing her long black hair away from her freckled face. Outside the giants howled and began to throw their weight against the door and she realised it was time to leave. There was nothing of use here.

She turned and tensed allowing power to flow from her hands as she sent her presence into the portal and pulled it open. She tried to gather some sense of what lay on the other side of the door, beyond the dark hole before her, set between the grey stones that formed the chimney. With effort she could almost visualise where she would appear but it was more a suggestion of shapes rather than an actual view. One had to be careful. More than a few people had opened doors that proved to be underwater or underground. She had heard that people in the other world had noticed the strange round sinkholes that appeared when doors were opened carelessly. Kya had been into the other world only a few times, and only fleetingly. She didn't like it much. But, that would come later. Her first destination was Suun-t-Marten. She stepped through allowing the sensation of disembodiment to overwhelm her.

Kya appeared inside some kind of dim and circular hut. She barely had a moment to absorb her surroundings before she found a man standing before her with a spear levelled at her throat.

'Who are you?' the man shouted. 'Riven? Are you Riven?'

'No!' said Kya. Then more gently. 'No, I am a friend.'

The man moved the spear tip back an inch but did not look sure. 'Who are you then?'

'My name is Kya. I have been sent here for the Great Line.'

The man lowered the spear and stepped back in wonder. As he did so he moved into a patch of light and Kya saw with surprise that his skin was completely green.

'It is you. We were told that you would come.' said the green man.

'You were? By who?'

'The Secret Keeper came. He said you would follow one day. I must tell the others. Please, follow me.' He turned and walked towards a door.

For the first time Kya was able to get a proper look at the figure.

His skin was entirely green. His head was shaved bald and he wore a mixture of green and brown clothing of a style that she had never seen before. Around his neck were a number of beaded necklaces and similar trinkets hung from his ears.

As they crossed to the door Kya also looked around at the building. The hut was round, with wooden walls and although simply made it was richly decorated with fabrics and tapestries hanging from the high ceiling. A fire in the centre of the space provided a little light, the smoke moving out through a narrow hole in the roof above it. Kya could see low pieces of furniture that looked like beds around the edge of the round room, interspersed with chests and cabinets. Behind her, an empty doorway, shaped by three large pieces of stone, seemed to indicate where the line hummed behind her. There was a smell of spices in the air and peering into a nearby bowl she could see what looked like a dish of green beans in some sort of broth. It appeared as though she had interrupted a meal.

'I am sorry for the welcome.' said the man over his shoulder. 'We do not see many visitors here and nothing good ever came out of that door. That is why it is guarded. Once a black-robed Riven came through and started killing immediately using presence to tear men apart. Over fifty died before we were able to stop him. To make matters worse we are in mourning as something terrible has just happened here.'

'What?' asked Kya.

The man stopped and turned to face her, with his back to the door. 'Two of our children were playing nearby when they heard a strange sound and they both disappeared. It seems as though a line of some sort opened up and they entered it not realising what it was. Before anyone could stop them the hole had closed again and is gone. It is unlikely that they will ever be found. They will have entered the other world but the chances of them arriving somewhere that is safe are slim. There is a lot of grief in the village. We Green Men have never known the barrier to act in this way before. We are worried that the barrier is being affected by something, or someone. The Great Line to the other world has always been stable, at least for as long as we have protected it. But we have never known another line to just appear near our village before. But I have already said too much. Come, the elders will want to meet you.'

He opened the door and Kya stepped into a world of an eerie light. It was as if the sun was still in the sky but had been hidden somehow, as if during an eclipse. She turned and looked up but could not see the source of the strange light. The noise of crickets filled the warm air as they walked over short grass towards a large group of the green-skinned people. Many were dressed in warrior garb and carried spears but there were women and children too. They were deep in conversation and did not seem to have noticed Kya approach.

Kya had the chance to study the strange new land and saw that behind the hut was a wide body of water, although it could not be water as it glowed with a faint phosphorescence that made it seem brighter than the grass that grew at its edges.

'You've probably never seen anything like this place.' said the green man as they approached the edge of the people. He pointed with an arm. 'In that direction the land is in permanent sun. It's a harsh lifeless place of endless heat, a desert of shifting sands. To the other side the land is in perpetual darkness and it is a place of savage beasts. Little grows there but glowing mushrooms and plants that take their energy from the ground rather than the sun. We Green Men must guard constantly against those borders to keep our families safe. No-one has ever crossed either expanse and returned to tell of it.'

They stopped at the edge of the group and now the people saw Kya and gasped in surprise. They parted for one of the warriors who had been at the centre of the group. This man was clearly quite old and particularly short. As he approached Kya's guide bowed low and Kya followed suit.

"Welcome daughter.' said the man 'We have been expecting your arrival. I am afraid that you reach us at a time of grief and uncertainty. But, I presume you will not wish to delay. Please follow me.'

Kya's guide bowed to her and set off back to his post, but the rest of the village followed her and the elderly man at a distance, whispering to each other.

Kya's guide led her past some more huts toward a small wooded hill. As they approached two round stone columns appeared from between the trees, one at either side of a narrow path. As they passed between the worn pillars the whispering crowd fell back so that Kya and the elderly man continued alone, up the hill. It was not long before they came to a slope that led down and Kya was led along a path to a huge set of metallic doors set into the side of the hill and covered in an elaborate swirling filigree. They stopped before it and Kya looked up at the gates.

'The lock has been designed in such a way that two people with presence are needed' said the green man. 'One person is not enough. I am the only one with presence in my village so therefore I always require a visitor to open this door. Similarly, a single visitor could not open it alone.'

'How many times has it been opened?' asked Kya.

'Once.' said the man. 'Come, place your hand here.'

He indicated a space and Kya pressed her hand against the cold metal. The man did the same in another spot on the other door. Kya sent her mind into the internal workings of the door, feeling the green man do the same. She was amazed to find how complex the inner mechanism was and it took some minutes for them to work the lock open. They worked together, one holding a hidden section apart while the other pulled or pushed at some catch. Then with a final click the lock was open and the doors swung inwards.

A domed brick tunnel led into the darkness of the inside of the hill. The green man produced a flint and had soon lit two torches that sat in a sconce on the wall. Together they walked down the passageway.

It was not long before the tunnel ended and they faced a dark open space. The green man let go of the flaming torch he held and using his presence lifted it out into the darkness. Looking into its light Kya could not see anything beyond but then the flame caught something else and with a whoosh a line of fire suddenly spread around a system of chandeliers that hung overhead and then the room was illuminated.

Before them lay the largest room Kya had ever seen. She could not see the sides or the ends. But that was partly because of the shelves. The room was full of rows upon rows of shelves and each shelf was full of thousands upon thousands of books. They stretched in every direction. Fascinated Kya walked towards the nearest row and touched the spine of the books there carefully. They were written in a language she did not understand. The letters were familiar but the words meant nothing. The first word on the spine of the first book was

'*Philosophiæ*'. Kya puzzled over the last letter. She had never seen that before. She looked to the next book '*Harmonice Mundi*'. Something about harmony perhaps? The green man's voice was startlingly loud in the quiet echoing room.

'A great store of knowledge.' he said. 'But there is something else here besides old books. That which you seek. A Great Line to the other world. Come.'

He led Kya along the centre of the room, down a wide aisle between two enormous racks of books, all the while Kya staring in wonder at the room around her. Eventually they reached a round space from which the rows of books led away like the spokes of a cartwheel.

'Here, the line.' said the man.

Kya could hear it, sense it, humming. The sound seemed to reach her mind without travelling through her ears. She looked around at the books again. How she would have loved to have stayed and searched for secrets amongst them. But time was not her ally. She sent her presence into the line and pulled it open.

She turned then to the green man 'Thank you.' she said.

'You are welcome.' he said 'I hope in happier times you will be able to return from the other world and visit us again.'

Kya smiled and took one last look at the books. 'I hope so too.'

Then she stepped into the Great Line and vanished.

She appeared at the crest of a hill, underneath a cloudy sky and a monument of some kind. A square pillar made from a pale grey stone stretched high above her. Looking at its very top she could see a blue-green dome which sat at the summit like a crown. Around her, in a circle, was a stone wall. She left the circle through a black iron gate and found herself on a grassy plain, not dissimilar to that across which she had so recently been pursued, albeit this seemed to be smaller. Ahead of her, down a steep bank lay a large town. Rows of box-shaped houses ran in long lines in various directions. The Great Line did not seem to have brought her somewhere particularly great, but there was no doubt that she was in the new world. She had been told to find Fort Amhurst, a small castle of some sort which lay nearby. Choosing a direction almost at random she set off.

Aleksy felt a veil lift from his mind like mists evaporating from a pond. It was like waking up slowly, as though his head was being turned on by a dimmer switch, but he hadn't been asleep. He blinked a few times, and tried to think about where he was but he felt extraordinarily tired and it was hard to hold a coherent thought.

He was still in his cell but a vague memory told him that he hadn't been in here recently. As his tired brain began to function more normally dull aches and pains began to filter through and memories of, he concentrated, memories of working with a pickaxe, hacking at rock, each blow sending a painful vibration though his hands and along his body. He looked down at his torso. He was naked to the waist; a sheen of sweat covered a muscular chest underneath patches of dirt and grime. He looked at his body more closely. It was thin but his muscles were bunched under the skin in a way they had not been before. What was going on? How long had he been insensible in this hell that his body should be so changed? He moved a hand to poke at his stomach muscles but as he moved his arm he felt a sting and tightness across his back. Cautiously reaching a hand behind him he gingerly touched his lower back. He could feel rough cuts there and he winced as his fingers explored what he couldn't see. When he brought his hand back before him he could see blood on his fingertips, dark against his pale hand in the dim light. His hands hurt too. Blisters dotted his palms and the soft area at the base of his thumbs was raw and weeping.

With another grimace Aleksy forced himself to his feet. His body felt as though it was made from lead, every movement was an effort. Turning he was startled to see movement. He was not alone in his cell.

A shape, huddled in a corner, began to form itself into a person. It was another man, grimier and thinner than Aleksy but similarly stripped to the waist. Where Aleksy was barefoot this man seemed to have fashioned himself a pair of shoes of sorts from something that looked like old leather and rag. A shaggy beard and long tangled hair made him look mad and wild but when he had forced himself into a sitting position he seemed fairly normal. The man pushed his hair from his eyes and stretched his filthy legs ahead of him in a stretch before crossing them at the ankles and making himself comfortable. He gave Aleksy a careful look as he scratched at his beard.

'It would seem that we are momentarily free of our mental capture. A changing of the guard. Do you speak English?'

Aleksy nodded and putting his hand to his own face was surprised to find a heavy stubble there.

'Excellent. How long have you been here? Do you have any news or messages?'

Aleksy shook his head.

'Come on man, speak. We don't have long before presence robs us of our clarity. Who are you?'

'Aleksy. I, I don't know where I am or how long I've been here. Am I, am I dead? Is this hell?'

'Ah, a new chap, eh?' said the man 'Thought so. Well,

at least it will be good to have someone to talk to I suppose. Alec was it?'

'Alek-see' said Aleksy.

'Alek-see. Hmmm. Well, my name is James Worson, but everyone here calls me Worsen. I can tell you that you are not dead, but, I'm afraid, you are not far wrong when you speak of hell.'

Worsen rose and crossed to the featureless bars and peered out into the gloomy corridor.

'Anyone else awake?' he called.

When there was no answer he turned back to Aleksy. 'Always takes a while for folks to wake up. I'm surprised that you were awake first. You must have a certain mental fortitude. Well, Aleksy, you wish to know what on earth is going on?'

Aleksy nodded.

'Well, the first revelation is that what is going on is not going on on earth, if you follow. We are currently hundreds of metres below a temple called the Rivenrok Complex and we are slaves to its residents. Whatever you were before, you are now a miner. We dig for crystals. Where and when were you captured?'

'London.' said Aleksy 'I was underground.'

Just then several quiet voices floated down the corridor and Worsen turned his attention back to beyond the bars.

'Who's awake?' he called softly.

A series of voices floated back, voicing names. Aleksy heard men and women call out, a mixture of accents. When it was quiet again Worsen called his own name before adding 'and Aleksy, new man.'

He turned to Aleksy again. 'There are usually new names but the old names get shorter. We're missing many people today, or tonight, whatever time it is. It sounds like we're down to a single Stonehenge hippie.' He gave a grim laugh then called 'Any sign of Middie?'

A deep gruff voice came back through the darkness. 'I'm here, Worsen. Took me a little time to find my voice, that's all. Who's the new guy?'

Worsen beckoned Aleksy forward. When he reached the bars Aleksy looked out but could see little in the faint light. The other cells must be to the sides he thought.

'My name is Aleksy. I am a labourer on the London Underground. I was in a tunnel when I saw a flash and I went to look. Then there was someone there I think. I was pushed into a, a hole of some sort. I ended up in this cell but I must have been here a long time. I don't remember.' He rubbed his heavily stubbled chin.

'And when were you taken Aleksy?' came Middie's voice.

'I don't know.'

'He doesn't understand, Middie.' came a woman's voice.

'I haven't had time.' interjected Worsen.

'Well, friend Aleksy,' came Middie's gruff voice. 'You are in a place that exists separately from our world. This place is run by a race of men called the Riven. They're magicians of sorts. They use telekinesis, telepathy and general brutality to keep a hold on this place but they're increasingly seeking to force their way into our world. Your world. There are pathways, lines, between our worlds and every now and then they cross over to collect a few slaves. Sometimes one or two, sometimes a whole bunch. You've probably heard of their actions, although you haven't realisssss...'

Middie's voice tailed off and Aleksy felt a thought come to him although he couldn't focus upon it. It was distant.

Worsen whispered in his ear. 'They're coming back. They must be changing shifts. Good luck.'

As the pressure of the thought in his head began to build Aleksy watched Worsen stiffen until he stood, immobile and slack jawed as though his mind had been removed. Aleksy felt his own mind grow increasingly clouded and panicking he fought against the presence that threatened to overwhelm him. He felt the pressure ease a little and had a vague impression of surprise before the pressure returned, much more intensely this time. He continued to try to keep his mind clear but the force seeking its way into his head was relentless. He felt angry and again pushed as hard as he could but the effort was exhausting. His last thought was that he would not let them beat him. He tried to shout out but the sound died on his lips and he slipped into a waking unconsciousness. He did not see the black robed figure stop before his cell and peer at him curiously. He did not see the thick iron bars bend as though made of cloth, pulled apart like a curtain. He did not see the black hood fall back from a misshapen and ugly face but then a little of his mind leaked back in and, although he could not move, Aleksy was startled to see a face so close to his own. Aleksy's mind was still present but he was unable to even flinch when the horror before him showed him a whip and began to lash his back.

CHAPTER EIGHT

Sam stared in terror at the beast before him. It had the build of a lean, but muscular man, standing on two legs. It wore no clothes but shaggy, matted grey fur covered its body. Its face was human but dog like too with a muzzle and round eyes. Werewolf. The word came into Sam's mind like a punch to the stomach. It snarled, revealing yellow canine teeth and then dropped onto all fours looking at Sam and the others in turn. It seemed to quickly decide on Sam and its muscles tensed ready to spring.

Weewalk darted in front of Sam and as the creature pounced he threw up his hands. The beast seemed to hit an invisible wall. For a moment it froze in the air, then Weewalk's shoulders slumped and the animal dropped to the ground again, getting ready to spring.

Sam had thrown his arms over his head, sure he was about to be killed. As he straightened again he saw, from the corner of his eye, that Hadan had moved into the kitchen area. There was a clatter of cutlery and then Hadan cried Weewalk's name.

The tiny bearded kobold tensed again, the muscles in his neck drawing taught, his face set in a grim expression. Sam could feel the atmosphere in the room change and the little man seemed to become a source of light and focus whilst everything else became dim. Time seemed to slow. Weewalk stood immobile with his arms out, his fingers splayed and his yellow dress moving softly in a breeze from the door. Hadan had grabbed handfuls of knives and forks and now he threw them towards the beast and time seemed to reassert itself on the room. The animal did not move. Hadan had not thrown the metal with much force and, although some of the pieces were sharp, none looked capable of inflicting any real damage from Hadan's underarm throw. Then a strange thing happened. Weewalk moved his arms and the blades which had, a split second earlier, been tumbling in a lazy arc through the air, suddenly twisted and sped up, darting towards the creature like a swarm of angry wasps. The animal yelped and tried to dodge but too late. Several of the knives struck it in the face. Weewalk moved his arms again, more implements turned and swung around to attack from behind, a squadron of little fighter planes.

There was a howl from the creature. Several pieces of cutlery bristled from deep within its face and blood began to drip on the floor. One eye was gone, a knife embedded in the socket. The beast raised a paw-like hand and began to rub at those blades that were embedded in its head.

They all saw the chance. Grabbing their bags they dashed towards the door at the same time, dodging around the flailing monster. Sam noticed that Weewalk seemed to be moving slowly, as if suddenly exhausted. Hadan burst through the open doorway first, Sam hot on his heels. Then there was a roar and a bang behind him and, turning, Sam saw that the beast had lunged as Weewalk had passed. Weewalk lay on his back. The creature's outstretched arm had caught his boot, two long claws hooked into the side. It roared again and adjusting its balance readied itself to make the kill. Weewalk seemed to have no energy left.

Sam stopped as quickly as he could and turned back, standing in the ruined doorway. 'Noooooo!' he cried, bringing his hands up to point at the terrible scene before him. Then he felt something. His hearing was suddenly muffled, as though his ears had popped. The beast, almost on top of the tiny kobold, flew backwards and cracked into the back wall of the shack with enormous force. There was an almighty smack as it hit the wall, punching part way through it so that splinters flew. The beast fell to the floor and lay still, its stare fixed, its remaining eye empty.

Sam grabbed the tiny figure before him, picked him up and ran, almost colliding with Hadan in the process. Together they escorted the little man outside and lay him onto the grass.

'Keep going.' he croaked 'I'm okay. I can walk.' They picked him up and set him on his feet and, with Hadan leading the way, the three of them hurried away.

They followed the line of the coast for half an hour or so, keeping to the tussocky grass rather than leaving footprints on the flat damp sand. The waves crashed endlessly on the beach. Gulls span overhead. Sam was wishing that he had never left home but with no idea where he was or how to get back he had little choice but to follow. Besides Weewalk had certainly saved his life. Surely he could be trusted. He noticed that Weewalk was studying him carefully. When they were far enough away that he felt able to break the silence Sam spoke. 'What was that? A werewolf?'

'Yes and no. It was a garoul.' said Weewalk who was limping slightly from the injury he had received from its claws.

'It's essentially the same thing.' said Hadan. 'They come from our world but the Riven have been sending them into your world over hundreds of years. It's where your legend of the werewolf comes from.'

'But I thought that they were just that, a legend.'

'There are few unexplained things in your world that do not have a basis in ours' said Hadan 'Name me a myth, a monster, a miracle, a civilisation that suddenly prospered and gained knowledge ahead of its time and chances are it will be something from Mu. It might be misunderstood or mis-explained or the reality may have been lost in the retelling but these things are real.'

Why do the Riven send things like the garoul through?' asked Sam, horrified but interested and pleased that Hadan was offering information.

'For fun. To kill.' said Hadan. 'They might bring one through to some remote village and turn it loose so they can watch it kill from the comfort of a rooftop somewhere. The legend of the garoul goes back a long time in Mu too. It's said they were men once but when Pyxidis came and scoured the world with magic they were created then. I don't think they were supposed to be so vicious then. They've become more monstrous, more beastlike, over hundreds of years, partly thanks to the involvement of the Riven King.'

'Who's Pixie dust?' asked Sam.

Hadan just shook his head.

'Pyxidis.' laughed Weewalk, 'I haven't told you about him yet. He was a great mage, some revere him as a God, who came to our world from the heavens many thousands of years ago. Our people lived differently then and were constantly at war. When Pyxidis saw the mess that we had created he burnt the world to the ground and clouded the skies. The impact of his wrath created the lines to your world that we still use now. Most of the people at the time didn't survive but Pyxidis allowed a few who he deemed worthy to continue to exist in Mu. These chosen few were given the seed of new powers in the expectation that they would develop these powers and grow to be better masters of our people. Over generations, the power, the presence as it became known, waned in some. In others it became stronger. But peace did not last and new wars were fought by those who claimed to be the most worthy to lead and the most pure recipients of the gifts that Pyxidis had given. The different races were created by Pyxidis too. Kobold and yeren and others, and the beasts, garoul, Sitecah, ropen and countless others. The powers that men acquired allowed them to shape some of those early creatures and turn them into weapons.

'So Ferus is one of these powerful people then?' asked Sam.

'Oh yes', said Weewalk. 'Legend tells that his ancestors were always powerful but when Ferus was born, the power grew dark. He is one of the Riven, a body of powerful men and women with great presence. They're zealots. They want to rule and conquer and see themselves as superior. You know they're the basis of your legends of black-robed magicians. They appear in all sorts of fiction in your world, don't they?

Of course, the Riven King is the most powerful of them all. Ferus is nothing compared to him. The Riven King rules Mu from the Rivenrok Complex. It is claimed that his presence is the most clear, that his ancestry can be traced back to the visitation of Pyxidis himself. As such he tolerates no challenge to his authority and seeks to weed out and destroy any who show the slightest degree of presence in order to keep the line of power clean. He is the most powerful being who has ever lived. Thousands of those showing potential have been recruited into the

Riven or killed at his command.'

Sam was silent for a moment.

'What kinds of powers does he have? The Riven King?'

Weewalk's face clouded 'It's best not to speak too much of him out in the open but the extent of his presence is mysterious. You've seen some of my power but that's like the power of a mere mosen to him. They say he can control energy giving himself impossible strength. He can move any object at will. He can speak directly into your mind. He sits, a silent statue, on top of an ancient throne. Above all he is malevolent and twisted and he never forgets, he remembers everything, he remembers everything.' Weewalk's voice trailed off and he hung his head with his eyes on the ground.

Sam had not expected such an emotional response from the otherwise cheerful character and realising that he had touched on the wrong subject Sam changed it quickly despite a burning desire to know what all this had to do with him.

'Where are we headed now?' he asked.

It was Hadan who answered. 'There's another line up ahead. Although they're fairly rare Dragsholm has quite a few of them dotted around. The one nearby will get us away from here and hopefully we can find somewhere a bit safer. For now we need to keep moving and hope that no-one is on our trail. We need to protect you from Ferus and the Riven King.'

Sam was about to ask why he needed to be protected when he became aware of a hum in the air. Weewalk spoke first.

'Nearly there.' said the kobold.

They heard the line before they saw it. Guided by Weewalk's compass which seemed to work like a lodestone they found the source of the low hum. Within a series of lichen speckled boulders they found an entrance to a small cave. At the back of the cave was the patch of darkness.

As before Weewalk tensed and tore the hole open. Hadan went first followed by Sam. This time having some idea of what to expect Sam had more of an opportunity to prepare himself and think about the feeling as he entered the void behind the dark portal. As he stepped through the world throbbed. The very air pulsed like the inner workings of some giant speaker emitting a deep bass note in extreme slow motion. And as it did Sam fell, not down to the floor of the cave but though it and to another place entirely.

'Welcome to Tongue's Scar.' Ferus spread his arms, pointing at the blank grey walls of the square room. 'I've made myself quite at home here, away from civilisation. I've set up a small prison here, not even the King can see us here I think. It gives me the space to work.' He ran his hands over the chains and serrated blades that hung from the wall.

'I've got some questions for you. Answer them and things will be less painful. I want the secret that you carry. This boy. Sam. He survived the fire. Does that mean that he is the subject of the prophecy? I want to know where I can find him? When was he born?' He stopped with his hand against a heavy hammer which had a little dried blood and matted hair on its head.

Tarak still seemed to be quite drunk, he lolled against his bonds and when he sat up to peer through his straggly hair at Ferus his neck looked like it was made of rubber and seemed unable to steady the weight of his stubbled jowls. He swore and then dissolved into a fit of coughing that threatened to choke him. After a moment he spat a gob of blood to the floor near Ferus' foot.

'So, we're going to do this the hard way then?' said Ferus to himself, drawing a box of matches from the inside of his cloak. He opened it and a single long match flew into the air and hovered before his face. He plucked it from the air and struck it against the side of the box so that it flared, bringing a quick scent of sulphur flashing in the room. The match floated back into the air and Ferus directed it towards the man's face.

As the match moved Ferus chatted amiably

'I only recently found this place you know. But I like it very much. I found a line that no-one else knows exists. It's well hidden. I took the line and ended up here. We must be far across the sea from the Rivenrok Complex. When I arrived I found a man wrapped in furs herding some strange beasts through the snow. He spoke a language I didn't know and the only useful thing he was able to tell me before he died was the name of the place, Tongue's Scar. Unusual isn't it? It's a bit cold, lots of snow, but, well, you know me, I'm always happy to light a fire.'

The match danced closer to the bound man.

'Now, where shall we start Tarak?' Ferus laughed 'Shall I make Tongue's Scar live up to its name?' The flame moved towards Tarak's jaw. Ferus made a movement with his hand and Tarak's mouth opened, his jaw muscles clenching as he fought to close it. He tried to blow the match out but only succeeded in breathing heavily, spraying spit over his chin. With his other hand Ferus put his thumb and forefinger together and cocked his wrist. Tarak's tongue slid over his teeth until it was held out ahead of him, the match hovering above it. Tarak made frantic noises in his throat, unable to speak. His eyes were wild as he stared at the yellow flame.

'No, you're quite right, of course.' said Ferus 'I need you to be able to talk.'

He tapped his chin in mock thought 'I could melt your eyeball. You know, that's what I did to your wife in the end. And she screamed and screamed. But still she wouldn't tell me what I wanted to know. I don't think you'll give me the same problem. Will you?'

The match moved close to the man's watering right eye.

'Hmmm, no, maybe we'll start with your nose first.'

Tarak Everune struggled but could not move. His eyes looked madly at the match as it moved down a couple of inches in the air. Then the flame entered one of his nostrils and he screamed.

Ferus held the match there a second, his head cocked to one side as if he were watching a scene of only mild interest. Then he allowed the match to fall out and he sighed.

'You really have lost your presence haven't you? I almost didn't believe it. Well, secret keeper. Let's see if we can't have some of those famous secrets of yours. Tell me where the boy is. What's his path?'

Tarak swore. A new match sparked and moved to his nostril and he screamed. After a few seconds the match burned out and the scream echoed and died.

'Okay, okay' gasped Tarak 'I'll tell you how to find him. There's a girl, she will find him. Follow the girl. The prophecy. The boy. It doesn't matter. Nothing matters. That's not what the secret is. Your precious King doesn't need to feel threatened. I've seen the future of their world.'

As Sam arrived, feeling the ground appear under his feet, his vision swimming into focus, he was aware of an enormous roaring sound and he felt a pressure across his chest. The noise of a huge heartbeat reverberated up from the ground, through his feet, into his stomach. TA-TAK

TA-TAK. Yellow lights flashed in his eyes. As he became aware of his surroundings he realised that his face was inches from something moving very fast past him. A blur of light whipped past. The roar was deafening. Then there was a loud pop and some of the light disappeared and there was a squeal of metal. He stayed motionless, unsure of what was happening and then the rushing stopped and he looked up to see an underground train slowing on a track next to him. He looked down to see Hadan's arm across his chest. Had Hadan not been there he might very well have walked into the side of the train.

'Thanks.' he said, unsure what else to say.

Hadan gave a rare smile. 'Don't mention it.' he said. 'I think we want to keep you alive a bit longer yet.'

Sam turned and saw that Weewalk was smiling too. 'This way.' said the kobold, setting off through the dark tunnels. As they walked away down a side passage Sam saw people on the train peer at them curiously and he could hear the gasps of the people inside. They turned a corner as the train powered up again and accelerated away. Weewalk explained that the nearby line played havoc with the electrical systems of the trains, causing them to stop and cut out.

London.

Sam felt his heart leap. It would be good to return to somewhere with lots of people. London felt a world away from magic and monsters and cold deserted beaches.

It wasn't long before they came across a station. They could see the lights long before the station itself came into view. Several times they had to press themselves into recesses set in the wall to allow trains to move past.

As a train pulled into the station they jogged up a slope onto the platform. A few people were around but no-one noticed that they hadn't simply stepped out of the last carriage. No-one even seemed to notice Weewalk's unusual appearance. It wasn't often one saw a small bearded man in a dress. But apparently London was used to the unusual and no-one stopped to bother them. Sam breathed a sigh of relief. He was with real people again. Ordinary folk in London for a day's work, tourists eager to see the sights.

Weewalk motioned them over to a set of seats.

'We need to work out what to do.' he said 'We can't just chase around for ever with no direction. I don't know how that garoul found us but you can be sure that the Riven were behind it in some way. Hadan, where shall we make for? I think it would be good to find somewhere properly safe.'

'Well,' said Hadan, 'there are other lines down here. We can get just about anywhere.' He twisted his mouth as he thought.

'Whatever we do we should take a train. If whoever sent the garoul is following us then we'll be harder to track.' Weewalk said hopping off the hard metal seat. 'Besides, I think I have an idea.'

They made a strange looking trio as they sat on the train in a row facing an opposing line of commuters. Weewalk swung his legs slightly, his hairy knees showing under his yellow dress. Sam felt a bit embarrassed but it was testament to the strangeness of people using the Underground system that no-one stared too hard. Sam tried not to catch anyone's eye. Instead he looked into the window opposite, over the shoulder of a suited, middle-aged man who had his eyes closed, his head back and his mouth open. The man's slumped position and the tilt of the window allowed Sam to see his own reflection. He gave a huge yawn to himself and realised that it was a long time since he had had any decent sleep. His eyes watered with the effort of stifling another yawn and his reflection blurred. He rubbed his eyes and looked at the reflections again. This time he studied Hadan, his handsome face looking disinterested and bored. Sam wasn't really sure how he felt about Hadan. Hadan clearly was not going to make much effort to be friends. *Perhaps he resents me joining their gang*, thought Sam. *But is that what I've done? Am I staying with them? Given what has happened so far I might be putting myself in more danger by staying with them. Or even putting them in danger by staying with me.* Sam resolved then to leave them. When they got to the line that Weewalk wanted them to take he would say goodbye and go out into the bright streets of London and not think of all this magic again. He would be sad to leave Weewalk though. He had quickly become quite fond of the little man. The train lurched to a sudden stop causing the sleeping man opposite to rock wildly from side to side with a snort. Sam turned his gaze to Weewalk's reflection and jumped. The reflection in the window was not Weewalk's at all. A ghostly pale face stared back at Sam but as quickly as he'd seen it, it disappeared and the window was blank. Sam could only see the top of Weewalk's head reflected next to his own. He looked around but could see no-one that resembled the face. Had the person been outside of the train?

He leant down to whisper in Weewalk's ear as the train began to move again. 'I just saw something odd.' he said, 'A pale face looking in the window.'

Weewalk looked up at him 'Are you sure?'

'It was only for a moment, but pretty sure, yes. Was it a ghost?'

'No.' said Weewalk dropping to his feet. Turning to Hadan he said 'Sam saw a yeren, looking into the carriage. We may have been seen. I think we're being followed. We should change trains or take a line.'

Hadan stood and the three of them moved to the doors of the train as they pulled into a station.

Weewalk spoke quietly to Sam as they waited for the train to come to a full stop.

'The yeren are with Ferus. Remember them from the fire at your house? They patrol the lines down here.'

The train stopped and the doors opened. They stepped onto the platform and a few other people left the train too and hurried away through archways towards the exits. The train doors closed and the train accelerated away leaving Sam, Weewalk and Hadan alone on the platform, several sheets of newspaper twisting in loops from the warm wind that blew along the tracks.

'I don't know which way to go', said Weewalk 'but I want to get away from here quickly, take a line, cover our tracks.' He went quiet and seemed to be listening. Then he pulled out his compass and studied it for a moment.

Sam listened too, at the edge of his hearing there was a faint hum, a chime. 'I think I can hear a line.' he said carefully.

'Really?' asked Weewalk 'Which way?'

Sam concentrated. He had to move his head slowly to identify the sound but it was coming from the tunnel into which the train had just vanished. He pointed 'That way, I think, but I'm not sure.'

'It's our best bet.' said Weewalk.

They moved along to the end of the platform, where several television monitors showed bright grey images of the station behind them. As they passed by the televisions Sam caught sight of a flash of movement in one, then it was gone again. Then there in another. Then gone. Sam turned to look back down the platform behind him. A black-cloaked figure stood at the opposite end, immobile, staring at them.

'Uh-oh.' he said.

Weewalk and Hadan turned and saw the figure too.

'Run!' said Hadan, and they ran.

'Wrath of Pyxidis!' cursed Hadan, as they jogged along the track 'Why do we always run? I wish we could fight!'

'I'd rather live.' said Weewalk.

They felt a rumbling behind them and then heard the screeching of a train pulling into the station they had just left. It was quiet for a minute and they continued to run. Then they heard the train accelerate behind them.

'I can't hear the line.' said Sam, 'It's too noisy.'

'There's a side tunnel up ahead.' said Hadan, looking over Weewalk's head.

Weewalk studied his compass 'I think it's in there.'

They ducked into the tunnel just as the train thundered past. Within a moment it was gone, the lights leaving images dancing in Sam's eyes.

In the sudden silence they could all hear the steady hum echo down towards them. They quickly followed the passageway towards the sound. Sam kept nervously looking over his shoulder but it was pitch black behind them. He had no chance of seeing a figure in a black cloak. He tried not to imagine a cold hand grabbing him from behind and he quickened his pace. Then they were there. The portal lay before them. Weewalk performed his trick, small flickers of electricity sparking brightly from his fingers in the darkness. The doorway opened and they stepped through.

They arrived in what looked to be a dim cellar. A candle on a shelf gave some light and Sam could see Hessian sacks against one wall, barrels in a corner and shelves stacked with jars and pots. The warm smell of freshly baked bread filled the air.

'Come on.' said Weewalk, 'Away from the line.'

He started up some stone steps towards a heavy wooden door.

'Hello everyone.' came a cold voice. They turned in horror. A single figure stood at the same spot at which they had just appeared themselves. Meaty hands pulled back a dark hood and the man's face came into view. Candlelight flickered in his eyes and he gave a grin. It was Ferus. He had found them.

CHAPTER NINE

Aleksy's mind had trickled back into his brain like tiny rivulets of water filling a glass as he had tried to throw off the mental control of the man he had come to know as 'Grim', the most brutal and by far the most regular of the jailers. As usual Aleksy had been the first to come round. Today he had found himself alone in his cell and when he had wandered over to the bars to call out to the people who had become his friends a few more names were missing from their roll-call.

Each time he had been able to resist Grim a little longer as though his ability to push the man away had increased over time. However, there were other jailers and Aleksy knew each of them by their mind control. Grim was the weakest and easiest to resist but he was also the cruellest. Aleksy's back was covered in scars as a result, but he refused to be broken by the jailer. If anything the beatings only made him more determined and more angry. He felt a deep hatred burning within him like a flame, always there, always hot. One day he would open the door on it and it would explode in rage. He would squeeze the jailer's throat until his eyes bulged and he begged for his life. Aleksy would offer him no mercy but first he had to break the control once and for all. He was not the only one who felt such anger towards their overseer but many had had their spirits or minds broken long ago. Aleksy knew of a few who were barely able to think for themselves any more, little more than husks waiting for Grim to fill their minds and set them to work. For them Grim's mind had become familiar, almost a comfort and they struggled to function without his presence. But a few, Middie and Worsen in particular, still had the presence of mind to look for a way out of the hell that had been imposed upon them. Down in the dark cells they always thought about a way out. However, not even the gruff Middie or the eloquent Worsen were able to achieve clarity in the way that Aleksy could. He wasn't sure how he did it but he knew he had to keep that flame of anger burning within him. He visualised it now. A steady light in a darkened room, held secret inside his chest where Grim could not touch it.

Aleksy had formed a plan. It wasn't much of a plan but his options were limited and he was desperate to escape. It would probably only get him as far as the end of the corridor at best, but he had to try. He would continue to push the boundaries that held his mind. One day he would break that bond permanently. He was sure that he would do it. He had been practising keeping his mind empty to fool the guards. He refused to be beaten. If he could just push away the grip on his mind for long enough to get close to Grim whilst pretending that he was still under control. Then when the bars were opened he could seize the jailer and force him to release them all. Grim was not a physically strong looking man, it was only the power of his mind that allowed him to hold them captive. Aleksy's time within the mines had developed his muscles in a way that he thought was never possible on the meagre rations they were given. His hands were used to holding a pick for hours at a stretch, his shoulders and biceps were bunched under his skin from continually striking the heavy rock.

He had tried and tried to resist the control and felt that he was almost there. Perhaps today would be the day. The prisoners had been able to relax for a few hours but, despite his tiredness, Aleksy felt unable to settle and paced his cell like an animal, restless and nervous. He ran his hands over his smooth head. He had shaved his head every day whilst living in London. He couldn't do that now, but at least he could finally admit that he didn't need to.

Worsen called out to him 'Hi, Aleksy, you really must save your strength. I know how dearly you would like to get us out of here, but it just isn't possible. Concentrate on surviving, man.'

Aleksy sighed and moved to the bars, running his hands over the smooth cold metal.

'I just can't rest. I have to get out of here. I have to see the sun. Lie on grass. Eat some proper food.'

He kicked the wooden bowl that had held the gruel on which they survived, sending it spinning across the rocky floor.

'You can try and try to resist Grim but one day he'll beat you to death.' growled Middie. 'I'm surprised that he's let you go this long.'

'He enjoys the beatings.' said Aleksy. 'I can sense how much he enjoys the violence. He doesn't think I'll ever beat him. It amuses him to watch me try.'

'Well, don't count on it that he won't get bored.' said Worsen. 'Somebody once escaped on his watch and Grim has been in the doghouse ever since. I'm surprised they let him live to be honest. He won't take the risk that you might confront him.'

'What?' said Aleksy. 'Someone escaped?'

'Yes,' said Worsen 'Only one lad has ever escaped. He was young. A fighter. He wouldn't be beaten.'

'Who was he? How did he escape?'

'We don't know really. He never said where he was from. But Grim hated him and punished him mercilessly. He was a young and handsome lad, and proud. Grim couldn't stand that. No matter how he punished him Grim could never break him, not inside his head. As to how he escaped? We're not sure. He was in a cell one minute, then gone the next. I remember waking up. I heard his voice, speaking quietly, and another voice coming from the same cell. I couldn't see anything but there was a weird feeling in the air. It made the hairs on my neck stand up. Then suddenly there was silence. He was gone. Disappeared. It must have been a line but who opened it and where he went, I guess we'll never know. I don't know what the Riven did but no-one has ever come through again. They must have sealed it off somehow. But it has given us hope. We're always hoping that someone will come for us. But no-one has ever come again. The lad always swore he'd have revenge on the Riven, that something he would do would bring them down. He believed it too. I hope he's out there somewhere, causing them problems. He was a good lad, for all his pride. I can't remember his name. Hey, Middie, what was that lad's name. The young chap who escaped?'

'Hmmm,' Middie grunted. 'Hadan. His name was Hadan.'

'So, it can be done. I will get out of here,' said Aleksy softly, more to himself than anyone else, 'I will get us all out and I will pull this entire place down around me as I leave.'

The flame inside him burned brighter than ever. Then

he felt it, the faint touch of a presence. 'He's coming.' he said. But the others had already fallen silent. Aleksy steeled himself, positioning himself near the front of his cell and, focusing on the image of a flame within his chest, feeling the creep of Grim's mind, he pushed back.

By the time Grim appeared at the bars Aleksy was sweating and shaking with the effort of keeping his mind clear. He forced a grin at the jailer, barely managing to shape his face. Then suddenly he allowed his body to go rigid and allowed a little more of Grim to enter his mind. Aleksy sank within himself, hiding his own thoughts deep within his head. Not thinking thoughts, as he had practised.

Grim smiled to himself and parted the thick iron bars with a wave of his hand. Instantly Aleksy leapt for him and seized the startled man by the throat. Grim immediately began to struggle and Aleksy tightened his grip on the man's windpipe. He held the jailer between the gap in the bars so that if Grim tried to cut off his escape route and close the space then he would be crushed. Aleksy's grip was iron and the struggling stopped. Grim shut his eyes and stood motionless. Aleksy had expected the mental attack but was stunned by the force of it. Grim pushed and pushed his way into Aleksy's mind until his fingers began to release their grip.

'Stop it or I will kill you.' Aleksy said through gritted teeth, managing to get his fingers a little closer again. He saw fear enter Grim's eyes and finally the man gave up allowing Aleksy clarity.

With his vision now clear Aleksy felt a brief moment of triumph. But as he looked into the corridor he was startled to see another man standing there. A man in a black cloak. The black cloaked man stood silently. Aleksy's stomach clenched. He had not seen him arrive. There was no way he could defeat another. The man stared at him, immobile. Hanging his head Aleksy released Grim who fell to the floor clutching at his neck. Aleksy closed his eyes and prepared himself for death as the man at the entrance raised an arm towards him. He had failed.

Hearing a sudden noise and a startled cry Aleksy's eyes flickered open involuntarily. Grim lay in a broken heap behind him, his empty eyes fixed on a heaven that he would never see.

'What's the point in a prison guard who cannot control the prisoners?' said the cloaked man, his voice a smooth purr.

Aleksy stood dumbfounded. He had been certain that he was about to be killed. He still wasn't sure whether he might.

'Follow me.' said the cloaked man. 'The Riven King has noticed you and wants to keep you close. You are of interest.' He turned and strode along the dark corridor. 'From today you are no longer a miner. You are a servant.'

Stunned, Aleksy rose and followed.

'Hey! What about the others?' he called after the man.

'We'll find another jailer soon enough.'

Every man and woman stared at Aleksy as he walked the corridor. Seeing Worsen, Aleksy touched his hands as he passed. 'I'll come back for you.' he whispered into Worsen's ear 'I'll be back to free you. Hold on.'

Ahead the cloaked man turned his head almost imperceptibly, a small smile touching the edge of his mouth, before opening a heavy iron door with a wave of his hand and leading Aleksy up, up towards his first sight of daylight in months.

Inside of Aleksy the flame of anger burned hotter than ever. He was going to gain entrance to the palace. His next plan would be justice for all and the death of the

King.

In the dimly lit cellar everything seemed to happen at once. Ferus immediately turned his attention to Sam. His arms came up and Sam felt a wall of air wash over him, ruffling his hair and clothes. Ferus flashed a look of anger over Sam's shoulder and Sam half-turned to see Weewalk on the stairs, his arms outstretched, concentration etched into his face. Meanwhile Hadan leapt towards Ferus, a large knife in his hand.

Without even looking Ferus lifted an arm in Hadan's direction and it was as though Hadan had been hit with an invisible fist. He seemed to bounce off empty air and he fell back. Ferus put his forefinger and thumb together as if he was going to pluck something from the air and the shadows in the room moved. Sam realised that he had used his presence to pull the flame away from the candle and it was now suspended in mid-air and moving towards Ferus who was gathering himself to strike, his shoulders hunching.

Seeing the danger Sam cried out in fear and alarm and felt another wave of wind rush along his outstretched arms, the material flattening against his limbs; snapping and fluttering. Ferus staggered, lost his balance and was forced to steady himself against a barrel. The flame he had been holding in mid-air vanished, plunging the room into pitch darkness. A crash came from Ferus' direction and a bark of annoyance. Sam felt a hand grab him by the shoulder and push him towards the steps. Hadan had found him in the darkness.

Sam tripped over the bottom step and landed painfully, his shins connecting with a stair. But he didn't hesitate and he was already a few steps up when the door ahead opened and he saw Weewalk's small silhouette dart through ahead of him. Hadan slammed the door behind them.

They had little time to absorb their surroundings. A huge thing that looked like an oven stood to one side and the smell of bread was stronger again. They stopped in the middle of the room and Sam noticed a dusting of flour coated the floor. Again, candles provided some light.

One of the candles bobbed ahead of them. Sam squinted into it. It was being held by a short man wearing old fashioned night clothes.

'What the bloody hell are you doing in here?' he shouted.

'No time. Get away!' said Weewalk and took off at a run almost knocking the man over. The kobold dashed to some stairs opposite, Sam and Hadan in hot pursuit. A moment later they heard the crash of the cellar door hitting the wall, not just flying open but flying off its hinges and spinning through the room.

Again the shadows in the room shifted suddenly and a bolt of flame shot past them as they made their escape.

A voice called down the stairs, fear evident in the tone.

'What is it, pa? What's happening?'

Weewalk bolted up the stairs and up another flight and into a room containing four scared looking people, a mixture of ages.

A woman let out a scream. Weewalk didn't hesitate but ran to a window. He ignored the strangers and beckoned Sam forward. 'Can you jump?' he panted.

Sam looked out and down. They were on the second floor above a cobbled alley. A sign swung beneath him.

'Thomas Farrynor of Pudding Lane, Baker.'

It looked like a long way down.

'Not down, across.' urged Weewalk pointing.

Sam had been so intent on looking at the height that he hadn't noticed that the next building lay only a few feet away, the sloped roofs above were nearly touching and the window opposite was open. By way of answer he took a few steps back, took a deep breath and ran at the window, getting his foot on the windowsill in just the right place so that he cleared the gap easily and flew through the window opposite.

He landed slightly off balance and allowed himself to fall and roll to a stop. He quickly jumped up and turned to see Weewalk standing on the window ledge of the house he had just left. Weewalk readied himself to jump and Hadan gave him a shove under his bottom that sent him up and towards Sam. He landed in the window and almost toppled back before Sam managed to dart forward and get a hand on him to pull him through. Hadan followed quickly behind, landing smoothly.

This house was much like the one they had left and, spotting the stairs, they dashed down and down where Sam flung open the front door, allowing them a view of the street.

Flames were clearly visible inside a window of the house they had just left. The lower floor already seemed to be ablaze. Hearing a noise above Sam saw the family above him were taking the same route as them to leap the gap. But, one girl had yet to jump and Sam heard her cry out that she was too scared. The others urged her on. She was just about to leap when she suddenly jerked back out of view with a yelp of surprise, as though she had been pulled back by a speeding train. Ferus' head appeared where the girl had disappeared. He looked across at the frightened family and then looked down and saw them.

They turned and ran up the narrow and dark cobbled street and quickly into a side alley. There was little light. No moonlight filtered between the tall buildings. Calls began to ring out, voices shouted 'fire' and a noise, like someone beating a metal pan with a spoon began, a loud clanging which reverberated between the tall houses. They moved on quickly, turning this way and that, racing down narrow streets that twisted and turned like the inside of a rabbit warren. Once or twice Ferus caught sight of them and leapt after them, but the narrow streets were such a maze that they quickly lost him each time. As they ran the streets looked wrong to Sam, old fashioned but not old. The people were even stranger than the houses, their clothes, their build, the way they moved. It all seemed wrong.

As they ran through the strange city more people began to spill onto the streets and then a muffled church bell began to sound. The din increased. Behind them a glow seemed to fill the sky.

'Have we lost him?' panted Hadan eventually.

'Think so. For now.' breathed Weewalk. 'In here.' he added, motioning to a small house from which three people had just hurried out.

They ducked through the open doorway, closing it quickly behind them. Hadan moved to the side of the window and looked out carefully. Sam put his hands on his knees and sucked in air.

'Weewalk.' he panted quietly, when he had regained his breath. 'Where are we?'

Weewalk didn't answer, just breathed heavily.

'Weewalk,' Sam said again, standing and fixing the kobold with a look. '*When* are we?'

'Ah,' said Weewalk 'Now. That is a very interesting question. But. If you'll excuse the pun. Perhaps now is not the time.'

Someone dashed past the window and Hadan shrank back. They stood in silence for a while. Then they moved on into the street again, and hid and then moved again before following a procession of people making their way into a church. Crowds were filing into the stone building with arms full of their belongings. One man even carried a pig. The vicar looked at him sternly but let him in anyway. They were all moving away from the fire which seemed to be quickly getting out of hand.

Weewalk, Hadan and Sam took up residence in a shadowed corner at the back of the church, away from other people. They collapsed, exhausted. As soon as they slumped onto the floor Sam felt the last of his energy drain away and his eyes began to close.

'I reckon we're safe here for a while.' said Weewalk.

'Tell me, what's going on?' said Sam.

'Please, give me a little time to think. Try to get some rest if you can.'

Sam scowled but slipped his rucksack from his shoulders and punched it into the most comfortable shape he could and stretched out on the cold stone floor. He closed his eyes and after a few minutes changed his breathing so that it would appear that he was asleep. He lay still and silent and strained his ears as Hadan and Weewalk hunched together and began to speak in whispered conversation.

'He's got the gift. A strong presence when he's threatened.' said Weewalk softly, pulling off a boot with a wince. He stuck two fingers through holes in the leather and then took a cloth from his bag and pouring a little water on it, wiped at the claw mark on his foot. 'It wasn't me that threw that garoul through a wall, or knocked Ferus off his feet.'

'I guessed as much.' said Hadan grimly. 'What have you got us into? If he's really that strong already, without even knowing it, then the Riven aren't going to stop until he's dead. The Riven King won't let him survive. He's too much of a threat. Even if he isn't the one, the Riven won't take any chances. We've been lucky. Ferus has underestimated him.'

'I know, I know.' said Weewalk, rubbing the bridge of his nose. 'There's no doubt that we need to get him somewhere where we can get someone else to have a proper look at him. You know how rare those powers are. I think it's about time we told him the full story too.'

'Agreed.' said Hadan, 'Now they've found him he will always be under threat. We can't leave him. He wouldn't last long.'

Weewalk gave a huge yawn 'Right now, I'm too tired to think about it.' he said 'Best get some sleep while we can.'

It wasn't long before Sam fell asleep too, despite the questions that squirmed in his head like a bucketful of eels.

Kya left the empty house and tried not to let herself be panicked. This was the fifth place she had tried since leaving Suun-t-Marten and taking the Great Line and still she was no further on with her mission. She had eventually found the ruined fortress and the line inside and now she was somewhere further north. But how was she to find one person when he could be in any place at any time? The directions she had been given had set her on a path but had not, probably could not, have told her exactly where to find the boy. She only had a vague idea of what he looked like. At least he was travelling with a mine kobold, that would make him easier to spot, but he would be keeping well hidden if he had any sense. She knew he was likely to be in this world, but where? Any leads she had managed to find had proved to be fruitless. Perhaps he had been found already. What would that mean for the future of her world?

The last inn she had been to had been burnt to the ground. She needed a better plan. She had decided to try the obvious places first but no-one had been able to be much help. She had hoped that the boy would end up in one of the known places that offered safety to those pursued by the Riven. There was one more place she could try. She had purposely left it until last, aware that she was likely to pick up some unwanted attention, but there she would be able to ask around, and if he hadn't been seen she could, at least, ask someone to keep an eye out.

When Sam awoke Weewalk and Hadan were already sitting up, chatting. His whole body ached from sleeping on the stone floor and Sam arched his back and stretched with a groan. Despite the pain in his neck and shoulders Sam decided that he felt infinitely better for some sleep.

Hadan moved closer and handed him a couple of cold sausages and a hunk of bread, before picking up a jug of water and pouring Sam a cup.

'The other people here have been generous' said Hadan, 'They're sheltering from the fire. It seems to be spreading across the city. Every time they put out one part another seems to spring up somewhere else. I suspect Ferus is trying to flush us out, but we're safe here for now.'

Sam felt his stomach rumble as the water hit the emptiness. He bit off some sausage and took a mouthful of bread. Food had never tasted so good. After he had eaten Weewalk and Hadan drew him further into the corner of the church and Weewalk began to talk.

'When Pyxidis came to our world many years ago and all but destroyed it he also created the lines. Over time we noticed the strange aura around these lines and we investigated them. Some who spent a lot of time near them and had been granted Pyxidis' gift of presence found that their powers developed. We learned to open the pathways and use them, and some of us from our world found themselves here, in your world. But we didn't just find ourselves in your time. We found some lines led to times in your past. There was a scramble to use the lines and find a better world than the one Pyxidis had almost ripped to pieces. Powerful individuals from Mu have travelled back and been seen to do what has been considered to be miraculous by your people. You've probably heard of them. They've passed into legend in your world. Whole religions have been based upon their presence.

There are other races in our world who live on islands separate from the lands around the Rivenrok Complex, far across the black seas and glowing fields who have gone through in groups and been worshipped as Gods by your ancestors for bringing what seemed to be incredible technology and mysterious powers. For example, there's a land far from Rivenrok called Shambhala and they've made regular contact with a race of your people. Tibetans I think they're called.

Mucking around in time is difficult though. Some of us may yet travel to your past which raises complicated questions. Have they already arrived? Your past has already occurred. Does that mean the people from our future can't help but go back and do what has already been done?'

'Hang on,' said Sam, 'This is confusing. Give me a minute. The sign on the bakers we arrived at. It said Pudding Lane. That's where the Great Fire of London started. We're in the year 1666, aren't we? Are you saying that we caused Ferus to follow us here, and if we hadn't then the Great Fire, which is going on now, would never have started?'

'Possibly, but you already know about it. It's already happened. So, did we always have an influence on its start, or did it, in an alternate past, start in some other way? We always thought we could only affect events in the future ahead of us but then we found the lines. Perhaps, like a pebble dropped in a pond, our existence sends ripples in all directions. Or is it all predestined, perhaps you can act in no other way. But that doesn't feel right, does it?'

'Okay' said Sam 'but if you can travel to other times then you know what will happen in the future.'

'We really don't. Things change we think. We're not really sure. But we've not yet been able to build a complete picture of what the future holds. Of course, stories and legends appear from ahead. Prophecies you might call them.'

Weewalk shook his head.

'Sam, don't worry if you find this hard to deal with. The greatest minds in both our worlds have studied this for as long as we have had a concept of time and no one has ever been sure of what happens. We just have to run with it.'

Sam lifted his hand and looked at it. He gave it a wave. 'Did I do that because I decided to, or was I always going to do it?'

Hadan laughed. 'Crazy huh?'

'Anyway, that is a mystery we may never fathom' continued Weewalk 'But now you get the power of the lines. People and creatures from my world are able to leave it and appear in different times in yours. The lines are variable. Some seem to lock two places and times together, they're more stable. Some can fluctuate. You might end up in the place you were expecting, but at a time that you weren't planning for. But, many of your legends and myths and unexplained phenomena are caused by us. Stories from the past develop over time. Your Loch Ness Monster is a species of sea creature that lives in the De'Aan Ocean in the far north of Mu. It moves back and forth between worlds. That's why it's so hard for you to find. I have a good friend back home called Squatch. Hairy chap, big feet. Every now and then he pops into your world. People have found the tracks, even photographed him. Your history is full of the tales. The technology of the Egyptians and the Aztecs didn't come from nowhere. I already mentioned how the Tibetans discovered a portal to the place called Shambala. The Dogon tribe in Mali met a fish-like race called the Nommo who taught them of the stars and planets well before the invention of the telescope. The Bermuda Triangle is riddled with lines to all over the place. Atlantis is in Mu that's why men have never been able to find it again. Lines are not always fixed. They come and go over years as the worlds move across one another.'

'Why hasn't anyone here ever realised any of this before?' said Sam.

'People from your world just don't understand. The visits from this world become stories and legends and myths and fairy-tales. Vampires, werewolves, goblins, pixies. These all have some basis in truth based on people and creatures from our world. Time may have warped what is accurate but they are real. Remember, we don't get here very often and our visits are spread throughout the entirety of history. The paths are fairly rare and many of them lead to a time when even the technology you have in your time would have been considered miraculous. And, yes, some have stumbled upon Mu by accident. Many of your people vanish each year. Have you heard of the Marie Celeste? I mentioned the Bermuda Triangle and you know all about that, I presume. Heard of exorcists? They're nothing more than people who are able to affect or close lines. Often they don't even realise they're doing it. But sometimes people do actually become aware of Mu and try to break through', said Weewalk. 'Once they even managed it in a place called Montauk. Normal men learnt how to create a bridge between worlds.'

'What happened?' asked Sam.

'Well,' said Weewalk 'The details are a little hazy but so far as we know in 1943 there was once an attempt to make one of your great warships invisible to enemies through new science using light. It was called the Philadelphia Experiment or Project Rainbow. By pure chance the tests were conducted near the entrance to a line. When the machine was switched on the ship did indeed vanish. But it wasn't simply invisible. The scientists had actually managed to open a door and the entire ship went though. But they couldn't control the power. They managed to pull the ship back, but not all the crew came back with it. I expect some of them survived their trip to Mu, and may even be there still. The scientists weren't sure what they'd discovered but they realised it was something completely new and powerful. However, the project was considered to be a disaster and the Government closed it and hushed it up. However, some men on the project didn't want to stop. They met years later to try to restart the project. They created a chair which amplified presence to incredible levels. In time they were able to open a line in a place called Montauk and begin to control some of that power, some of the presence. Some of the scientists and crew from the original warship were seen years after they were thought to have died. Some people even absorbed a little of the power of the line and began to be able to control objects and even other people with their minds, but it is said that those people soon became unstable and destroyed the equipment effectively ending the project. The lines that men made were different somehow. Dangerous. Rough.

And they conveyed too much power.' Weewalk gave a grim laugh. 'You know, the scientists even thought they had made contact with aliens from another planet. It was people from Mu who they saw. There are still holes in Montauk which lead to Mu, and I know there is a line to a place in our world called Icut, but it's not been used in a long time. It is possible that your people realised there was a hole there many years before that experiment. I can't think of any other reason why that area is called Connecticut. In fact, the hole may have opened again. I heard that a monster of some sort was found washed up on the beach nearby.'

'You said that people absorbed some of the power from the lines.'

'Yes, it seems that people in either world can, over time, absorb a little of the magic which the lines emit, more from those few man-made lines. It doesn't affect everyone but it means that some people in your world find they are able to move things with their minds, bend spoons, think of a friend a minute before he knocks on the door. This is presence. Where the barrier between our worlds is at its thinnest people can have an impression of the world on the other side and experience what they call ghosts. These are sometimes echoes as if the sights or sounds from the other world are travelling out of a long cave, but sometimes we create the illusions to keep people away from areas that are useful or dangerous. These are the legends of abandoned haunted houses!

Only a very few people in every thousand years show any real level of power, the ability to move enormous weights with the power of the mind, the ability to manipulate fire or to heal another by just touching him. You've seen that my presence is pretty limited but I am stronger than most. Those with real ability are often recruited into the Riven as children and brain-washed. It's like a cult. But, did you ever learn about King Herod and his bid to kill the babies who might one day threaten him? Same story. Different time. If you don't join you're as good as dead. The Riven King who rules from the Rivenrok Complex, wants to eliminate anyone with any significant power so that there can be no future challenge. He wants to rule a defeated, simple population, without the power to resist his authority. So, anyone with any power, or with little or no power but rebellious tendencies like me and Hadan, who don't join the Riven, are in for a visit from one of the Riven King's generals, like our friend Ferus. The Riven are also using the lines to infiltrate your world to gather slaves. There are very few people in your world with presence and so most are easily controlled. The other thing you should know about is the prophecy as it occupies the mind of many Riven. It is said that a mighty warrior, with a legendary presence, will save us from the Riven King The King is taking no chances, although no-one seems to know if the prophecy is true. That is the one aspect of the unknown future that persists, and the part that worries the King the most. That someday he will be challenged. Which brings us to you, Sam.'

Weewalk turned and looked directly into Sam's eyes.

'Sam, how was it that you were able to throw that garoul off me and hurl it through a wall?'

'What?' said Sam, 'That wasn't me. You did that.'

'How did you manage to hit Ferus with such a powerful block that he staggered and lost his hold on the flame? I've not seen people who've trained for decades be able to fend off that terrible sorcerer. He's being rather cautious around you, Sam.'

'That was you too.' said Sam, 'It wasn't me, I don't know how.'

'Show me.' said Weewalk.

He placed a sausage on the floor, out of sight, where no-one else in the church would be able to see it

'Move it.' he said.

'Weewalk, this is stupid. I can't move it.' said Sam.

'Try.'

'I don't know what to do.'

'Put your hands out towards it. Then just concentrate on it and will it to move. Roll it into the corner.'

Sam sighed and shifted so he sat cross legged, his back to the people behind him. He stretched out his arms, and splayed his fingers. He concentrated as hard as he could. He thought he might be able to feel a strange heat running up and down his spine but nothing moved. He tried harder, but nothing.

'I can't do it.' he said.

'Hmm, we'll see.' said Weewalk.

Sam slumped feeling gloomy. For a moment he thought he might have managed it, that he might be special. Then suddenly he realised something and beamed.

'I just thought.' he exclaimed happily 'My grandfather. He knew!' Sam clapped his hands, delighted. 'He knew. He wasn't going mad, ha! He knew about Mu. When he talked about other worlds he knew.'

'Who was he?' asked Weewalk, 'What was his name?'

'Adam Hain.' Sam said happily and a weight he hadn't realised had existed seemed to lift from his shoulders.

'Hmm, I don't know him' said Weewalk. He looked across to Hadan who creased his eyebrows but shook his head.

At that point a disturbance at the other end of the church drew their attention. Two men were pushing one another and raised voices could be heard.

'It's you bloody foreigners startin' these fires.' one

shouted, 'It's you bloomin' Dutchies.'

'I ain't Dutch, you idiot, I was at school with your sister.' roared the other and gave the other man an almighty shove.

Others pushed their way between the men and hustled them outside where shouts could still be heard.

A woman sitting nearby looked over to Sam and the others. 'I'd best be careful if I was you. People are nervous, they say the fire's spreadin' faster than it should, starting afresh in new houses. They say foreigners, French or Dutch, most likely, been seen sending firedrops out across the roofs. My cousin swears he saw a man throwing fireballs through doors, but then my cousin likes his ale if you know what I mean. Either way I'd say it were best if strangers like you kept themselves to themselves, 'specially if you're going to stare at sausages.' She eyed Weewalk's dress and beard at this point before turning away.

'She has a point.' said Weewalk quietly. 'We do need to get away from here and we have been getting some strange looks. We might have to try to get back to the same line if it's still there. Hopefully Ferus has moved on and his attention is elsewhere and the fire may have been put out there.'

'Where do we go after London?' asked Hadan.

'Hmm, good question.' said Weewalk, 'How about The Island of the Pelicans?'

'Too hard to get to.' said Hadan.

'Yonaguni?'

'Underwater.'

They were silent for a while.

'What about the Mermaid?' said Hadan.

'Good idea.' said Weewalk. 'We'd be safe there and old Vallalar hangs out there sometimes. It'd be good to talk to him. See what he makes of our young friend.

Actually, now you say it, I seem to think that it's exactly where we need to be.'

They quietly packed up and crept around the edge of the people and their possessions. They came out of the front door to find an official looking and portly man in discussion with other men on the steps.

'We need action, Mr Bloodworth', said one of the men nervously as they looked at the thick pall of smoke above the roofs ahead of them. It looked like the end of the world.

'We need firebreaks.' said another.

'Pish!' said the portly man 'A woman could piss it out.'

The other men laughed nervously, but didn't look sure.

Sam and the others skirted them carefully and made off down a side street.

Aleksy smoothed out the grey tunic he had been given to replace the dirty ragged trousers he had worn below. The world above the dark mines could not have been in starker contrast to the pits below. The high echoing halls of the Rivenrok Complex were light and clean. The people who moved around above ground, both slaves and magicians, were orderly and neat. Aleksy was still struggling to see well after so many months in near total darkness but he stared at every detail, drinking in the space and freedom. For a moment his heart felt light but then the black-robed man who had taken him from the hell beneath his feet turned to him and Aleksy's mood darkened. His situation might be better but he was no more free than he had been before. As he had got closer to the surface he had felt another mind touch his own, interested, mocking, twisted and evil. The Riven King. Aleksy had felt his mind explored by the presence and had been able to hold almost nothing back in the way that he had with Grim. The mind pressed against his own like a blind man's fingers exploring a face. It did not see every detail but it had been able to explore closely enough that it had built a pretty good picture. Aleksy shuddered.

'You will not speak unless spoken to.' said the black-robed man in his smooth voice. 'You will keep this section of this level clean. You will work until you are told to stop, then you will go to the slaves' quarters on the bottom floor. You will stay there until you are summoned. You will obey any command immediately. You will be watched.'

The man tapped a finger against his temple 'We can see you. Always. Any mistake, any attempt to do other than I have told you, will be dealt with most severely.'

The black-robed man extended an arm casually to point at a slave who was carefully sweeping a corner at the end of the corridor in which they stood. The servant suddenly froze, looking around in terror. His eyes found them at the same time as his hands flew to clutch at his head. Then with a look of startled horror he dropped to the floor, blood trickling from his ears and nose. He twitched a few times and then fell still, his eyes unseeing. He had not made a sound.

The black-robed man straightened his sleeves. 'Your first job is to clear that up. You *will* behave.' He strode away leaving Aleksy alone in the corridor, anger coursing through his veins and the Riven King's thoughts at the edge of his mind, amused by the futility of his emotions.

Daylight allowed Sam a better look at the City as they moved through it, trying to track back the way they had come. The narrow streets were cobbled for the most part, packed earth in places, a muddy maze of narrow alleyways and tall thin houses that leaned out over the street, almost touching in places. The streets were clogged with people on the move, not necessarily going in the same direction. They pushed wagons and carts laden with goods and sometimes animals. Men shouted information to each other about the path of the fire. Several times Sam and the others had to divert around large areas that were aflame or places where the seething mass of people had ground to a halt unable to decide which way to turn. The haze of smoke was everywhere, its smell mixing with the stink of sewage from the gutters at the side of the street where dogs, cats and rats nosed through rubbish.

After having to detour around a particularly large fire they came to a wall which seemed to run around the City. They followed it until they came to a large gate but it was locked and barred by guards. A crush of people jostled and pushed before it, shouting and screaming at the guards to open the gate to let them through. But the guards only shouted that the people should go back to fight the fire. As Sam and the others stood trying to decide which way to go the crowd pressed more tightly and Sam saw an elderly lady fall, the crowd surged over, no-one sparing her a glance. Indeed, no-one seemed even to have noticed.

'Hey, hey!' he shouted and fought his way through the sea of people to the place she had disappeared, pulling at arms and clothing to get through. His foot touched her before he could see her beneath him. He looked down and was just able to see her hand poking up through the crush, an elderly hand with a ring bearing a red stone. Sam pushed and pushed at the people around him until he had made a little space. As he touched the woman's hand he felt like he'd had an electric shock but he managed to grip her arm as the crowd jostled him. He was barely able to haul the woman to her feet before the crowd surged back into the gap, threatening to crush them again. With one hand under her armpit Sam shoved his way back to where Weewalk and Hadan were moving people aside to let him through.

Sam and the lady came out of the crowd like a popped cork and all but collapsed as they suddenly cleared the edge. Sam sat the woman on a nearby step and crouched down beside her. He could see that one of her eyes was already starting to blacken and swell but otherwise she seemed unhurt, although she gasped for breath.

'Thank... thank... thank you' she managed. 'I am ... thank you.' She gave him a weak smile.

A man hurried over a concerned look on his face. 'Mrs MacGuffin, are you okay? Thank goodness this gentleman was there to help.'

'Yes, I'll be fine. Thank you young man. You saved my life. Here.' she slipped the ring with the red stone from her finger and held it out to Sam. 'Take it as a thank you.'

Sam smiled. 'No, honestly. I don't need anything. I'm just glad you're not too badly hurt.'

The sudden caw of a large crow sitting on a roof nearby made them all jump and turn.

Weewalk patted Sam on the shoulder. 'I think she'll be fine. We should move.'

People were again starting to notice them and, despite Sam's actions, angry mutterings could be heard here and there. Sam stood, giving the lady a nod and a smile as he stepped back, suddenly feeling shaky and wobbly as adrenaline coursed through him. He rubbed his hand where he had touched the woman, his fingers still tingly from the strange sensation of touching her. Perhaps she had a presence, he thought. As he turned to leave Hadan whispered into his ear.

'Now, I wonder who she is, what she will become and whether she was supposed to die today. How will tomorrow be different, now that you have saved her? Or was she always going to make it out of there?'

Sam looked at Hadan in momentary horror.

'Not much you can do now.' grinned Hadan. 'You can't throw her back in. Don't worry. You did the right thing.'

Sam rubbed at his forehead, the momentary elation at his good deed quickly lost in a whirl of confusing thoughts, the end of which he could not seem to reach.

Weewalk took them back a little way before turning in again, towards the fire.

Presently they came to an area that had been entirely burnt. The charred and blackened shells of buildings and unrecognisable piles of woods and stone still smoked. Small fires flickered here and there but the blaze had eaten just about all it could. This part was deserted, everyone's attention focused elsewhere. After a couple of streets Sam recognised an alleyway they had taken the night before by the slope and twist of its cobbled surface. Now, more certain of their direction, they moved towards the bakery.

The building had gone. Hardly anything was left other than ashes and crumbling beams. The ground was hot underfoot and Sam could feel it through the soles of his shoes. After some searching they found a space where the dark maw of the cellar was visible. Pulling away a few beams with blackened hands they were able to make a space large enough to drop into. Much of the cellar was full of burnt wood. It was almost impossible to breathe with all the charred ash and smoke in the air but they found the line, its hum filling the air, and Weewalk was soon able to open it.

CHAPTER TEN

The cool dark tunnels of the London Underground were fresh after the smoke of old London. They walked for some time, Weewalk never allowing them to stop and, only occasionally, when there was no other route, taking them through the brightly lit stations. Eventually he paused before a door in a dark tunnel. There was no handle or keyhole. Weewalk moved his hand over the door, using presence to release the hidden mechanism inside and open the way, ushering them through before closing it carefully behind them. A stone archway lay ahead of them, a symbol of a mermaid etched into the stone at the point of the curve. Darkness hugged at the walls.

'Here we are.' said Weewalk, 'We'll be safe in no time.'

At the sound of his voice a shadow detached itself from the wall to the side of them. Sam immediately thought of Ferus and tensed, ready to run, but as the figure stepped into the faint light of a bare weak bulb hanging from the middle of the ceiling Sam saw that the stranger was small, a similar height to Weewalk, but less stocky. The figure spoke in a gruff voice.

'Oose dere, ooo are ya?'

Weewalk spoke 'Hödekin, is that you?'

'Owd Hob?' exclaimed the stranger and immediately bent to one knee.

'Weewalk.' said Weewalk sternly and the stranger rose sheepishly and came forward to grasp hands with him.

'Sorry. Old habits.'

Sam could see that they were both kobolds but where Weewalk was thick set Hödekin was slim. Hödekin wore more common place clothing than his mine kobold cousin, but still the clothes looked as though they had been taken from a young boy. He wore a red cap firmly pulled down on his head. His round eyes peered out from under the peak.

'Off to the Mermaid are ya?' he said looking at them in turn 'Well, you'll be welcome there sure enough. J?ran is taking in lots of folks at the moment, calling them all in, he is. Not safe for us no more. Riven are up to something. Yeren are prowling around. Yes, J?ran will see you safe at the Mermaid.'

'But what are you doing here, old friend?' asked Weewalk.

'J?ran decided to post a guard, he did. Heard a rumour someone was coming through here. We take it in turns to watch the doors to the Mermaid. There are many paths to the Tavern.'

'Here, let me introduce you to my friends.' said Weewalk. 'This is Hadan and Sam. This is Hödekin, a good friend of mine. A house kobold from the old days.'

Hödekin shook their hands, giving both of them a broad grin as he looked up into their faces.

'Well,' he said, 'from the looks of you a hot bath and

hot food is what is needed. Don't let me keep you here.'

He turned to the archway and waved his hands. The line immediately sprang into life, sucking at what little light there was in the room. After giving their thanks they each stepped through the portal and away from the London Underground.

Arriving after Hadan, Sam found he had appeared in the middle of an enormous fireplace. Stretching apart his hands he could not touch the sides and he was able to walk out without ducking. He was thankful that no fire had been lit, it would have been the size of a bonfire, and he guessed that maybe that was one of the defences for this place. Surely no one, with the possible exception of Ferus, could use that line whilst a fire was burning here. The room he stepped into was empty of people, other than Hadan and Weewalk, and was not dissimilar from the old pub that his grandfather had sometimes taken him to back in the village at home. Sam turned on the spot, looking around. A long bar ran down the wall opposite the fireplace, dried hops hanging along its length. Latticed windows to one side allowed sunlight to creep across a deep red carpet. The room was full of tables and benches. The walls and ceiling were white with dark wooden beams set into them. Old iron weapons hung here and there and Sam saw a pair of crossed pikes on one wall and a spiked mace on another. A murmur of conversation came from a corridor to one side and mixed with the pleasant sound of tinkling water. Immediately Sam felt as though this was a place of safety and tranquillity.

'Welcome to the Mermaid Tavern' said Weewalk. 'The owner is a man named J?ran. When you meet him, try not to stare at him. He's a good man, and friendly, but he can get touchy about certain things. He's not someone to mess with so we'll be safe here for as long as we want.'

'Is he on our side?' asked Sam.

'He's not on anyone's side.' said Weewalk, 'But he'll allow no trouble or harm for any of his guests.'

'How can we pay him?' said Sam, 'I didn't bring any money.'

'Let me worry about that.' said Weewalk.

At that point a man entered the room. He was the biggest person Sam had ever seen. A giant. He barely fitted through the door behind the bar. He straightened up and looked at them, a slight scowl on his broad face. He held a glass in one enormous hand and he rubbed at it with a rag. He wore a dirty apron over rough brown clothes. He was bald but the forearms which stuck out of his sleeves were covered in thick black hair.

Weewalk spoke, looking smaller than ever before the huge man in front of him.

'Hello J?ran. Do you have room for three?'

The man considered a moment, then gave a slow nod. He set the glass he had been wiping on a shelf above the bar and tucked the rag into the front of his apron. He raised a flap on the bar and strode out, stooping to avoid hitting his head on the low ceiling and turning sideways to squeeze his huge frame through the opening. He walked past them towards the corridor giving Sam a hard look as he passed. Sam realised that he had been staring, his mouth slightly open, and he hurriedly swallowed and looked at Hadan who was also looking at him, but with a smirk. J?ran gave a jerk of his head, motioning them to follow him.

They entered a long wood-panelled corridor but turned straight away to a set of steep rickety stairs which groaned under J?ran's weight as they climbed. They came onto a twisted corridor, the floor sloped noticeably. Taking a bunch of keys from a pocket the giant unlocked a door and held it open for them to enter. As he passed

Sam could not help but notice that his head did not even come up to the height of the huge arm that held open the door.

The room contained four single beds and other assorted mismatched wooden furniture. More latticed windows looked out onto a lush green garden where the sunlight of what seemed to be a warm summer's evening threw the shadow of large trees across a beautiful lawn. J?ran nodded at them and backed out of the doorway, closing the door behind him.

Weewalk immediately hopped onto a bed, his dirty boots hanging over the edge and sighed. 'It'll be good to sleep in a bed again.' he said happily, bouncing up and down.

Sam pulled off his shoes and chose another of the beds.

'J?ran doesn't say much does he?'

'He hasn't spoken a single word since his wife died.' said Weewalk, 'They were closer than anyone you'll ever meet. He named the Tavern after her.'

'The Mermaid?' said Sam confused.

'Yup,' said Weewalk, 'She loved our giant friend just as much as he loved her. One of the Nommo, she was. A Selkie. They say she was a beauty the like of which has never been seen.'

'But she was a mermaid?' said Sam, still trying to catch up.

'She was a Nommo tribeswoman from Mu. But, yes, in essence that is a mermaid if you're talking about human mythology. I wouldn't mention her around our host, if you know what's good for you.'

Sam sank into a steaming hot bath up to his chin. It felt amazing. He hadn't felt clean in days. He'd let Weewalk and Hadan use the bathroom first so that he could have as long as he wanted in the hot water. A fresh set of clothes waited for him on the soft bed back in the room. He used his fingernails to scrub at the dirt on his legs and arms and he kneaded his tired muscles with his knuckles. He studied a number of blisters on his feet. It would be good to rest here for a while. The Tavern seemed so tranquil and friendly.

Eventually, he rose from the water, leaving it considerably dirtier than when he had entered it. He wrapped himself in a fluffy towel and forced a comb through his brown hair. He dressed and took the stairs down to the room with the giant fireplace. The smell of food filled the space and Weewalk and Hadan were tucking into large plates full of chicken and potatoes. A wicker basket of freshly baked bread was in the middle of the table and Sam took a piece as he sat down. It was delicious and still warm, the top coated in poppy seeds. A few minutes later J?ran placed a plate of chicken in front of him and Sam attacked it hungrily. Eventually sated he sat back happily, rubbing his stomach. The sun had set and the last rays of the evening light showed through the window.

None of them spoke. There was no need. They were all full and content. It wasn't long before they silently trooped upstairs, dropped into their beds and fell asleep.

For a week Sam, Weewalk and Hadan simply enjoyed good food, plenty of sleep and the sun in the gardens. It was a simple life but Sam felt incredibly content. He finally had time to take stock of what had happened, the death of his grandfather, the destruction of his house, the pursuit from Ferus, the fight with the garoul and the bizarre events in old London. He even thought about the beautiful girl in the painting that had hung in the house and how the fire had curled its edges and destroyed it.

Sam and Weewalk talked more about his presence and Sam continued to try to make things move using the power of his mind. This was the only time when he felt unhappy. He was still unable to do so much as lift a feather and Weewalk's calm confidence made his failures all the harder to bear. Sam was trying for what seemed like the hundredth time to have some effect on a leaf which floated in the pool under the tinkling fountain in the central courtyard when Weewalk told him that he would meet someone new on the following day.

'His name is Vallalar', said Weewalk, watching the leaf for any sign of movement. 'He's particularly good at seeing potential in others. Hödekin told me that they're expecting him to arrive tomorrow. He's been guarding another of the entrances for a while.'

'It's no good, Weewalk.' said Sam, 'I still won't be able to do it.'

'We'll see.' said the kobold. 'Let's leave it for today.'

Kya sat on a long bench, an empty plate before her on the pitted wooden table. She eyed the others in the room. An odd bunch. This clearly wasn't the most salubrious of places. Two shady figures were in deep conversation in one corner of the room. In another corner the hairiest person she had ever seen was hunched over a flagon of beer. She wasn't entirely sure he wasn't part Yowie.

A shadow fell over her plate and Kya looked up. A woman stood before her, long dark hair covering much of her face. The newcomer looked around at the others in the room warily.

'Scusi, you are Kya?' she asked quietly.

'Depends who's asking.' said Kya carefully.

The woman sat down opposite Kya. 'My name is Eusapia. Aye ave a message from J?ran at the Mermaid Tavern. The boy you are looking for. Ee is there.'

'How do I know I can trust you?' asked Kya.

The woman looked around hurriedly. Satisfied that no-one was watching she extended a hand over the table between them. Her hand hovered above Kya's plate which, after a moment, span on the table then lifted into the air and hovered a couple of inches above the stained wooden plank.

'You go. Find him.' said Eusapia. The plate dropped back onto the tabletop with a thunk and Kya saw one of the shadowy men in the corner look over quickly.

'Must go.' said the woman and held out her hand again, but palm up. She nodded at Kya

Sighing Kya reached into a pocket and took out some Murian gold. She placed a single piece in the woman's hand.

Eusapia stood quickly and, with a last look around, drew her coat tightly around her and hurried from the room. Kya leaned back and stretched out her legs. So, he was at the Mermaid. She'd make the journey as soon as she could. Right now she had more pressing things to deal with. She was being followed.

Kya left the inn and stepped out onto the moonlit crossroads. She looked each direction and choosing one set off at a slow walk. She sent her presence behind her and sensed the man step out of the shadows of the stables and pad after her. She kept her eyes forward and tried to walk casually, which was surprisingly difficult once you began to concentrate upon it.

The path turned a corner into some trees and, as soon as she judged that she was out of the sight of her pursuer, Kya darted behind a large tree.

She did not have to wait long. The man crept between the trees on the opposite side of the road, even more cautious now that he had lost sight of his prey. Kya waited until he was level with her hiding place and then stepped out from behind the tree, simultaneously raising an arm and shaping her hand as if she were grasping a cup. The man froze, his back to a tree. His face began to flush, visible even in the pale moonlight.

Kya strode towards him. He was a weasely sort of man, with a pinched face and wide staring eyes. Kya had him by the throat and he was unable to move.

'Why are you following me?' she asked.

'Not following.' managed the man, struggling a little to breathe.

'I'll ask again.' said Kya 'Why are you following me and who sent you?'

The man only grinned, although the pressure on his windpipe made it come out as a grimace.

Kya sighed and lifted her arm slightly higher. A look of panic crossed the man's face and he lifted a little higher in the air until the tips of his boots were only just touching the floor.

'I'm dead if I tell you.' he managed.

'You must be confused about what's happening here.' said Kya coolly.

The man slid further up the tree trunk. He was now unable to touch the ground and he began to choke and struggle. Kya held him firmly although she was already beginning to tire. She tried not to show it.

'Ferus.' the man groaned, trying to push against the invisible bonds that held him aloft by the throat.

Kya did not relieve the pressure.

'Looking for the boy too.' he gasped, his face flushing darker, his lips parted in a snarl.

Kya lessened the pressure on his neck and he took a great gasp of air before entering into a fit of coughing. She kept him held against the tree for a moment. Then, looking up, she raised her arm again. The man was lifted into the very top of the tall tree his legs kicking as he rose. Kya placed him on a branch that she judged was just strong enough to hold his weight, provided he didn't squirm. She called up to him.

'Stop following me!'

Then she turned and walked away through the wood, quickly disappearing into the black night.

The man looked around wildly, gripping on to the branch as it bounced and creaked under his weight. The nearest branch was well out of reach. He was stuck.

Sam didn't feel like getting out of bed and stayed there for most of the morning. He knew that Weewalk wanted him to meet the mystic they had discussed the previous day, but he hated the thought of having to show someone else that he was completely without talent. Around midday Hadan forced him out, all but dragging him from beneath the sheets.

'Come on.' he said sternly 'You're to meet Vallalar. Weewalk wants him to have a look at you.'

'Why do you care anyway? What difference does it make to you?' said Sam grouchily.

'The Riven want to kill you. That's their idea, not ours. You should be grateful that we've helped you this far. Vallalar might be able to take it further and actually help you defend yourself. Although I'm not entirely convinced that you deserve it! Perhaps we should just throw you to the garoul! Now get out of bed!'

Sam felt so miserable that he never wanted to move again but eventually he found himself in the room with the fireplace. J?ran wiped at glasses with a dirty rag and Weewalk was deep in conversation with an elderly man with wrinkled brown skin, a light grey beard and long white hair. They turned as Sam and Hadan entered the room.

'Goodness me, but he is skinny isn't he?' said the man

in an accent which might have been Indian. His eyes twinkled kindly and Sam could not help but feel a little of his trepidation trickle away. 'Come here, young man and let me take a look at you.'

Sam stepped forward. Vallalar rose and walked around him in a circle, stroking his beard as he did so. He turned to Weewalk 'And you say he threw a garoul through a wall hard enough to kill it?'

'Yes,' said Weewalk. 'I'm sure of it.'

'Was there anyone else in the room?'

'It was just the three of us.'

Vallalar turned his attention to Hadan. 'So, you were there too were you? Hmmm,' he studied Hadan carefully, 'Ever showed any power yourself, Hadan?'

'No.' said Hadan softly 'It definitely wasn't me.'

'Are you sure?' said Vallalar.

Sam had never seen Hadan look anything other than confident and composed even to the point of arrogance, but here he looked distinctly uncomfortable and unhappy.

There was an edge to his voice when he answered 'Vallalar, it wasn't me, alright?' He kept his eyes on the floor.

'Well, if you're sure.' said Vallalar with a nod of his head, turning again to Sam. 'Must have been you then.' he said happily. 'Come with me.'

Sam followed the elderly man into the small courtyard that sat at the centre of the building. The sky above was blue and the midday sun pushed down into the stone square. The fountain tinkled and goldfish swam in lazy circles in the pool underneath, bright orange against the dark water. Vallalar led them to a patch of shade against one wall. He sat down crossed his legs and closed his eyes with a sigh.

'Good.' he said, almost to himself. Opening his eyes

he beckoned Sam to sit next to him. 'Please, Samuel, sit down.'

Sam sat, crossing his legs too.

Vallalar spoke 'Please close your eyes.'

Sam did as he was told.

'Samuel, one of the powers that is possible with presence is the training of the mind to sense many different things around you and inside you. I have practised meditation for many years and can set my mind to wander free. As well as moving some objects with my mind, by telekinesis, I can study things that are not usually visible. I am going to send my mind into your body and sense all the things inside. You may feel some odd sensations.'

With a start, Sam realised that the last sentence had not been heard by his ears. The words had been spoken directly into his head.

He opened his eyes to check that Vallalar was still there. The man sat motionless, his eyes closed.

The voice came again within his head. 'Please Samuel, close your eyes.' Vallalar's mouth had not moved.

Sam closed his eyes again and tried not to feel nervous. As he sat as still as he could he began to feel a strange fluttering in his chest and stomach, then a funny pressure behind his eyes. After a few minutes Vallalar spoke, normally this time.

'Thank you, Samuel. Please be so good as to take off your shoes and lie down.'

Sam did as he was told. Vallalar moved so that he could see the soles of Sam's feet. He picked up the right foot and kneaded it with his soft but firm fingers. After a moment Sam began to feel a warmth running up and down his spine. His back seemed to ripple against the cool stone slabs of the courtyard.

Vallalar stopped. 'All done, you may sit up, thank you.'

'Is that it?' said Sam.

'Yes, what did you expect?'

'I don't know. Something grander, more magical I guess.'

Sam raised himself into a sitting position and the warmth in his spine flowed away. Other than feeling rather relaxed he didn't feel any different. But Vallalar seemed very pleased.

'Samuel,' he said happily, 'It *was* magical. I unlocked your presence. And I think it might be rather strong. Now it is time to begin. You could be an important ally to the rebels. But tell me, have you ever been to a desert?'

There were several lines that existed in and around the tavern. Hadan and Weewalk had shown Sam their locations on the second day. The building was widely believed to be haunted. Indeed, Sam had heard that it was rumoured to be one of the most haunted locations in the country but he knew that the strange sensations and 'ghostly' happenings were caused by the effects of the lines that lay here and there, invisible to those without presence. The feelings that were caused by these lines no longer troubled Sam now that he knew what they were, no more than passing any other closed door would. The Tavern, although odd in places, felt comfortable and familiar.

The particular line that they needed was behind a shed in the garden. Vallalar opened it in a moment and he and Sam stepped through. Vallalar had instructed Sam to wear warm clothing which had confused Sam given that they were, he thought, travelling to a desert. But when he felt the ground form beneath his feet Sam understood why. There was no doubt that this was a desert, and as such suffered extremely high temperatures, but they had arrived at night and the rocky sand was cold under the dark star-studded sky. The wind sighed and moaned across the featureless landscape. A light blue tinged one horizon but Sam could not yet tell whether it was an approaching dawn or the disappearing day. The moon hung above them, out-shining all but the brightest stars.

'Well, Samuel, here we are.' said Vallalar. 'Time for us to move mountains. Have you ever heard the mystery of the rolling rocks of Death Valley?'

Sam nodded his head. By chance he had heard of the mystery. Rocks in a desert had been found to have long tracks in the sand stretching away behind them. The land was flat and the rocks were too heavy to be moved by the wind, or even by a man or animal. Yet apparently the rocks did move across the desert although no-one had ever seen it happen.

Vallalar continued 'I am confident that you are about to become part of that mystery. This way please.'

They walked up a slight rise until they could see a flat sandy plain below them. Vallalar seated himself at the crest of a dune facing towards the empty space. Tiny streams of sand trickled away at every movement. Looking again Sam could see that the area before them was not empty. In the moonlight he could see a number of boulders of varying sizes. Most were roughly spherical. He sat down next to Vallalar.

Vallalar pointed out a smallish rock, the size of a basketball. 'Samuel, I want you to move that rock.'

Sam began to stand up and Vallalar gave a laugh. 'No, Samuel. Like this.'

He took a slow deep breath and Sam saw the rock begin to roll. It was quickly rolling across the plain like a remote-controlled marble, twisting, turning. Sam gaped. The old man moved it with such ease.

Vallalar brought it to rest in front of them and turned to Sam.

'Now you try. Reach out to it with your mind. Imagine your mind wrapping around it. Once you feel that you are holding it, move it. It is more straightforward than perhaps you are thinking.'

Sam had tried this many times with Weewalk but had not been able even to move a sausage. How would he move something a thousand times heavier? But he did as instructed and imagined he was holding the boulder before him.

'Raise your hand if you find it easier.' said Vallalar from one side.

Sam did as he said. He raised his arm and immediately felt a change. He concentrated with all his might and then the warm feeling came to his spine. His arm began to shake. The rock moved an inch. Sam tensed even more, his jaw aching from straining.

'Aaaaarghhhh.' a cry escaped his mouth under the strain but then the rock moved properly. As if it had been given a sudden shove by an invisible hand it rolled three feet away from them.

'Ha!' shouted Sam joyously. 'I did it! Wow! I moved it!'

'Yes Samuel,' said Vallalar 'You have a presence.'

Sam and Vallalar spent another few hours in Death Valley. Sam found he was increasingly able to control the movement of the rocks and by the time Vallalar called a halt there were tracks in the sand behind many of the boulders, even some of the larger ones. They eventually had to leave as the sun had come up and began to beat down with an intensity that was completely at odds with the chilly night. Sam arrived back at the Tavern exhausted but happy.

It was evening at the Tavern when they got back. Sam

couldn't see Weewalk or Hadan and Vallalar excused himself so Sam ate alone before the giant fireplace. Having finished an excellent chicken pie he sat alone, too tired to go to bed, fingering the puckered scar on his right hand.

What now? Not long ago he had been an ordinary boy in an ordinary world. When his grandfather died his life had been thrown into chaos. Now he was sitting in a tavern, with a strange power which allowed him to affect the world with his mind. A power that, grown strong enough, might allow him to stop Ferus from hurting anyone else. A scowl crossed Sam's face as he sat there alone. Tired as he was, he sat, working out what to do. Eventually he nodded to himself and left the room.

Back in the bedroom Sam was almost ready to fall asleep when Weewalk came in alone. He was beaming at Sam in the candlelight. Sam slipped from between the sheets and walked over to Weewalk. He dropped to his knees in front of the small figure and gave him an enormous hug. Surprised Weewalk gave a laugh and put his arms behind Sam's back, returning the embrace.

'Thank you,' said Sam quietly. 'For everything. For getting me here. For saving my life. For showing me what you have. I want to help you.'

Weewalk looked at him fondly. 'Sam, this is just the beginning. Welcome to the resistance.'

CHAPTER ELEVEN

Over time Vallalar and Sam worked hard to build the strength and control of Sam's telekinetic powers. After one particularly long day in the kitchen of the Mermaid Sam found he was able to bend a metal spoon in half, and back again, so that there was hardly a ripple or mark on the stem. At one point J?ran came into the room to see a large pile of buckled cutlery on his big oak table. His eyes widened in shock and Sam was suddenly terrified. Then with an enormous beaming smile he clapped Sam on the back so hard that Sam nearly fell over. J?ran had marched from the room still smiling.

Another day saw Vallalar break an egg into a large glass full of water. By the end of the day Sam was able to separate the yolk from the white and even lift the yolk from the glass without breaking it. That night every guest had enormous cheese omelettes to eat, cooked in a massive frying pan by a still smiling J?ran.

After a week or so of moving things, big and small, Vallalar said that he wanted to try a different sort of exercise.

'Samuel, this is about building a barrier around yourself.' he said. 'You have seen Ferus walk through an inferno. He is no more impervious to fire than you or me but he is greatly skilled at control. As you are able to separate yolk from white so he is able to push away flame and heat and hold it millimetres from his body. Were that hold to break the fire would rush into the space and he would be consumed as any other man. It is an enormously difficult thing to hold something as abstract as heat. Have you ever heard of spontaneous human combustion? That's what happens when it goes wrong. Today we will practice.'

Vallalar moved to the giant fireplace. To one side a small fire was burning, the first time that Sam had seen one lit in the massive space. Even with the fire burning steadily at one side there was enough room for a man to ride through on horseback should the line be opened.

Vallalar closed his eyes and stretched out a hand towards the fire. A glowing coal lifted from the centre of the fire, a dull red in the air as it moved towards him. He sat perfectly still as it moved. Then he opened his mouth. The coal floated between his teeth and seemed to come to rest on his tongue. As Vallalar breathed the coal pulsed red, then yellow until it was almost white hot. He opened his eyes and looked at Sam.

It was a bizarre sight to see this man with a white hot fire burning in his mouth. The coal lifted back between his teeth and Vallalar used his presence to toss it casually back into the fire.

'The trick, Samuel,' he said, 'is to create a barrier that you do not allow the heat to penetrate. The difficulty comes in making that barrier as thin as possible. We are, I confess, reaching the limit of my powers. I cannot move the flames with any skill. But you should not assume that you are bound by my own limitations.'

Sam spent the morning trying to manipulate the fire that crackled in the grate. It seemed to be impossible. Every time he tried to focus on a tongue of flame it flickered away and another took its place. The fire was never in one spot. It was immensely frustrating, like trying to pick up a pin wearing boxing gloves. Even where a single flame seemed to persist it twisted and moved so that Sam could not grasp it.

In the afternoon Sam practised holding a glowing coal above a sheet of paper without the paper burning. By the time they stopped the smell of smoke filled the entire tavern and there was a large puddle before them where J?ran had had to rush in with a large bucket of water to douse a fire on one of his tables.

Having had a few days of success Sam felt dejected from the day's failures. That evening he sulked through a meal with Weewalk and Hadan.

Weewalk gave a knowing smile. 'I've got an important errand to run tomorrow. Would you like to come with me?'

'Yes.' said Sam quickly, eager to escape lessons for a time.

'I thought you'd say that.' Weewalk's grin broadened.

The next day Sam and Weewalk set off early. The other residents of the Tavern were still asleep. Only J?ran was up, busying himself with pounding some fresh dough with his huge hands. Before Sam had had enough time to properly wake up and ask where they were going Weewalk had led them to a line within a small room on the second floor. He focused his presence on the barrier, tearing it open, his shoulders hunched with the effort.

'After you.' he gestured to Sam with a small bow. 'Keep quiet once you arrive.'

Sam found himself in a bedroom in a typical looking

home. The lights in the room were off but a little light filtered through the window. It looked as though the sun had set some time ago and the sky was fading to black. Sam could hear the noise of a television somewhere below.

Weewalk tapped him on the back, making him jump. Sam turned and Weewalk motioned for silence before leading the way to the bedroom door. As they came onto a landing Sam could see that the top floor of the house was in darkness, but lights were on downstairs and the flickering white-blue light of a TV shone in a doorway at the bottom of the stairs.

Together they crept down the stairs towards the front door, checking each step for squeaky floorboards as they moved. As they reached the bottom Weewalk gestured with his hand and the handle turned and the door swung quietly inwards. They hurried the last few feet into the cool evening air and as they moved down a path through a neat suburban garden Sam let out a breath he had been holding. As they neared the garden gate he heard the front door click shut behind him.

Weewalk led them along the street. Lights shone in many windows and the kobold looked around carefully as though he was trying to remember his way.

'What are we going to do?' asked Sam. Weewalk had said nothing of what he actually intended.

'We just need to give a quick bit of help to someone very dear and important to me. Ah, here we are.' Weewalk came to a house and looked up at the sky. 'Come on, we don't have much time.' he said.

This house had no lights on that Sam could see and Weewalk led them around the side where he unlocked a gate and led them into a large garden.

'Hide yourself in that bush.' he said pointing at a group of small conifers. 'Quickly now.'

Sam squeezed himself between two trunks. The smell of pine filled the evening air and he felt sticky sap on his fingertips. He turned and looked out into the garden. Weewalk jogged over to a rotary washing line and after looking into the cloud of clothes above his head he jumped and pulled down some piece of material, leaving two pegs swinging round the line. He tucked it under his arm and scurried back to Sam and squeezed in next to him.

'Stay out of sight,' the kobold said. 'I don't need you to do anything. Just watch.'

As he finished speaking Sam became aware of a noise off to their left, behind the high wooden fence that bordered the garden. The commotion grew louder until there was a loud bang as something hit the fence, making Sam jump. As he looked a familiar bearded face, straining with effort, appeared above the wooden panelling. The figure wrestled an arm over the top and then another before heaving himself up and falling over the fence to land with a thump in the flowerbed below. After a huge sigh the figure forced himself to his feet and began to run across the garden, towards the opposite fence.

Sam stared in amazement. The tired figure running across the lawn was Weewalk, yet Weewalk still crouched next to him, his hand on Sam's arm, holding him back in the shelter of the bushes. The other Weewalk was almost completely naked. He was only wearing a pair of grubby Y-fronts. It was difficult to see in the dark but Sam thought he looked younger, his beard slightly shorter.

Another noise drew Sam's attention back to the fence. As he turned his head he saw a large shape clear the fence in a single bound. Sam recognised it as a garoul, the same kind of beast that had attacked them in the cabin in Dragsholm. In a moment it was at the heels of the naked

Weewalk, reaching out with its claws.

Just as it was about to catch the kobold, the Weewalk with whom Sam was hiding, flew out from the bushes shouting. He aimed a powerful blast of presence at the monster, knocking it through the air and into a football goal where it tripped over and tangled itself in the netting. A moment later Weewalk had tossed the spotted dress from the washing line to the naked Weewalk and with another blast of presence pushed the other version of himself up and over the next fence. As the figure flew through the air Sam heard him shout a string of numbers, and his Weewalk shouted another set in response, adding the word 'Mermaid' before darting back into the bushes next to him. The beast was back on its feet now and, unable to see them in the undergrowth, continued the pursuit, leaping the fence. The garden was suddenly quiet. The whole thing had taken seconds.

Chuckling softly Weewalk shook his head. 'That dress was the most comfortable thing I had ever worn. I'd never had anything fit so well.' He smoothed his own spotted yellow dress, which was a considerable amount grubbier than the one he had thrown to his younger self.

'How did you know when and where to be to help him, to help yourself, I mean?' asked Sam.

'You heard us call dates and times to each other. And I knew where to hide as I'd seen it happen once before. I should have realised sooner, back when we were escaping from Ferus, that we'd need to come to the Mermaid. I knew I'd need to be here, to go back to help myself out. That, in some ways, had already happened so we probably couldn't have done anything differently. Still, it's hard to keep it all in your head sometimes. Especially when you're on the run! Most of the time it's better not to try to think too hard about these things and just go with the flow. It usually works out in the end.'

Sam had been trying to think hard about it but realising that understanding the finer points of time travel were perhaps beyond him, he resolved to simply accept the order of events henceforth and, as Weewalk had put it, go with the flow. Seeing that he had given up on his internal struggle Weewalk clapped him on the shoulder and, squeezing out of the conifers, they set off in search of the line back to the Tavern.

The next day Vallalar came to Sam and brought with him a man Sam had not met before.

'Today, Samuel, something different. The time is coming when you will need to use your presence to defend yourself and fight. From now on you will practice how to block and counter-attack. I am not the best person to teach you this. Odhar, here, will be your instructor.'

The other man stepped forward to shake Sam by the hand. He was not much to look at. Muscular but not particularly strong looking, more wiry than anything. He gave Sam a nod and motioned for Sam to follow him as he turned away. And that was where it began. Sam soon realised that he had underestimated the man. Odhar showed Sam new skills and tricks and ways to use his powers that he would never have considered. Sam found that his slight frame made him more agile than he had expected and he was soon confident in throwing himself through the air by pushing off the ground and walls with his mind. He could twist as he flew but Odhar always seemed able to find a way through his defences so that he would end up being knocked to the floor by a blast of energy. After a while Sam was better able to make a defensive barrier, in much the same way as Vallalar had shown Sam how to protect himself from the heat of a fire, and Odhar threw pulses of energy like invisible punches at his defences to test them. After another two weeks Sam felt like he knew how to fight.

People came and went at the Tavern but one day, as he sat down to dinner, Sam realised that there were a few more people than usual staying tonight. Several had arrived separately throughout the day. Sam looked at one of the new arrivals from the corner of his eye.

The newcomer was a girl, with long straight black hair which she kept across her face. Sam hadn't been able to get a good look at her but he had the impression that she was about his age. She was, Sam felt sure, very pretty underneath that mask of hair and he found it hard not to look at her as Weewalk and Hadan chatted about various things. Once or twice Sam thought that she might be looking at him, but he was never sure whether she was looking out from under her hair, or past him, or indeed at Weewalk, who frequently received odd stares. Either way, she left the room before Sam and the others had finished eating and he did not see her again that evening. Sam watched her as she left the room and Weewalk broke off his conversation with Hadan to look at Sam accusingly.

'What?' said Sam guiltily through a mouthful of apple crumble.

After another day of training Sam's thoughts returned to the girl he had seen the night before but he had not seen her around the Tavern that day and so he presumed that she had moved on. So, he was surprised when he turned a corner and, exhausted after another long session with Odhar, collided with someone coming the other way. Sam had been so absorbed in thinking about what he and Odhar had been doing that he ran into the other person quite hard, hard enough that the force of it knocked him backwards and he sat down heavily on the floor.

He looked up. It was her, the girl from the night before. He looked into her face as she swept her black hair away from her face obviously completely untroubled for being hit hard enough for Sam to fall back. It was her. Not just the girl from the night before. It was the beautiful girl from the painting at his grandfather's house. The realisation hit Sam like a punch to the stomach and he gasped. How was this possible? He knew her face as well as his own. He had fixed his eyes on that face every time he had felt the prickle of the hairs rising on his neck as he had climbed those haunted stairs. The hairs rose now as he looked up into her face and he realised that this time the feeling was because she had used presence to protect herself as he collided with her. Then as she looked down at him, a slight smile on her lips, her face seemed to change and as sure as he had been a second ago Sam became completely unsure that this was the same girl.

Sam realised that he was sprawled on the floor his legs apart.

'Sorry,' she said, offering him a hand, 'Are you alright?'

'Yes, er, sorry about that. I wasn't looking where I was going.' He took her hand and shook it at the same time as he scrambled to his feet.

'Kya.' she said, 'You're Sam, right?'

'Sam, er yes, I mean, how do you know my name?'

A look of relief seemed to appear on Kya's face. It was there for a moment, and then gone. 'I saw you training. Vallalar says you're very strong.'

'Oh, really? He never....' Sam realised he was still shaking Kya's hand and dropped it hurriedly.

'I have a presence too, if you ever wanted to practice together.' said Kya.

'Well, yes. That would be er... great.'

'Good.' Her face turned serious. For Sam it was as

though the sun had gone behind a cloud 'I need to talk to the kobold that's with you. It's urgent.'

'I think he's at the bar.' said Sam. Weewalk had been looking lovingly at a pewter tankard of ale when Sam had arrived back.

'Thanks.' said Kya 'See you soon, I hope.'

And with that she headed off past Sam. He turned and watched her go. For a moment he had been certain it was the girl from the painting. But it couldn't be. There was no doubt that she looked similar, but the likeness was not exact. It was just a coincidence. There was no way the painting could have been of her. Deciding it was nothing more than a coincidence Sam headed to his room. Even if it wasn't her there was no doubt that she was just as pretty. He groaned inwardly as he thought how he must have looked sitting slack-jawed on the floor. Still, what had she said? See you soon, I hope. That had to be good.

After an hour or so Weewalk stumped into the room, a grim expression on his face as he sat on a bed opposite Sam. Hadan appeared a moment later and sat down too. He looked pale. Turning to Sam Weewalk said something which Sam had been dreading.

'It's time for us to leave.'

Sam had been worried about this for some time. 'Where will you go?'

'Not us.' smiled Weewalk pointing to himself and Hadan, 'Us!' he said, this time swinging his finger around like he had a lasso so that he pointed to all three of them. 'We have to stick together.'

'You didn't think we'd leave you here, did you?' said Hadan.

Sam shrugged his shoulders, feeling slightly better. He didn't want to leave the comfort of the Mermaid behind and say goodbye to Vallalar and Odhar and J?ran but if he was going to leave then at least the others would be coming too.

'We're pretty confident that Ferus knows that we're here and we've had some incredible but important news this evening which means that we need to put ourselves in some danger.' said Weewalk. 'We can't stay here anyway. With Ferus close the Riven may even be bold enough to try to attack the Tavern, even though they'd have a serious fight on their hands.'

'What's the news and how do you know he's close?' asked Sam, looking around nervously.

'There has been a yeren watching the place for a few days.' said Hadan, avoiding Sam's first question. 'If you go out into the garden after dark you might see him hiding in the bushes. We can only presume that he is feeding information back to Ferus.'

'What? I thought we were safe here.' said Sam.

'Ordinarily I'd say we would be.' said Hadan. 'It doesn't really make much sense to fight us here. There are enough lines in the building that we could easily escape any attack but Ferus is definitely up to something. We're better off getting away before he puts whatever plan he has into action.'

'Fine by me.' said Sam, thinking back to the oppressive menacing feeling that had washed over him when Ferus was near. He shivered at the thought of it. 'So, where will we go?'

Weewalk spoke up. 'We're going on a rescue mission. A dangerous one. We're going to rescue Tarak Everune, the secret keeper. The Riven have him captive but he has a message for us and we have to hear it before it's too late.'

'But I thought he was just a drunk coward.' said Sam remembering an earlier conversation.

Weewalk gave a sigh and a small nod before replying.

'It seems Everune may have misled us all.' he said grimly. 'Friend and foe alike. He carries one last great secret. A secret that may determine the entire future of man, Murian, Riven and koboldkind. If this goes wrong then we're doomed.'

Sam miserably stuffed his meagre possessions into his rucksack whilst Weewalk and Hadan prepared their bags too. Just a few hours ago he had felt happy for the first time in what seemed like a lifetime. Learning new powers. Living comfortably with friends around. Sam added a set of warm winter clothes that J?ran had given him as a gift to his bag. You never knew when a line would take you into a wintry place and it was best to pack for all occasions. The conversation with Weewalk and Hadan had not gone on for much longer. Sam had tried to pry more information from the kobold but Weewalk had promised that he knew nothing more. Sam couldn't tell just how Kya, for he presumed that the information had come from her, had persuaded Weewalk that Tarak was worthy of saving, but whatever she had said had utterly persuaded Weewalk and Hadan that this dangerous mission was necessary. Sam had also discovered that Kya would be coming with them, guiding them to where Tarak was held captive in Mu. At the moment Sam wasn't sure how he felt about that. Part of him already wanted to remain close to Kya, his stomach lurched when he thought of her, but another part of him felt a little resentful that she was joining their group and that she had set the path that they would take. He couldn't believe that the four of them were the best ones for the job. Surely there were stronger people out there, with a more marked presence, who could complete Tarak's rescue much better. There was something going on here, thought Sam to himself. He knew he was usually too trusting to a fault but something about this situation just didn't fit.

It was clear that Weewalk and Hadan had not really had much of a plan before. They were used to moving around fairly frequently and spending their time being a general nuisance to the Riven wherever possible. And yet they had let Kya persuade them that they should put themselves into mortal danger for the rescue of Tarak Everune. It seemed like madness to Sam. He could not see the benefit in taking on the Riven to save the drunk, broken man who had once held the secrets of all those that were good and pure. They would be leaving the Tavern the next day. Sam's training was over.

Sam sighed and looked out into the moonlit garden. A light wind rustled the leaves on the trees and bushes, as though the trees were sighing softly. Then something caught his eye. As he looked he realised that a figure was standing motionless in the shadow of a tree looking deeper into the garden. Sam followed its gaze and saw another person there, and another.

'Weewalk,' he breathed 'There are lots of people in the garden.'

The kobold hurriedly blew out the candles and the room fell dark. He hurried over to the window, jumping onto a bed to be high enough to look out.

'Yeren.' he said, 'Lots of them.'

Hadan came to join them and gasped. Something else pushed a bush aside.

'What's that?' asked Sam.

'A nandi.' said Hadan.' Where has he come from? And look there, garoul.'

The three of them stood silently at the window watching as an army of their enemies gathered in the darkness below.

CHAPTER TWELVE

By his best reckoning Aleksy had spent a month above
ground, tending to the needs of the magicians who lived
and worked within the Complex. All the while he had
allowed himself to appear cowed. He had dutifully
mopped and swept, carried and obeyed, pausing only to
sleep, eat or to hang his head whenever the swish of black
robes or the echo of voices could be heard in the
otherwise still air. Life was infinitely better than it had
been in the mines, but still Aleksy was not free and still
his anger burnt inside of him.

He had met other captives but the other slaves were
reluctant to talk. Many were little more than mindless
zombies. Aleksy had seen some whose minds had
eventually completely gone. They were taken away and
never reappeared.

Rather than cultivate friendships Aleksy had used the
time to find his way around the Complex when he could.
At first the King's presence in his mind had been quite
regular but now, he felt as though he was often free of it
or at least that it was different somehow. When he was

certain that his brain was his own he tried to build a plan of escape and form a map of the complex in his head. He had found the main entrance but it was always well guarded. He had also been able to pass the door to the throne room, although it had been closed. He could feel the King behind that terrible door, silent and waiting. It was the discovery of this door that had really excited him. If he could get in then he might be able to kill the King or at least hold him hostage in some way. It would throw the entire building into disarray. The King's mind seemed to affect everyone and without that stabilising presence Aleksy was sure he could lose himself in the confusion. It wasn't much of a plan, but he had nothing else to go on and he felt the need to escape with a fierce desperation, like a drowning man fighting for the surface. One day he would gain access to that room, at just the right moment, and slit the King's throat where he sat. He would end this cruel tyranny. But first he needed more information.

Aleksy sat at the long bench where the slaves ate their meals. A dozen or so sat at the table in silence. Although there were no magicians in the room still no-one spoke. Aleksy had tried to strike up a conversation when he had first arrived but whenever he had tried to talk to someone they had looked scared and had moved away without even acknowledging him. They all seemed scared of him. They all seemed scared of everything for that matter. But there was one man who Aleksy thought might speak to him. Aleksy looked over to him now. The man was black and fairly old to Aleksy's eyes. He had grey hair and pockmarked skin on his cheeks, with large bags under his eyes. Whilst everyone else sat with their heads bowed, intent on the thin porridge before them this man sat straighter. His head up, relaxed.

Aleksy picked up his bowl and began to walk over to him, not daring to leave his food behind. He always seemed to feel so hungry, although it always seemed somehow distant. As soon as he moved the others in the room looked uncomfortable and shrank back. They had become wary of Aleksy's attempts at conversation. But the black man looked at Aleksy as he approached and gave a small nod and a smile. Aleksy sat down opposite the man.

For a few minutes neither of them spoke. Then Aleksy steeled himself and whispered.

'My name is Aleksy. You don't seem like the others here and I could do with a friend.'

'Well, friend, my name is Allende. What would you like to discuss?'

'Where are you from?'

'I am sorry but I do not wish to speak about my past. I am here now. That is what is important. That is why I am called 'All End'. I do not discuss the start."

'Okay. Well, where do you work? Here in the Complex?'

'I work within the throne room. Inside that terrible room, where the crystal whirlwind turns.'

Aleksy felt his heart rate quicken.

'I would like to see inside that room. I want to see the King.' he said.

Allende looked at him carefully. 'It takes magic to open that door but some servants are admitted. I have been here a long time and I have some influence. I could arrange to have you allocated duties that would take you into that room. But why do you wish to go in? Most are only too keen to stay away.'

Aleksy stalled giving himself time to think. 'How would you get me in? Do you, do you speak to the magicians?'

'I do. As I say I have been here a long time.'

'Well. I just want to see the King' said Aleksy. 'He's

always here inside my head. I just, I just want to see what the room is like. Then perhaps, perhaps I could ask the King to let me go.'

It sounded weak to Aleksy even as he said it, but he was not ready to trust this man and he could think of nothing else to say.

'I do not think he will let you go. But I will see if I can persuade one of the Riven to allow you access.'

With that the man got up and walked from the room, leaving Aleksy alone with the silent slaves.

An hour before dawn they came. A silent signal saw the yeren rush forward first, heading for the doors and windows. The night had allowed the Tavern residents some time to prepare. J?ran had sent messengers along the lines that led from the interior of the building and a dozen people or so had come to protect the building. J?ran had also apparently positioned others at the entrances to the lines which led into the property. The disadvantage of having so many portals and ways into the building was suddenly stark.

Sam, Weewalk, Hadan, Vallalar, Kya and Hödekin were standing shoulder to shoulder in the room with the giant fireplace when the first wave came. The yeren flung themselves at the building; their spindly arms scrabbled at the windows looking for a way in. Hödekin raised an arm and pointed a hand at one of the latticed windows. It exploded outwards sending flying glass into the face of a yeren who had been scratching fingernails down the pane. The creature fell back howling.

The others all turned to look at Hödekin.

'They were going to break the windows anyway.' said Hödekin with a shrug 'Besides, I hate that noise.'

Two more yeren filled the open window. They all raised their hands at once and hit the creatures with a blast of presence at the same time. The figures flew back from the window with such speed it was as though they'd been pulled away by a jet plane. Sam felt the warmth of power up his spine. He might just be able to enjoy this, he thought, a little of the fear he had felt since first seeing the host in the garden leaving him. But uncertainty settled in again when, not for the first time he heard Weewalk mutter to himself 'It just doesn't make sense. Why attack here?'

Then the door, which was still locked and barred, was hit by something which made an almighty crash. Whatever was on the other side seemed to continue the pressure and the wood bowed inwards and began to make loud cracking noises to accompany the growling squeal from whatever monster was behind it. They all focused upon the doorway and as the wood finally gave way and splintered they all sent a blast at whatever was there. There was a roar and before anyone could see what had tried to get in it was gone and the door was empty.

After that the attack intensified and the onset of the invaders was fierce and sustained. Sam saw endless yeren and garoul try to force their way through the windows and doors. It seemed as though hours had passed but still the sun had not risen and Sam realised he had completely lost track of time so intent was he on sending blasts of presence at the attackers. It was an odd attack though, the beasts never really seemed to gain any ground. They would throw themselves at the building but few actually made it inside. Those that did were quickly dealt with by those within. But still the attackers came. Then suddenly realisation dawned on Sam.

'Weewalk.' he shouted over the din 'It's a distraction. They're not trying to get in, just keep us busy!'

At that moment the door behind them flew open with a giant crash and J?ran stumbled into the room. He swayed for a moment and then collapsed, like a tree falling, smashing through a table before landing face down on the floor. Sam could see his hair was matted with blood and as he drew closer he saw the burns on J?ran's huge arms. Sam, Weewalk and Kya all crouched over the giant as he lay unconscious. Then his eyes flickered and the massive man lifted his head to look at Weewalk.

'Ferus. Cellar.' he said in a deep voice before losing consciousness again.

Weewalk shouted orders.

'Kya, you look after J?ran. Sam, with me. Everyone else keep those creatures out of this building.'

He dashed away, Sam hot on his heels. Weewalk called over his shoulder. 'Sam, you were right. It was a distraction. There must be a line here that Ferus needs to use. The attack was just a way to keep us busy. We must get to the cellar immediately.'

They all but flew along the corridors and through rooms to reach the cellar door. Burns marked the walls and the entire door frame leading to the cellar flickered with fire making the darkness beyond look like a portal to hell. Weewalk didn't pause, running down the stairs as fast as his short legs could carry him, Sam close behind.

After the roar of the battle the cellar was eerily quiet, but the hum of the line was obvious. As quickly as he could Weewalk pulled the line open and he and Sam dashed through.

Sam and Weewalk appeared on a misty, dark and deserted country road, bordered by trees and bushes. They looked around them. There was little light save for the moon above.

'Keep quiet.' said Weewalk softly. Then they both

heard the sound of a car. Sam looked up as a pair of headlights appeared on the road ahead of them. The car crested the hill and Sam found he was rooted to the spot. Everything happened too quickly. In a second the car was upon them. He had a momentary vision of a man and woman in the front seats as the car hurtled toward him. For the briefest of instants he locked eyes with the man in the driving seat and saw the man's eyebrows lift in shock. Sam stared at his father.

Then time reasserted itself and he felt himself shoved roughly to the side. At the last second he saw his father wrench the wheel, fear etched on his mother's face, and the car began to slide, just clipping his arm with a wing mirror, spinning Sam onto the floor. Then it was past them. The car's wheels seem to catch on something unseen and it suddenly flipped, rolling over and over with a sickening crash that sounded impossibly loud in the still night. The car smashed into a low stone wall and came to rest. Lying on the cold dark tarmac, Sam saw a hot spark drop into the spreading petrol. Flames licked at the car, the petrol tank was alight.

Before Sam could recover, Weewalk was moving to the car. The kobold threw open the back door and quickly reached inside. He emerged a moment later holding a bundle of cloth and dashed away from the burning wreckage. Sam was on his feet then and sprinting towards the car when the force of the explosion lifted him and threw him backwards, smashing him into the middle of the road.

He screamed in despair as a ball of fire rolled up into the tree carrying the souls of his parents with it.

A second later Weewalk was with him, holding him awkwardly as Sam struggled for breath. Hearing a noise Sam looked down and through his tears saw that Weewalk held something. Within the bundle of cloth was a baby. It let out a tiny cry and Sam could see it had a cut to its forearm. Still choking back sobs he lifted his own sleeve to look at the faint scar that puckered his arm, Sam touched the baby carefully. 'Hello, Sam.' he said.

Weewalk touched his shoulder gently. 'We have to go, Sam. You know how this scene goes. Look.'

Sam followed Weewalk's gaze. An indistinct figure dressed in a dark cloak was disappearing across a field. A flashing blue light was approaching along the road. Together Sam and Weewalk struggled to their feet. Weewalk gently laid the crying baby at the side of the road and, taking Sam's arm, steered him back through the line and back into the cellar of the Mermaid Tavern.

Sam saw the hole close and disappear behind them. 'He killed them', he whispered to himself. 'Ferus killed my parents all those years ago. Now I'm going to kill him.'

Sam marched up the stairs into the Tavern. Vallalar, Kya and Hadan all turned in surprise as Sam entered the room behind them, tears still wet on his cheeks. The battle was still raging and the yeren and garoul were still fighting their way into the room. But there, anger and hate coursing through his veins, Sam unleashed his presence. The beasts were flung away by his fury and within moments the battle was over. Those that had survived fled as dawn pinked the horizon.

Aleksy started from sleep. The room was dark, there was no sound other than the soft noises of the other servants sleeping nearby. Without moving his head Aleksy narrowed his eyes, peering into the room. He could see nothing particularly unusual. But then he sensed someone was moving behind him. He rolled quickly onto his back ready to grab whoever it was. A figure loomed over him.

Aleksy was about to lunge forward when he saw it was Allende, the strange dark-skinned man who worked in the throne room. Allende put his finger to his lips and knelt next to Aleksy.

'It is arranged.' he said. 'From tomorrow you will carry out duties within the throne room, in the King's presence. I have organised this for you. I feel there is something different about you Aleksy and I felt that one day someone like you would come, and that things would change. Here is your chance. Do not waste it.'

With that Allende rose and walked softly away, stepping over the other slaves and was gone.

Aleksy lay quietly looking at the ceiling above him. This seemed too good to be true. What did this mean? How had this man made these arrangements? What would the throne room be like? And, most importantly, how would he kill the King?

Two hours later, as they were getting ready to go, Vallalar came to Sam.

'Samuel,' he said kindly 'There is something I wish to show you before you leave.'

Sam was exhausted after the violence and emotion of the night. His ears were still ringing from the noise of it all. His head swam and his spine felt hot and stiff, like a heated metallic bar had replaced the bone. He got up from where he had been staring into space and stumbled after Vallalar through the wreckage and debris of the Tavern.

Much of the damage was only cosmetic. The attackers had never truly breached the defences. They had simply thrown themselves at the building again and again to draw the attention of those within. More worrying were J?ran's injuries but Vallalar had looked him over and done what he could to heal him. Sam had been reassured that he would recover soon enough. He had saved Sam's life by alerting them to Ferus' presence. Sam had only brought destruction to his home. He felt hollow.

Vallalar led Sam to a line in an unoccupied bedroom. The line sat inside a wardrobe so that when one pushed aside the old coats that hung inside and opened the doorway it was as though the back of the wardrobe disappeared. It felt faintly familiar to Sam as though he had read about it in a book once.

'Where does this line lead, Vallalar?' asked Sam.

'I do not know, although I have been there before. Please, come and see.'

Vallalar ushered Sam though the line and they found themselves in the strangest place Sam had ever seen.

The entire world around them was grey mist. There was no ground beneath their feet, giving Sam the impression that he stood on a sheet of glass within thick cloud. He stared around in amazement. They were in a world where nothing existed.

'What is this place?' Sam said.

'I do not know for sure.' said Vallalar 'But I have a theory. Samuel, I believe this is the distant future as yet unformed. I think that something is to happen. Some choice will be made which will determine the shape of this place. For now, I think, it exists only as pure possibility. I wanted to show it to you so that you could see that everything is not mapped out for you. Yes, much of what we do seems predestined but this place, if I am right, shows there are still choices to be made which will affect the entire world. It is my belief that the Riven King knows of this place. That he has seen it too. He knows the future is yet to be decided and that is why he seeks to wipe out any who threaten his own future.' Vallalar lowered his voice. 'Sam, there is tell of a man who will save us all. Whether it is a prophecy, a whisper of something someone has seen in the future, or mere wishful thinking, I do not know. But it is enough to have the Riven King worried, I think. There are not many who have presence and he seeks to kill us all. Should he succeed I believe mankind is doomed.'

Vallalar closed his eyes
'A fiery dragon will cross the sky,
Six times before the earth shall die,
Mankind will tremble and frightened be,
For the six heralds in this prophecy,
And when the dragon's tail is gone,
Man forgets and smiles and carries on,
To apply himself – too late, too late,
For mankind has earned deserved fate.'
His masked smile, his false grandeur,
Will serve the gods their anger stir,
And they will send the dragon back
To light the sky – his tail will crack,
Upon the earth and rend the earth,
And man shall flee, king, lord and serf.'
'What does it mean?' asked Sam.

'Well, it is part of a very old prophecy by a lady called Mother Shipton. She was born sometime around 1488. Either she used lines or somebody told her of the future, I suspect the latter. She made many prophecies which people have interpreted as having some to pass. It is said that she foresaw motorised travel, instant electronic communication, aircraft, large-scale farming, television and submarines but she also spoke of a number of disasters which would befall the world, certain wars and the rise of particular tyrants. The passage I quoted is one that it is believed has not yet occurred. It is thought the fiery dragon refers to a comet with a red tail. Beware such a sign Sam.'

Sam took a step closer to Vallalar.

'Thank you for showing me this place, and for everything you have done for me. Despite the threat of the King, seeing that there might be a future that is undecided has given me hope.'

Sam turned to leave. But Vallalar stopped him.

'Oh, and Sam. Keep an eye on old Weewalk. Although he likes to play the lowly kobold he is more important than you know. Maybe, one day, he will take you to the Palace of Kalapa in Shambhala, which you might know as Shangri-La. Then you will see.'

Vallalar turned away signalling the conversation was at an end and Sam slipped from the room wondering what secrets Weewalk kept.

Jak appeared in a stand of trees, the line behind him closing but the hum still ringing in his ears. He grinned and flexed his long claw like fingernails. The sound of a battle reached him between the trunks of the trees around him. He had been drawn to this place. He was always drawn to places like these. He could smell the fear and death. He crept to the edge of the copse and looked out onto a sea of mud. To one side he could see a large force of men, clad in a dull green. They fired rifles at other men that he could not see. Smoke and fog obscured large parts of the hummocked battlefield. Every now and then a large explosion threw large clods of mud through the air. One impact was close enough that small stones rained down on Jak, tinkling against the dull metal helmet that he wore. He brushed grit from his black cloak and continued to watch. A unit of several hundred men appeared out of the whiteness making for Jak's hiding place. He smiled to himself and ran his tongue over his sharp teeth and then shrank back into the trees to wait.

The men came into the trees at a trot. Jak heard snatches of voices.

'...come on, men...quick smart....through the wood...Gerry won't know what hit 'im....form up'

Then through the trees they crept.

Jak readied himself. Stretching out with his presence he pulled fog and smoke around and into the woods so that the men could see little as they moved forward. Jak waited until they had moved slowly past then scampered up behind the last man. The man was wearing a flat green cap and carried a pistol. Jak clicked his long claws together. Hearing the noise the soldier stopped, allowing the others to move on into the fog. Jak used a flash of presence against the ground and leapt over the soldier and landed in front of him. The man's eyes widened in shock and his mouth dropped open beneath his thin moustache. Before he could move Jak had slashed at his throat with silver fingernails. The man died on the spot, slumping to the ground like a dropped sack of potatoes, a pool of deep red blood soaking into his uniform and the carpet of leaves and earth. Jak licked his fingers. He opened the line nearby and with a quick burst of presence he flung the man's limp body through the portal. The blood-lust was on him now, the other men didn't stand a chance. Shrieking with glee he leapt high and threw himself into their midst and the carnage began.

A short time later Jak stood panting in the foggy wood, his eyes closed. He felt the blood drip down his face and from his hands. A voice behind him startled him and he was ready to leap and attack before he recognised it.

'Hello Spring-heel.' said the voice.

Jak turned to see a figure emerging from the mists.

'Been busy, I see.' said Ferus, stepping over the tattered remains of what had once been a man. 'I have a job for you. There is a young boy who I am particularly keen that you should meet. He has become rather elusive.' This last sentence was said with such anger that even Jak quailed for a moment. Ferus continued in more measured tones 'I don't want anyone to know about this. It is starting to become an embarrassment to me that this boy still lives. The secret keeper tells me that I don't need to worry about this boy, but I don't trust Tarak Everune. The boy must not survive. Find him. Kill him. You will be rewarded.'

Jak grinned, showing his pointed teeth. As much fun as killing in numbers was there was nothing he enjoyed more than the thrill of the hunt, the challenge of a single elusive target.

He and Ferus spoke for a short time. Jak listened carefully then led Ferus back through the line into a grisly scene. Jak had flung a large number of the dead soldiers down the line and into a room. The bodies lay in bloody heaps. He crouched atop a pile for a moment, grinning wolfishly.

Then with a nod to Ferus he climbed through a window and out into the night. Using his presence to push off from the ground, he travelled in large leaps across the town below him. Every now and then he would drop to the ground in front of a person just to delight in the look of fear on their faces. Ladies fainted. Gentlemen in tall hats raised their canes in defence. But Jak stared down at them with his red, flame like eyes and they all quailed in fear.

In the darkness of night, on the shore of a lake in a wooded Romanian valley, a young gypsy girl knelt before the still waters, a candle in her hand. Tonight she would complete the ritual, for tonight was ' Sânziene ' night. Tonight a gateway to the world of the ghosts would appear and she would be able to see the future. She was hoping for a vision of her husband. The old lady from the village had taught her how to perform the rite, on this evening when there was magic in the air. As she solemnly said the correct words she was startled to see that something had begun to happen. She hadn't expected it to actually work. The old lady was a bit mad, everyone knew that. The girl's eyes grew wide as some kind of doorway opened just off shore. Was this the vision of her husband which she had so hoped for?

There was a splash and she heard a deep voice utter a loud and extremely rude sounding curse. More splashes reached her and then a figure appeared. This must be him. Her dream man. Her breath caught as she peered into the mists, holding the candle aloft.

Her dream man had a bushy beard, round eyes and a large nose and ears. He was only a few feet tall and he was wearing, well, this couldn't be right, he was wearing a yellow spotted dress and big black boots as he squelched from the lake. He stopped and sat on a thick log at the edge of the shore. He pulled off each boot in turn, pouring lake water from them as he muttered. Then he continued his way towards her.

He growled a greeting as he stomped past. He was followed by a girl who gave her an apologetic smile, then a young man who gave her a quick and perfunctory nod and finally a slightly younger boy. The last she smiled at. He was particularly handsome. She wouldn't mind him as a husband.

He said something to her and gave her a sympathetic smile but she could not understand the language. The four figures trooped into the dark trees behind her and the girl found herself alone again, the candle flickering in her hand.

Now that the anger had been burnt out of him by the events in the Mermaid Tavern Sam felt hollow and empty. When the time had come to leave J?ran to repair the damage he had left with a cold determination in his stomach. But the trip he had taken with Vallalar had made him feel substantially better, like suddenly life was less futile. Like there was something be could do. But still he thought he might never get over seeing the death of his parents. Ferus had killed them in an attempt to kill him. He could see that Weewalk kept giving him quick glances to check that he was alright.

'So, where are we headed?' Sam asked as they walked along a quiet lane which meandered away from the lake and woods and into open countryside.

It was Kya who answered 'We're going to see someone who studies Mu. We need to get to Tongue's Scar, where Tarak is being held, and this man might know how to reach it. His name is Professor Keel. His home is quite close to here. He lives close to a line to the Tavern as it's such a good source of information for him. J?ran told me about him.'

'Wait, J?ran told you. I thought he couldn't speak.' said Sam.

'No-one ever said he *couldn't* speak.' said Weewalk, 'Only that he didn't. He seems to have changed his mind since the Riven attacked him. I've never seen him so angry. Ferus has made himself a powerful enemy.'

As they walked Sam had the chance to consider Kya. She really did look remarkably like the girl from the painting. She caught him looking and Sam quickly looked away trying not to blush. They walked for half an hour or so before reaching a narrow lane which ran towards a house, only partially visible beyond a stand of trees. A postbox at the start of the lane bore the single word 'Keel'.

'I guess this is it.' said Hadan, eyeing the letters which overflowed the box. 'Should we take him his post?'

'It seems like the polite thing to do.' said Kya.

They waited for a moment while she gathered up the letters into a bundle and then they walked down the track to the house. As it came into sight they could see that it was quite large and rather unkempt and ramshackle. They climbed a step to the big front door and Sam pushed a button. They heard a chime sound within the house.

When no-one appeared after a few minutes Sam pressed the button again. This time, from deep within the house, a thump could just be heard. After another couple of minutes the door swung open in a rush. A strange smell emanated from the doorway.

The man who had opened the door scowled at them, but when he saw Weewalk his expression softened. He ran a hand through his shock of white hair and pulled a pair of goggles away from his face, nestling them in his frizzy hair, leaving deep pink lines around his eyes.

'Murian folk?' he said excitedly.

Weewalk nodded and smiled and introduced them all in turn.

'We need your help, Professor Keel. May we come in?'

'Of course, of course. This way, please.'

The scientist ushered them into the fusty smelling house and led them along a corridor to a large bright room at the end of the hall which clearly functioned as some sort of laboratory. Sam had the impression that Professor Keel spent the vast majority of his time in this room. Where the hall had been dim and slightly unkempt, this room was full of light and piles of stuff lay everywhere. Papers, odd pieces of equipment and books covered every surface and much of the floor. Shelves around the sides of the room held oddly shaped contraptions. In the middle of the room a black box, the size of a shoebox, emitted a strange hum which seemed to dominate the air.

Professor Keel gestured to the room.

'Welcome. Come in come in. Have a seat.'

As he mentioned seats he swung an arm around as if gesturing to some chairs which he couldn't quite locate amidst the debris and clutter of the laboratory. Sam couldn't locate the seats either and shifted nervously for a moment, anxious to be polite and obey the instruction but finding it an impossibility to do so. Eventually he settled for leaning against a table, deciding that was as close as he could get.

The man before them dashed around the room for a few moments, moving piles of papers and books as though needing to reassure himself that he had done something to improve the mess. All he did was move it around. Eventually, apparently satisfied, he stopped, or perhaps gave up, and turned to face them. He looked excitedly at Weewalk.

'So, you are a kobold? A mine kobold? Yes, how very interesting. What brings you here?'

'We need your help, Professor Keel. J?ran said that you might know of a way we can reach a place called Tongue's Scar. We are in something of a hurry.'

'Tongue's Scar. Hmmmm.' The scientist scratched at his head. 'I can see why J?ran has sent you here. I have studied Mu for many years and have made many attempts to map the lines which you folk are so fond of using. But, I am afraid that I do not recall any mention of such a place. I will check my notes though. My memory is not what it once was.'

He stepped over to a shelf and brought down a large book. He thumbed through the pages.

Whilst he searched Weewalk looked around at the others nervously. If the scientist could not help then they were stuck. They had no idea how to begin to find the place.

Eventually Professor Keel turned to them with an unhappy look on his face.

'I am afraid that I can find no reference to it. Do you have any more information?'

'No,' said Kya 'I just know that we need to get there. The message I received had only the name of the place, nothing else on how to get there or where it is.'

'Well, I'm sorry, my dear. But it seems that I cannot help.' The scientist looked genuinely unhappy, like it was a personal failing.

'It's not your fault, Professor.' Kya said. 'We'll find another way. Here, we collected your post from the road.'

'What? Oh, thank you.' Professor Keel took the bundle of papers glumly and flicked through them idly.

Weewalk turned to Kya 'Is there really nothing else that you know? What can we do now?'

'I just don't know.' said Kya 'We need to hurry, but we don't know where to hurry to.'

She looked so sad that Sam moved a step closer to comfort her, but couldn't quite summon up the courage to say anything. They stood in silence, brooding.

'Um.' said Professor Keel. 'Um. Excuse me.'

Weewalk looked over 'Yes, Professor.'

'Um. I have received a letter. Look.'

He passed a single sheet of paper to the kobold. Weewalk looked at it as the others crowded round. Sam could see it was a page torn from some kind of journal. He read it over the kobold's shoulder.

Entry 79

Strange. Today during my research I wandered away from my usual section of the library and came upon a book of philosophy called The Grandfather Paradox. It caught my eye as it was sticking some way out of the shelf. I opened it and a separate piece of paper fell out.

On that page was a poem. A poem I remember well for it led us on the path to Montauk and Tongue's Scar. I copy it here:

Down in the dark, beneath the Deeps,
A line lies where the Cyclops sleeps,
A man-made line which full of power,
Will help you in your darkest hour.
That door will also lead to doom,
For beyond its gate; that dreaded room,
Yet do not falter, do not dismay,
To Tongue's Scar you will find your way.

Even as I write this I realise what this page before me means. I know what I am supposed to write. Do I have the power to change things now? I could leave a warning. Dare I write something different? But what if I'm wrong and altering events leads to a worse tragedy. This is torment. What should I do?

Ha! Without meaning to I realise I have written what I should have all along. It is settled then.

They looked at each other in utter amazement.

'Professor, can I see the envelope?' asked Weewalk. He turned it over carefully in his hands. It was blank apart from the Professor's name on the front. There was no stamp, no postmark and nothing else inside.

'Weird.' said Sam 'What does it mean?'

'I don't know but it is our best lead.' said the kobold. 'Montauk. Who would have thought we would need to go there!'

'It could also be a trap.' said Hadan 'The problem with time travel is that someone might already know our movements and have sent Professor Keel this page knowing we would arrive here and follow the clue.'

'I don't see what choice we have.' said Weewalk 'If we don't follow these directions then we have no chance. And we don't know how long we have to rescue Tarak. If they knew we would be here then why not just attack?'

'But the Deeps.' said Hadan, shaking his head, 'There must be some other way.'

'What?' said Sam 'What is the Deeps?'

Weewalk sighed 'It's a network of caves and caverns. It's dangerous, there's no doubt about that. There are not many that could cross those paths, but I've done it, once. We kobold know how to move through the earth's heart. It's safe so long as one is quick and quiet. But this Cyclops. What threat that poses I do not know.'

'And what about the wendigo?' asked Hadan.

'As I said,' Weewalk replied, 'quickly and quietly and we have nothing to fear.'

At that moment the black box that Sam had noticed earlier began to chatter. Sam peered at it curiously. It was about the size of a shoebox. Wires trailed from it along with a roll of paper that looked to Sam like the roll of paper you saw in tills in shops. Some kind of data was printed on it and more figures appeared as the machine worked. The Professor quickly moved to it and studied the figures. 'Hmmm, interesting,' he said, 'Interesting.'

'What is that Professor Keel?' asked Sam.

'This, young man, is a random event generator. It makes predictions. It has recently begun to predict something very troubling, but I need to do more research before I am ready to announce the results.'

The machine jittered again and the Professor remained hunched over it.

'So,' said Kya 'We're going to the Deeps then.'

CHAPTER THIRTEEN

The next morning they used more conventional means for the first part of their journey to the entrance to the Deeps. Professor Keel took them in his battered car to a tumbled down and deserted ruin of a castle on the crest of a lonely hill. Weewalk spent a short time showing Sam and Professor Keel how to open the line that was there. Then the Professor bid them goodbye as they took the line to arrive in an alleyway in London. Weewalk then led them along city streets until they came to an area which Sam recognised from a school trip. He had been surprised that the entrance to somewhere as fearsome as that which they had discussed should lie beneath the streets of London but he was more surprised to hear that the relevant doorway was in a conventional newsagents. They stood nearby now. Weewalk pointed out that many people went missing each year on the streets nearby and besides, the Deeps themselves were not under their feet, merely the line that would take them to that place. They stood at the junction of two roads near an apparently disused Underground station. Dark red tiles fronted the building and black letters on cream gave the name 'Aldwych.' Weewalk gathered them against it; a concertina metal grill covered the entrance.

'We go in here.' he said, nodding to the station. 'But we won't get in this way. There's another entrance around the corner, but it's guarded. We'll have to get past the Old Witch.'

'Did you say Aldwych, or Old Witch?' asked Sam putting a slightly different inflection on the words.

'Sharp.' said Weewalk, 'I kind of said both. The entrance is through a newsagent which sits next to the other door to the station. The newsagent is run by an old woman. She's been here a long, long time. She's not one of the Riven, and she has no powers, but she is one of their spies. A familiar if you will, like the old vampires used to have, and she guards this door for them. I think she's always wanted to have some of their power and has become bitter and twisted that she doesn't have it. She hates everyone and she's called the witch with irony. She's no witch, just an old lady. But we don't want her to see us.'

'Well, can we just wait until the shop closes?' said Sam 'And get in then?'

'24 hour.' said Hadan with a wry smile. 'The old witch never sleeps. She might not have a presence, but nor is she entirely normal.'

Sam crept to the corner of the street and carefully looked around it and down the hill. He could see a small road sloping down towards the Thames and could just make out a little of the frontage of the newsagent, but not much because of the angle. As he watched two men approached from the opposite direction, walking towards him. They wore black suits, black ties, white shirts, long black trench coats and both had sunglasses on. They walked in step. Something about them immediately gave

Sam the creeps. He moved back from the corner.

'Two guys, walking up the hill. Take a look.'

Weewalk and Hadan looked around the corner together, taking care not to be seen.

'Riven.' said Hadan, 'They've gone into the shop.'

'This might be a chance.' said Weewalk. 'This isn't just an entrance to the Deeps. Actually, people almost never go that way. This is also a general doorway into parts of the underground that the Riven use. There are sealed off parts that you can't get to from the public side. When men built the Underground network they tunnelled into all sorts of places that had long been forgotten. There's a way through here to the 'Old Gate East'. And there are key lines to Mu there. But if those Riven are heading into the underground then the witch will be distracted. She'll be fussing over them. We might have a chance to slip in.'

'Or they might just be stopping for a packet of crisps and we'll bump into them coming out.' said Kya glumly.

'Let's go and see.' said Hadan and stepped around the corner. The others hurried to catch him. They came to the shop front and tried to look in the window. This wasn't easy. Metal grills covered the windows and the glass was covered in posters advertising travelcards, cheap international calls and a series of cards on which people had displayed items for sale. One caught Sam's eye. It had a picture of a mangy crow with leathery wings and the words 'Money for old ropen. Enquire within.' He shared a look with Kya who had read it too and they both renewed their attempts to see in the window.

'It looks empty.' said Hadan. He walked to the door and began to push it open.

'Wait!' said Sam, and grabbed the handle, stopping the door from swinging any further.

He looked up at the top of the door. A small brass bell

had been lifted by the door. Another inch and it would have slipped back, rung and alerted anyone inside the shop that the door was opening.

'Wait a minute.' whispered Sam. He reached out with his mind and took hold of the bell. He held the clanger away from the side of the bell as Hadan carefully pushed the door the rest of the way open. Once they were in and the door was closed again Sam slowly let the bell fall back into place. Satisfied that it would not sound he released the clanger and the bell remained silent.

They stood in a fairly grimy and sad looking little shop. There were a couple of aisles of shelves, but they were mainly bare. A few loaves of bread and some canned goods of the kind that no-one could ever really want were all that sat on display under the strip lighting. One wall had a fridge which was mostly empty with just a few cans of soft drinks and some milk on display. At the opposite end from the door there was a high counter. A selection of chocolate bars covered its front and cigarettes were stacked behind it. At one end a flap was raised which allowed one to walk behind the counter and to an open door, beyond which voices could be heard.

They crept along the shop and squatted in front of the counter to listen to what was being said. The voice of an elderly lady could be heard.

'Yes, sirs. Very careful. No-one's been this way, no-one at all.'

A deep voice sounded.

'Stop pawing me, you old hag'

'Sorry, sirs, sorry. Just you are so powerful and magnificent'

'Get away from me. Just make sure that no-one follows us through or Ferus will hear of it. We are travelling to the Old Gate on the King's direct orders.'

'No sirs, I'm sorry. No-one will pass. Already burned

me once Master Ferus has. I've no wish to see the fires of his eyes again.'

'Then see to it that this door remains guarded.'

The sound of another door opening and closing reached Sam and the others, crouched by the confectionery. A moment later they heard the sounds of footsteps approaching from behind the counter, and then the creak of a stool as someone sat down very close to them. The four of them held their breath, pressed against the rows of chocolate bars. Sam looked to Hadan who was sneaking a bar into an inside pocket. Sam stared at him and he shrugged with a smile.

The old woman's voice reached them from above as she began to mutter to herself.

'Tell me what's what. I've been here longer than them. Knows it all I does. Don't need them Riven to tell me what to do. Know full well they need to keep the King happy and ready those in the pit for his attention. Yes.'

Sam looked across to Kya. She had her eyes closed and he soon realised why. A sharp tap came from the window and as he looked between the cluttered notices Sam was just in time to see a stone which had been frozen in the air drop to the floor outside.

'What?' called the woman's voice behind them and Sam heard the legs of the stool rock against the floor as she stood up. 'Who's there?' she barked.

Another tap came from the window as Kya willed another stone to hit the glass.

The woman rushed past them down an aisle. She was so intent on looking at the window that she didn't notice them pressed against the high counter as she raced down the shop. Sam had a strobe-light vision of an old woman, hunched over with wispy grey hair and a pointed nose and chin. A witch without a tall hat. She went to the door, opened it and stepped out, the bell jingling as she did so.

'You bloody kids!' she called into the street shaking her fist. With no time to lose, and not believing their luck, they slipped behind the counter and into the back room, closing the door quietly behind them.

They paused a moment, holding their breath, but there was no call from the woman. Seconds later they heard the bell tinkle again and her voice drifted through the door.

'Bloomin' kids. Wait till I catch one. Then they'll be sorry. Yes, put them in the cellar I will. See if they can throw stones then.' The voice got louder as she moved closer to the door and they quickly moved away from it, crossing what seemed to be a storeroom. Carefully they went through the door at the other end.

Once inside that room they found a narrow and steep circular staircase set in a hole in the floor. The hole, only a couple of metres across, had a brass rim. As they stood looking into down the steep stairs Sam noticed words etched into the brass. He had to walk in a circle to read them. They said

'The forthcoming end of the world will be hastened by the construction of underground railways burrowing into infernal regions and thereby disturbing the Devil.'

Weewalk was the first to move. Kya and then Sam followed him into the narrow opening. Hadan brought up the rear. They moved quickly down the black wrought iron staircase and into the darkness below.

Behind them they did not hear the Old Witch mutter to herself, as she sat hunched over the counter of her shop. She opened the drawer of her till with a clatter and selected a coin. She placed it in a certain slot and released it. It rolled away through a carefully concealed tube, down towards the caves below. It could not cross through a line but the alarm would be sounded. 'That's it. In you go, into the Deeps. Jak will be along soon enough to make sure you stay there. If the wendigo don't get you first.' she cackled.

The stairs went down and down and down. Sam kept a good hold on the metal handrail, his hand warming as it ran over the smooth metal. It was dark, almost no light filtered down from above as they descended into that pit. He could not see below him into the blackness but the shaft was so narrow that, if there had been any light, he would have seen little but the top of Kya's head and shoulders. They descended for a long time. Little sound reached them apart from the intermittent rumbling of what Sam guessed were Underground trains passing nearby. It was like climbing down into the belly of a hungry giant. Then, as Sam's knees and thighs were starting to feel quite sore, Weewalk called softly up to them.

'I'm at the bottom.'

Sam came out of the narrow rock tube to find Weewalk and Kya standing in a roughly hewn tunnel, a blank wall behind them and a long echoing passageway before them. Hadan arrived a moment later, pulling a lantern from his bag which he lit carefully. A deep but distant rumbling noise swirled down the passageway.

'Now we're out of that staircase we can hear the trains better.' said Weewalk. 'I think we're pretty far below them.' He rubbed his thighs looking back up the stairs. 'But perhaps the sound is amplified in some way.'

Belatedly Sam realised that the stairs must have been even more tiring for Weewalk with his shorter stumpy legs and he felt a twinge of guilt for thinking about how much his own legs ached.

They walked softly down the passageway, careful to make no noise. Weewalk had given them a stern warning about the need for silence. The line they needed was nearby but the Riven had come this way too. Then, once they arrived in the Deeps proper, they would be in the lair of a race of mysterious beings called wendigo. These horrors had cadaver like bodies with fiery eyes and could shift their shape into beast like forms. They had found a line into the tunnels and had made it their own kingdom in the darkness, rarely venturing above into the light.

There was little sound in the tunnel as they walked, the occasional plink of dripping water as it filtered through the rock, the scratch and rustle of rats or other small creatures and the ever present distant rumble of trains from far overhead. Hadan's lamp provided the only light. He led the march, Weewalk brought up the rear.

As they walked Kya came up alongside Sam. The passage was wide enough that they could just about walk side by side. She touched Sam's arm and then stopped as if adjusting her shoe. Sam stopped too and Weewalk edged between them. Once they were at the back Kya started walking along, tugging Sam's arm so that he was walking beside her again.

She whispered into his ear. 'Thanks for doing this. Trying to save Tarak, I mean.'

Sam was immediately aware of her breath on his neck and the light touch of her fingers on his arm.

'Oh.' he said much too loudly. Weewalk turned and shot him a glance.

'Sorry.' hissed Sam sheepishly. Turning back to Kya he said 'That's okay, I mean, I've got nowhere else to go and Weewalk and Hadan have, you know, really helped me. And I want to fight Ferus.'

Sam groaned inwardly. That had sounded so stupid. He closed his eyes in silent frustration and immediately caught his foot on a stone and stumbled. He opened his eyes again as Kya tightened her grip on his arm.

She gave a quiet chuckle. 'You okay?'

'Yeah,' whispered Sam. 'I'm fine. I mean, look Kya.

Right now, even though we're walking through a dark tunnel towards a place full of evil mythological creatures that probably want to eat our skin or something, this, this just feels right. I feel like I'm supposed to be here. And I would never have learnt what I have if I hadn't got involved in all this. The things I can do. I can feel the power running through me. I feel good, great, and if I can make a difference and help some people then so much the better.'

Kya's hand tightened on his arm again and suddenly she was uncomfortably close. In the dark Sam couldn't see what she was doing and the movement startled him and he ducked away, leaning his head away from her.

She laughed softly again and drew him to a stop. He felt her use her presence to hold his head still. It was the strangest feeling. His entire head felt as though it was enveloped in a warm blanket. She kissed him softly on the cheek, gave him a wry smile and whispered 'Well, thank you.' Then she turned and walked away down the tunnel.

Sam stood a moment, surprised. Then he hurried after her.

After a while the tunnel began to slope downward. Then other passageways began to appear to the sides allowing cold air to swirl into the tunnel from the dark openings. One must have held a line close by as Sam heard the distinctive hum as he passed. He was surprised to see static electricity flicker on his fingertips, bright blue in the darkness. The hairs rose on his neck and he gave an involuntary shiver.

Eventually, Weewalk selected one of these side tunnels and took them down it and through a line which led to an almost identical underground passageway.

'This is the Deeps.' he said 'There'll be no Riven here I think and the wendigo live deep enough that we shouldn't be troubled by them.'

They followed the new tunnel for a time before it suddenly widened and they found themselves on the edge of an enormous cavern. The small part of the floor they could see was uneven and littered with tumbled rocks. The ceiling and walls were out of sight. Hadan's light barely made a dent on the echoing darkness. They turned to look at Weewalk.

'Koschei's Hall. It's almost straight ahead.' he said.

'Who's that?' asked Sam.

"Koschei the Deathless' he's called. But I don't know anything about him, or if he's here now.'

'Is it safe to show our light?' asked Kya quietly.

'We're not deep enough to be in any real danger yet.' said Weewalk as Hadan set the lamp on the floor next to them. 'We should rest here. It will take us some time to cross this cavern.'

They sat in the yellow pool of light and stretched their legs. Sam sat with his legs dangling over the edge of the tunnel facing into the darkness. It was strange to sit there. The dark was almost tangible. It felt as though it were pressing against him. His eyes had nothing on which to focus unless he raised his hand to catch the weak light coming from behind him. Sound moved strangely in the enormous space and odd echoes rumbled back towards him. Not long after sitting down he wished he hadn't chosen that particular place. It was unnerving not being able to see ahead of him, but at the same time he didn't want to move in case the others thought he was scared. After a few minutes Kya came to sit next to him and the two of them sat in silence together staring into the void.

Sam felt his heartbeat echo in his chest to match the distant rumbles that echoed from the dark cavern in front of them. Every time Kya was near his stomach fluttered. He was trying to pluck up the courage to speak to her when he suddenly realised he was already talking.

'It's strange but I think, I think I knew you before we even met. Did you ever know someone called Adam Hain?'

Kya shook her head. 'Who is he?'

'He was my grandfather. He's dead now. When I lived with him there was a painting in our house, a painting of someone who looked a lot like you. Whenever I felt scared, well, not scared, unhappy I used to look at it.'

'And did it make you feel better?'

'Yes,' said Sam. 'Every time.'

'Time to go.' whispered Weewalk, his voice startling Sam. They packed up their things and climbed carefully down the tumbled stone onto the jumbled rocks of the cavern floor. It could only be thought of as a floor because it was beneath them. There were few flat horizontal spaces. As they pressed forward they were climbing more often than not, sliding over rocks, using their hands to pull themselves along. But all the while their passage sloped downwards, deeper into the earth. It was not very long before the ceiling came lower and lower. Soon the feeling of claustrophobia was hardly bearable as the space between roof and floor became less and less. Sam felt as though he was being crushed between two enormous slabs of rock and he had to force himself to not panic.

Once they passed a great chasm which dropped away suddenly to one side. Sam edged to the side of it to peer in but the bottom, if there was one, was well out of sight. As he looked over the edge his foot dislodged a rock which fell out into the space, cracking and making echoing '*pock*' noises as it bounced off the walls as it fell. He tried to grab it with presence, horrified at the sound but it fell away too fast and was invisible in the darkness.

'Sorry.' he whispered when he had finished cringing.

'Don't worry.' said Weewalk 'Rocks crumble away here all the time. This pit is said to be bottomless.'

They sat by the pit for a moment. Then Sam thought he heard the rock land again. A very distant noise swirling softly out of the chasm. Then it came again and they all heard it.

A distant boom danced out of the darkness, like the far off beat of a large drum, a giant door thrown back on its hinges. The sound echoed around them, making it impossible to guess at its direction. Sam saw Weewalk's face turn to horror.

Then another sound reached them. A distant chattering began, like a far away troupe of monkeys. Sam noticed the darkness begin to lessen to one side and then yellowish firelight was clearly visible.

'The wendigo.' said Weewalk with fear in his voice. 'We must run.'

The spell was broken. They jumped to their feet and keeping the faint firelight behind them they dashed into the darkness ahead, the chittering of high pitched voices at their backs.

They clambered over the tumbled rock as quickly as they could, keeping as low as they could in the enormous dark cavern. Hadan had extinguished the lantern and so they stumbled in near darkness, the wendigo's fires behind them were all that illuminated their way in the gloom. As they hurried along as best they could the sounds of pursuit fell away, and then rose again as the creatures searched for those who had disturbed their lair. Several times Sam and the others were forced to stop and seek shelter in the shadow of jagged boulders as animalistic shapes dashed nearby or birdlike shapes flew overhead. The chase went on for what seemed like hours and they quickly tired from climbing. All of them bore bruises and scrapes from colliding with the edges of the rocks. Sam was sure his shins would be blue from the endless impact of stone on skin, but he didn't care so long as they stayed ahead of their pursuers.

Eventually, Weewalk pulled them into a large recess under a rock and drew them around him. He was sweating despite the cold air.

'I don't know where we are.' he confessed in a whispered voice, 'And we can't run forever. We might be going in circles for all I know. Let's rest a while. I don't think they're near at the moment.'

So they spent a short time crammed into the small space to catch their breath. At one point some small rocks tumbled to their feet from just overhead but if it was from a passing wendigo they never found out.

Eventually Hadan climbed from their hiding place for a look around. He climbed one of the higher piles of stone before returning to the group.

'The wendigo have lit a number of fires, so there's a bit more light now, but I don't think any are nearby. If we need to keep moving downwards then we should head in that direction.' He pointed away to one side. 'The ceiling seems to be coming even lower that way.'

Cautiously they emerged from the rocks and crept in the way Hadan had pointed. They could see that the cavern did seem to be getting smaller as they moved forwards, narrowing to a point. The rocky ceiling became lower and lower and soon there was little space between the rocks on which they climbed and those above. They were now moving lying down more often than standing and they all felt the panic and chill of claustrophobia. This would not be a good place to be caught by the pursing wendigo thought Sam, trying to calm the terror caused by the rocky embrace of ceiling and floor. Eventually the cavern wall began to come into view and they hurried towards it. Reaching it however left them with a difficult choice. Left or right.

Weewalk suggested they head left since again, the floor seemed to slope downwards that way. As they moved down the ceiling moved away again, allowing a little more room although it did not rise far above their heads. They crept on again for what seemed like hours, following the wall as best as they could until, eventually, they could see a dark opening up ahead.

Reaching the doorway they saw that it was a rough archway, which seemed to have been crafted by design, made by someone or something. Casting a look around Hadan carefully lit the lantern and raised it to make out the rough letters that were etched into the stone around the opening. They looked as though they had been chiselled in a hurry so indistinct were they. Weewalk read them aloud.

'Here you will find us, cyclops.'

'Well.' whispered the kobold. 'We don't have much choice. And the name of the Cyclops means that we might be on the right track.'

At that moment, as they faced the opening, they heard a scrabbling on the rocks behind them. They turned to see what they had been dreading. A grey humanoid sat upon the rocks grinning at them. Its large yellow eyes stared at them unblinking. It leered at them, its dry papery skin tight over its bony gaunt face. Bloody, tattered lips parted like flesh being ripped from bone and it raised its head towards the ceiling and gave a long echoing call.

Suddenly the wendigo flew away from the rock as though it had been smashed by an enormous invisible fist. Its cry echoed as it tumbled away broken, into the darkness.

Sam looked in surprise at Kya who had her hands raised towards the place where the beast had been a moment earlier.

'No point in hiding now.' she shrugged. 'Guess we'd better meet this Cyclops of yours', she said to Weewalk.

They dashed into the tunnel. Sam stopped after a few paces.

'Wait, I've got an idea!' he said.

He closed his eyes and extended his arms.

'Whatever it is, do it quickly!' hissed Kya, and Sam heard the chittering of the wendigo rushing towards them. He lost his concentration then regained it. He sensed the rocks beyond the tunnel entrance and, using his presence, he picked them up and pulled them towards him.

'Quick!' shouted Weewalk.

Sam heard and felt the stone hit the tunnel entrance a few feet ahead of him and sensed that the wendigo had arrived at the same time. He heard a yelp and felt one of his larger rocks crush a body as the tunnel sealed, plunging them into silence.

He opened his eyes and turned to look at the others.

'That was well done.' said Hadan, with respect in his voice.

'And not an easy thing to do.' said Weewalk going back to look at the newly created barrier. 'These stones have been set perfectly. I've not seen such a neat wall this side of Cuzco.' He ran his hand over the wall. The stones fitted together like pieces of a jigsaw.

Sam shrugged as if it had been nothing but relief washed over him. He hadn't been sure he was going to complete it in time.

'Well.' he said. 'The only way is forward.'

Hadan raised the lantern and they started their way along the rough rock passageway.

Jak walked confidently through the cavern. He had no need to fear its inhabitants. At first a few came close, sniffing at the air, wary of someone who strode through with such purpose. These few, Jak killed and flung their bodies towards the others. After that none drew near and he heard their chittering dwindle as they scurried back to the depths from which they had come. It was unusual to see them this high in the tunnels of the deep. The old witch had done well in sending her coin to alert them but it did not seem as though the wendigo had caught their prey. The others had a good head start on him, but he was in no hurry. He enjoyed the hunt.

CHAPTER FOURTEEN

The tunnel wound down and down into the cold darkness. How it had been crafted none of them could guess and neither Weewalk nor Hadan, despite their extensive travels, had heard of the Cyclops whose lair they were about to disturb. Sam had told them all he could remember of the Greek myth of the one-eyed giant but Weewalk and Hadan had not been able to tie what Sam had said to any denizen of Mu that they knew of.

The tunnel was sometimes narrow, and sometimes it widened as they crossed caves but the route was always clear. As they marched Sam studied the young man who walked just ahead of him. He had not been sure he was going to like Hadan when first they had met. Sam had warmed to Weewalk almost instantly and had quickly come to respect him as a leader and a friend. But Hadan had been aloof almost to the point of unfriendliness at the start. Sam wondered now whether it was a lack of presence that had so shaped his character. Weewalk had hinted a few times at Hadan's past and Sam had the impression that Hadan had been some sort of prisoner or slave in the place where the King dwelt. But neither Weewalk nor Hadan seemed willing to expand on what had happened or how Hadan had been liberated and, anxious not to offend, Sam had let the matter rest. Anyway, he had to admit that he felt very differently about the young man now. As Sam's powers had strengthened Hadan had seemed to find new respect for him and the bond between them had become closer. Sam often noticed Hadan studying him with a twinkle in his eye and they shared jokes more and more often. He reminded Sam of somebody but like a half remembered dream Sam could never quite put his finger upon who. Hadan must have felt Sam's eyes on him for he turned his head and glanced over his shoulder. He dropped back half a step and put his hand on Sam's shoulder for a moment and gave him one of those rare smiles of his. They had already been through a lot together.

After another hour or so they reached a cavernous chamber with a sandy floor and a high ceiling. The musty ammonia smell of bats wafted over from one corner of the space but Weewalk felt that it was a good place to stop and take a rest. They had been walking for the best part of a day he thought. One part of Sam was surprised at how long they had been underground. It was hard to keep any sense of time in the endless night. But another part of him felt sure they hadn't stopped walking for weeks. His legs ached and he was extremely grateful for the chance to sit on the soft sand and eat some of the food that they carried. Rubbing his legs he thought about the lessons that Vallalar had given him.

'Weewalk, do you think I could use my presence here?' he asked. 'It won't cause any problems will it?'

'I think it's safe.' said Weewalk looking at Hadan, who nodded.

Sam closed his eyes and turned his focus to the aches in his legs. He concentrated on each muscle feeling its size and shape, noting where it ached and where it was tense. He tried giving each part a little massage by applying a little pressure with his mind. As he concentrated on each part in turn he felt some of the tension in his legs ease and his tired muscles felt soothed. After a few minutes his legs were noticeably different.

He shuffled on his bottom over to where Weewalk sat with his short legs outstretched, checking the contents of his bag. Sam sat opposite the kobold.

'Weewalk, can I try something?'

'Sure,' said the kobold, 'What's up?'

Sam closed his eyes and sent his mind out to sense the small legs pointing towards him. He moved his mind into them, again feeling the muscles as he had his own. He heard a gasp from Weewalk and opened his eyes quickly worried that he had hurt the little man, but Weewalk was looking at him in surprise, not pain. Weewalk gave a nod and Sam reached out to put his hands on the short stumpy legs before him. He closed his eyes again and continued. It was much more difficult than doing it on himself, and Weewalk's legs did not seem to have quite the same anatomy as he own, but the basic principle was the same. Sam was amazed to feel just how tight the knots in Weewalk's leg muscles were and again he felt a flash of guilt that he had forgotten that Weewalk had to take several steps for every one of his. The clamber over the floor of the rocky cavern must have been incredibly arduous. It was testament to the hardiness of kobolds that Weewalk had not shown any tiredness.

After a while Sam felt he had done as much as he could and opened his eyes again. Weewalk looked as though he had almost fallen asleep. Sam realised Hadan and Kya had been watching him and he grinned sheepishly. Weewalk stretched and then stood up and did a little dance, twirling in his spotted dress.

'Now, that feels better!' he said.

'Who's next?' asked Sam, pleased.

Hadan declined Sam's offer. 'I don't want anyone else's presence invading my body.' he said. 'No offence.'

Sam shrugged and moved over to Kya. As he was about to start Hadan called from behind him.

'Weewalk and me are just going to have a look around the cave and see how far it goes', he said and Sam heard them move off into the gloom. He had an uncomfortable feeling that they had purposely meant to leave him alone with Kya.

He sat opposite her and looked into her eyes. She gave him a coy smile and took his hand and placed it on her bare leg. Sam felt as though his stomach was doing somersaults. He could feel his heart hammering in his chest. Kya lay back and closed her eyes.

Sam moved his hand slightly on her leg, feeling the smooth soft skin slide under his fingers.

He sent his mind into the muscles as before. He placed his other hand on her leg and slid his fingers underneath so all eight rested on her calf, his thumbs near her shin. He massaged away the tightness that he found in that part before moving on to the next part. After a while he realised that he had become caught up in the healing process and had run his hands all over Kya's leg. He dropped it hurriedly and she sat up with a smile on her face.

'Weewalk's right.' she said, staring deep into his eyes, 'That feels much better.' She took his hands and placed them on her other leg and he repeated the process. When he had finished she stood and pulled him to his feet. Then, in the darkness, she kissed him on the cheek, shyly.

'Thank you.' she said softly as she held his face in her

hands.

They heard Hadan and Weewalk making their way back over and, embarrassed, they quickly stepped apart from one another.

Hadan looked into both their faces and grinned.

'We've had a good look around. This cave seems fairly safe. We think we should get some sleep here and move on in a few hours. We'll post a watch and take it in turns. I'll go first.'

And so, they pulled out blankets and made themselves as comfy as they could on the sand. Sam lay awake for some time, staring into the flickering lantern. He could hear Kya breathing softly in the gaps between Weewalk's snores and all he could think about was the feel of her lips on his own.

Eventually, he must have fallen asleep for Weewalk shook him gently by the shoulder.

'Your turn.' the kobold said quietly.

Sam stood and stretched, brushing sand from his clothes. He walked around in large circles for a while staring into the darkness whilst the others slept. The cave was almost silent. The sound of the sleepers and the rustling of the bats were the only noises that filtered through the black air. Once Sam tensed when he thought he heard the rumble of rocks from far back the way they had come, but there was no further sound and, dismissing it as his imagination, he continued his watch and no further sounds, real or imagined, reached him until a short while later when the others awoke.

They had walked for an hour before they came across the first set of bones. They had left the cave feeling rested and reasonably fed and had continued on through the next part of the passageway feeling more positive. The tunnel had continued to descend into the depths of the earth through a twisting, winding and uneven subterranean world, devoid of life. They were all grateful for Hadan's lamp which he checked regularly and topped up with oil when needed.

The skeleton lay in the dust, its arms stretched above a yawning skull as if it were trying to crawl away from the direction in which they were headed. There was no way to tell how long it had been there, no clothes or jewellery, just old, dead, grey bones.

After another hour they had passed two more. One lay on its back, its jaw wide as if screaming to the sky, miles above. The other was the same as the first, stretched out as if it were clawing itself away from the depths. This one had no legs below the knees although whether the bones had been removed before or after death none of them wanted to guess.

Not much further on echoes began to sound from beneath them, rushing back up the tunnel, distorted by the crumpled rock walls. They slowed their pace and moved more cautiously and Hadan was careful not to let the light travel too far.

After a while the passageway began to widen again and then they were at the entrance to another cavern but this was like nothing that any of them had ever seen before. They stood in silence at its edge, stunned by the sight that lay before them. The cavern itself was impressive. They could see a good way in. Light filtered in from somewhere, despite how far underground they were. Long thin stalactites hung from the ceiling and were matched by similar stalagmites which rose from the floor. At some point some of the roof must have collapsed because there were long rocky spines protruding from the walls as well. It was like being inside the giant mouth of some terrible beast, a maw ringed by fangs. But it was what was held in those monstrous, needle-like teeth which was the most remarkable.

Sam found his mouth was hanging open in surprise. He ran his hands through his hair. In the middle of the cavern, sitting in what looked to be a few feet of water and only just visible in the gloom lay an enormous grey warship of the kind that he had only seen in films he had watched about the First World War in history class. They stood opposite its starboard side, somewhere near the bottom of its hull. They could see its front end in the pale light. The rear end was lost in shadow.

So incongruous was the sight that none of them spoke for a few minutes. They simply stared. It was Hadan who spoke first. He pointed across to the lettering on the side of the warship.

'I think we've found our monster.' he whispered.

Sam followed the line of Hadan's finger to where he could just make out some words that he had not noticed amongst the patches of rust on the ship's side.

'USS Cyclops'

'The words on the arch.' said Hadan. 'Not us, but U S S. Here you will find United States Ship Cyclops'

'How in Mu did it get here?' said Weewalk in awe.

'There's a line.' Sam said quietly. 'There must be. Away back behind the ship. It must have gone right through, crew and all, and disappeared, and arrived here. The crew must have had quite a shock.'

'I don't think they lived to be surprised for long' said Weewalk. 'Electrical equipment often fails around lines. They might have had no light and my guess is that, down here in the darkness, the wendigo made short work of them.' He pointed to more bones that lay amongst the rocky teeth and shallow water on the floor. 'The wendigo must have had a party when such an easy meal landed in their laps.'

They stopped a little longer imagining what terrors those sailors must have faced in the darkness.

Kya broke the spell.

'Should we take a look around? We need to find the way out of here.'

They climbed down the cavern and picked their way amongst the pointed stalagmites. Each tooth was taller than Sam and needle sharp at its tip. They protruded from every surface and Sam felt like dental floss as they picked their way between them towards the smooth grey hull of the USS Cyclops. They splashed their way through shallow pools of water until they got close to the dull metal, here the stalagmites were broken and jagged from where the ship had run aground and smashed through them. Progress was more difficult so they went back a few steps before they turned toward the front of the ship, hoping to skirt it.

Water dripped steadily from the teeth on the ceiling, a monster's saliva running down its fangs. It landed with plings and plongs on the enormous grey beast held within its mouth, regurgitated from some watery depth. There were plenty more bones sticking out of the pools and puddles of the floor that they passed. All picked clean of meat.

They came to the front of the ship and continued around the other side. There they found that ladders had been thrown over the side and they stopped, wondering whether there was any merit in climbing them to explore the ship or gain a better vantage.

Sam thought he could hear at least one line nearby and thought the view from the deck might help to identify the quickest way towards it. As well as the now familiar hum of the line through which the Cyclops had arrived he thought he could feel some other line. It seemed to resonate on his senses pulling at his mind in an almost hypnotic way, a tugging at his presence, a low rumble to the growl of the main line. That, he thought, must be the line to Montauk. He tried to recall what Weewalk had said about that place...

'It took them another forty years to reopen a hole in a place called Montauk and begin to control some of that power. Some of the scientists and crew were seen years after they were thought to have died. Some people even absorbed a little of the power of the hole and began to be able to control objects and even other people with their minds, but it is said that those people soon became unstable and destroyed the equipment effectively ending the project.'

Who knew what they would find there? What point in history? Would it be in ruins already? As Sam stood, lost in thought, he became aware of a faint clanging noise somewhere behind him. As he listened he realised that he had been hearing it for a few moments. He looked around him. The others were still debating where to start looking but as he looked past them he could see the rope and wood ladders hanging over the side of the ship had begun to tremble as if in a strong breeze. The wooden rungs were clanging softly against the grey steel of the hull. It took a moment to realise that there was no wind here to disturb the rope lines. In horror his eyes travelled up the ropes and up and up. Grey bodies were swarming over the side of the ship, inching down the ladders, head first like insects.

Sam shouted and pointed. The others turned to look. The wendigo had found them again but this time there were hundreds. Their nest had been disturbed and they poured out like spiders. Their chittering voices began to sound.

Tarak Everune hugged his knees. He sat on a small pile of wet, dank hay that served as his bed in the small dark cell. Above him a single shaft of sunlight came in through a barred window illuminating a patch of stone above his head. But little light filtered down into the dark square of dirty floor. Flies buzzed around a wooden bucket in one corner of the room. They were all that moved. Not even rats bothered to cross his cell. There was certainly no food to be found here. He had sucked every last drop of the cold grey porridge that had been slopped into a bowl hours or perhaps days ago.

He kept his head down. His forehead resting on his knees, his lank bedraggled hair hanging in a dirty curtain around his face. He wiggled his cold bare toes but the movement brought no warmth and only made him feel even more weary.

He heard footsteps approach but he did not move even when the small hatch in the door was slid back. He knew someone was now watching him. He schooled his expression and looked up, through his grimy locks.

'How are you enjoying your stay?' asked Ferus with a laugh.

Tarak allowed his voice to waver. 'Please, let me go. I've told you everything I know. I promise.'

'Oh I know you have. You are a Secret Keeper no more. We shall have to think of a new title for you. Abject Coward. Traitor. There are so many to choose from.'

'Please, let me go.' Tarak hung his head again.

'No.' said Ferus. 'I like having you here. You might be useful yet. You might encourage others to my door.'

Tarak heard the small window clang shut and Ferus' footsteps receded into the distance. He kept his head down. You could never tell whether someone was still watching. He had taken an enormous risk. It all came down to Kya. He just had to wait and hope that she succeeded. He just had to hope that the rescue would come and come soon or he would be too weak to fight. Too weak to reveal the greatest secret of all.

Weewalk, Sam and Kya moved at the same time throwing energy upwards towards the advancing wendigo. There was no need to hold back. They threw burst after burst of presence at them and some fell screaming onto the sharp teeth of the cavern below. Sam and Kya were able to hurl others sideways or up causing those wendigo still coming to scream in rage. But for every one they hurled away to fall broken onto the rocks, another three took its place.

Hadan called to Sam. 'Try the lamp.'

It took Sam a moment to realise what he meant. Hadan had opened the lamp so that the flame was visible. Sam tried to catch it as Vallalar had shown him all that time ago at the Mermaid Tavern but still he could not grip it. He tried again and again. Still he could not hold the flame. The wendigo edged closer.

Kya screamed at him 'I can't hold them off by myself.'

Weewalk and Kya were doing what they could but it clearly wasn't going to be enough. Glancing round quickly Sam could see that Weewalk was trying to do something to dislodge the ladders, but without success.

Sam tried the flame again. Still nothing.

Hadan grabbed Sam by the shoulder and looked him in the eyes. 'I believe in you. I know you can do it. Focus.'

Sam tried again and this time, unbelievably, the flame flicked out towards him. For a moment it was a couple of inches longer than it should have been.

Sam tried again, and this time he wrenched it free from the wick and felt his mind take a hold of it. Once he held it there was no stopping him. He stretched it into a rope and whipped it in a fiery line at the advancing wendigo. Any that it touched were immediately burned but their fury only increased.

Sam lay the thin line of fire down across the floor between his companions and the advancing creatures using his mind to hold it in place. It smouldered on the wet floor. Sam steadied himself and took a deep breath. He leaned back and then threw his arms and his mind forward. An inferno sprang from the fiery string. A wall of flame lit the entire cavern so that every pointed tooth cast a thousand long shadows. The fire rolled up the side of the ship, hissing away the water and searing away the wendigo in a single blast of power like a volcanic eruption. Sam felt their bodies blast away like dried leaves in a furnace.

After the wave of fire had gone he blinked in the sudden darkness. Sam noticed that a tiny flame still flickered on a piece of hanging rope and he carefully plucked it away with his presence and drew it through the air to float back into Hadan's lamp.

He looked back at his companions. They were all fixed to the spot dumbstruck. If any wendigo remained they were hiding back inside the belly of the Cyclops.

Sam could feel the line more clearly now.

'This way,' he said and walked past a line of blackened and charred rock and gore towards another corner of the cave. 'They won't bother us again.'

Sam stood before the portal. This line would take them to the place called Montauk. There they would find another line which would complete their journey to Mu, where they would try to find a way to rescue Tarak, the Secret Keeper. With the information he held they might be able to think of some way to fight Ferus and the Riven

King's oppression. Standing here now it all seemed too difficult. They had already gone through so much and had got nowhere yet. But what else could he do?

Although Sam stood there, suddenly doubtful, it was Hadan who voiced his concerns.

'I don't know why but I've got a bad feeling about this one.'

Behind them the Cyclops creaked and planged as the metal cooled again from the fiery blast that had rolled over it.

'Come on.' said Kya, 'We need to save Tarak.' She opened the portal and they stepped through.

Jak watched them pop out of existence one by one. The lamp went with them plunging that part of the cave into darkness but he could still see in the blackness that enveloped him. As his eyes adjusted he could see that parts of the big grey ship still glowed a dull red from the heat of the blast sent out by the boy. No wonder Ferus wanted him dead. Someone as powerful as that could pose some real threat to the Riven King's rule. People would rally to him. It was only Jak's own malevolence and show of loyalty that had stopped him from being hunted by the ruler of the Rivenrok Complex. This boy was interesting. Very interesting. He had presence but could not always control it or will it forth. It was time to carry out the task that Ferus had set him. Jak clicked his long metallic fingernails together and strode to the line. He stepped through.

Immediately Sam was aware that this line felt considerably different. Normally the passage through the ethereal pathways was smooth but this one shook and bucked like it wanted to spit him out. He landed with a crash that knocked the wind from him, rather than the usual gentle realisation that ground was forming beneath his feet. He panicked for a moment when he realised that he couldn't see. He tried to open his eyes but found that he had already opened them. He called out to the others and Weewalk answered.

'It's okay. We're all here I think. My vision's clearing.'

'What's going on?' called Sam, as his vision turned from black to a blurry dark grey.

'These paths are different remember? These are manmade. Experiments by scientists trying to render objects invisible. It would seem they are not as smooth as the lines created by the God, Pyxidis.'

Sam rose and tried to stare into the room, his vision still very hazy. He saw movement. Something appeared before him and he had a sudden vague impression of a demonic face with glowing eyes, but a split second later, it was gone and as he blinked Kya's face swam into focus and he couldn't understand what he had seen as her pretty face appeared before him, a smile on her lips.

'I saw something strange for a moment there.' said Sam softly.

'This whole place is pretty strange.' she said.

Sam turned and looked around the room. They were in a long laboratory of some sort, long enough that its ends dwindled into shadow and could not be seen. Lights were only illuminated above their heads and Sam guessed that they were on some kind of motion sensor. He realised too that the walls were curved giving the appearance of being inside a very large doughnut. Blank television screens filled one large section of wall nearby and more hung from the ceiling. Big, chunky, old-fashioned computers took up much of the space under the bare concrete roof. The walls were painted white and were plain. There were no windows and, turning, Sam realised that he could see no door. No conventional door anyway. A dozen or more metallic archways were visible in the part of the room that Sam could see, set out around him at irregular intervals, each looking like some strange alien shrine. Within each of these Sam could feel a line buzzing with power so that if he opened his mind the room felt like the inside of a wasp nest.

'I never guessed they might have made this many.' said Weewalk in awe. 'No wonder the project eventually collapsed. There's no way they should be able to hold this many lines open. Can you feel the power?'

'How do we know which one will take us to Mu?' asked Sam.

'It's a good question.' came a high-pitched maniacal voice from the edge of the part of the room that was lit. 'I don't expect you'll ever find it.'

Sam turned in horror as a man strode into view. Not a man, a thing. He had red eyes which glowed beneath a metallic mask that covered the top part of his face. He wore a long black cloak on top of what looked like tight white leather body armour. He clicked his fingers as he stepped into view and Sam could see long metallic claws that caught the light as he moved.

There was a sharp intake of breath from Hadan. 'Spring-heeled Jak.' he said.

Jak merely grinned and kept his eyes upon Sam.

As the figure stepped under the bright lights, Sam noticed that Jak was flickering, almost hazy. A faint chime, like the sound of a line came from him. Suddenly Sam realised why. A thousand tiny pieces of metal floated around Jak, spinning so quickly they looked like floating orbs. Jak raised his arms slightly and gave a short laugh. The metal ceased its spin and the hum fell silent. His arms dropped and a storm of metal flew at Sam, a blast of jagged death, impossible to dodge. Instinctively, Sam threw his arms across his face and fell to his knees as the world turned white.

CHAPTER FIFTEEN

When Sam opened his eyes again Jak was staring at him angrily, his fiery eyes narrowed in hate. Sam chanced a quick glance over his shoulder where the pieces of sharp metal were embedded in the wall behind him. A perfect circle in the middle was clear. He had instinctively, with his eyes shut, grabbed each piece and thrown it past him.

Then everyone moved at once. Sam, Kya, Weewalk and Hadan dashed towards Jak but he pushed away from the floor with presence, arms outstretched and flew over their heads, brushing the ceiling with his cloak. He threw an arm sideways towards one of the metallic archways and a line opened. To Sam's horror Murian beasts began to enter the long laboratory. First came the fast wolf-like garoul, then a huge nandi, then another bigger than the first, then a flock of ropen.

'We have to get out of here.' shouted Kya as she dodged a garoul that leapt for her throat. She used her presence to push off the wall. She twisted as she flew and slashed at it with her knife.

'We can't.' shouted back Sam who leapt over a nandi. 'We have to stop this Jak here. He'll only follow us.'

Weewalk had his back to the wall as a nandi towered over him. 'Sam, you and Hadan try to stop Jak. Kya and I will try to hold off the rest and shut that line.'

Sam focused his presence on a garoul, holding it mid-air with his mind. He threw it at Jak who laughed and dodged allowing the garoul to smash through one of the television screens after which it fell to the floor and did not rise again.

For every one of the monsters that was flung to break against the wall or stabbed through by Hadan or Kya's knife another seemed to take its place and, through the melee, roared the nandi like angry rabid bears, relentless, using massive claws to slash their way through the throng not caring whether they eviscerated human, kobold or animal. More beasts entered every now and then almost as if they had been caged just the other side of the line and were finding a pathway through.

The battle raged as Sam and Hadan tried to edge closer to Jak. In the fight Sam found new respect for Hadan. Despite his lack of presence he fought with a skill and determination that Sam had only guessed at before. He ducked and dived, swirled and all the time flicked out with his knife, slicing ropen from the air and causing the garoul to fall back in panic.

Sam was able to use his mind to pick up and smash their enemies to the ground or wall. He found that was the most effective. But he was also able to use the tricks that Vallalar and Odhar had shown him during his training. He leapt and pushed himself from floor, wall and ceiling so that he flew around the room. He was a pinball in a machine, cannoning off surfaces and smashing through foes, but never landing in one place for longer than a moment.

He and Hadan made progress until they came to where Jak stood, apart from the battle, arms crossed, a smile on his face. Motion sensor lights clicked on above them as they moved towards him. Then they had cleared the path and he was before them. Sam could hear Weewalk and Kya fighting the snarling beasts some distance behind them but ahead stood only Jak. Sam pushed off the wall behind him moving his arms towards Jak, ready to lift him and dash him against a wall. But Jak uncrossed his arms, almost lazily, and suddenly Sam felt as though he had slammed into a brick wall. He was held in mid-air. From the corner of his eye. He could see Hadan similarly immobile. He tried to push away from the ceiling to get back to the floor but he only dropped a foot before Jak held him again.

'Oh, you want to get down do you? Fine.'

Sam's arms flailed as Jak swung him down through the air to crash into the concrete floor. He felt his head connect with the ground and ricochet off. He must have lost consciousness for a moment for when he opened his eyes Jak was closer and Hadan was lying next to him, pinned to the floor as he was.

Sam tried to move and felt something sharp inside his chest complain. His head felt like it had been hit with a sledgehammer and his whole body ached despite the adrenaline that flowed though him. He felt a trickle of blood run down his forehead, and then it met his eye causing him to blink as it stung his vision.

'I had hoped you would be a better fight.' said Jak.

Sam tried to move but could not. Again and again he pushed with all his might at the concrete floor beneath him trying to rise, but Jak held him firmly.

As he struggled he began to feel the pressure increase, a terrible force that threatened to crush him, to break every bone in his body. His entire frame seemed to scream in protest. Blood began to run from his nose.

Then Hadan stirred next to him on the floor, a dull moan escaped his lips and the pressure on Sam's body lessened, although he was still held immobile.

'Ah yes, Hadan. Well, we have no need for you any more.'

Jak strode over to Hadan and bent so that his mouth was near Hadan's ear as if he was imparting a secret, yet he spoke loud enough for Sam to hear.

'You see that doorway over there?' A metallic claw indicated one of the archways, a line hummed within it. 'Well, that particular line was certain death for the idiotic men that opened it. You see it leads to a point on the ocean floor, hundreds of metres beneath the surface. Anyone who went through found themselves immediately drowning in dark cold water, destined to become bones on the sea bed for ever, once the fish had eaten the jelly from their eyes and picked the flesh from their carcass.'

Jak straightened again and walked towards the portal. Hadan slid along behind him leaving a smear of blood on the smooth grey floor, pulled on an invisible string of presence.

'Would you like to see it Hadan? Must be a nasty way to die.'

Jak stepped to one side and rested an arm on the edge of the archway as Hadan continued to slide towards it. Sam could see Hadan's face. There was no fear there. Hadan looked him in the eye and smiled and nodded. Sam could only guess at the force of will that had allowed him that small gesture against the terrible power of Jak's control.

At that smile Sam felt some emotion inside him snap. He pushed and pushed against Jak's hold and shakily his arm moved. It felt like he was trying to lift a mountain but he managed to bring up an arm.

Jak's attention was still on Hadan who was almost at the entrance to the door. The line hummed.

'Nooooooo!' screamed Sam. 'Argggghhhh!' He blindly sent as big a blast of presence as he could at the moment Hadan reached the door. There was a huge crash as the metallic archway collapsed. The force of Sam's push sent objects flying away, lights flickered on further into the room as debris span under the sensors, and the concrete wall cracked and popped. But when Sam looked up, and the dust cleared, Hadan was gone. Sam could see a number of archways lay in ruins but the young man who had fought so bravely beside him had been pushed through the portal and was gone.

Jak, who had been staggered by the blast, turned his full attention back to Sam.

'Nice try, but too late.' he said. His jaw clenched and Sam felt the incredible pressure return as Jak brought his full force to bear.

Sam felt anger burn white inside of him. And he felt the entire room. He felt the power of the lines buzzing all around him. The power of the lines. As he felt some of the smaller bones in his hands and feet begin to break and more blood flow from his nose Sam found new strength in his anger at Hadan's death. The power of the lines.

He gritted his teeth and began to push.

Kya caught the odd glimpse of the ongoing battle with Jak away down the room but every time she tried to get a proper look she had to parry another attack. Sometimes it seemed as though there was a wall of claws determined to bar her view. She quickly gave up; she had to concentrate on her own fight. The only attention she was able to spare was every now and then when she saw a ropen or garoul head in that direction. These she grabbed and pulled back towards her, anxious to keep them away from the real danger that Sam and Hadan were facing, even thought it meant more danger to her.

Weewalk fought beside her bravely. Despite his size and stocky build he was quick and deft and fought in a way that was clever and made best use of his skills. He had nowhere near as much power as Kya but he was just as effective, lifting small objects and driving them at the beasts that attacked them.

At one point he was able to get enough space to open a line and Kya was able to shove a dozen ropen through the portal before it closed again. This allowed them the luxury of not continuously having to watch for airborne attacks from the sharp beaks and talons of the ropen.

The garoul were fearsome and relentless. It was no wonder that the legend of the werewolf had generated such fear throughout the history of this world, thought Kya. They were vicious and agile, constantly snarling and biting and more intelligent than a true wolf. Their weakness was that they did not have the sense to co-ordinate their attacks and often snapped at each other when they got in the way. This allowed Kya some freedom to push and jump between them and deal with one or two at a time. She raked her sharp knife across bellies and snouts; she severed paws and sprayed red blood across floor and walls.

More difficult were the nandi. Their size made them much more formidable. Only three had entered at Jak's command but that was enough. Under their mangy fur dense muscle bunched as they sprang surprisingly quickly through the chaos. Kya's knife seemed to have little effect. Most of the time she was not even able to get close enough to attack them and for a while she concentrated on keeping her distance and trying to whittle down the number of garoul whilst, at the same time, keeping an eye on the brave kobold who fought beside her. Several times the intense training she had received from Tarak Everune saved her life, her reactions honed to a point where she almost saw attacks before they came and was able to dance through a mad lunge from a nandi or push and twist in the air, allowing her body to flow through narrow spaces as claws and teeth flashed around her.

But, she was not invincible and after what seemed like an hour of fighting, although it had likely only been a few minutes, she felt herself beginning to tire. Hot tight lines across her back told her that she had been raked by claws at some point, although she could not remember when.

She looked across to Weewalk and was again impressed by his determination and courage as he faced a nandi, one of his arms hanging limp. He moved quickly to once side, diving onto the floor with a grunt as a huge fist sailed past him. Broken glass, thrown by Weewalk's presence, flew at the nandi's eyes and it backed away, clawing at its face with a roar.

In a rage it began attacking the first thing it encountered, another nandi. Blinded, it lashed out at the other beast and the two became involved in their own battle, smashing through desks and chairs as they fought like mad dogs. Both were quickly bleeding heavily and soon enough only one could still walk. It limped away to nurse its wounds and Kya and Weewalk were happy to let it go.

Still lying on the floor, Sam thought he felt Jak's hold on him weaken. Was it weakening or did it just have less hold over him? He put one shaking arm out towards a line which still hummed in its metallic arch. He felt the power flood into his body and the arch exploded in a cloud of dust and debris like a smashed neon bulb. The line winked out. He pressed his other hand to his chest and he sensed his broken ribs. Concentrating for a moment he moved them so they no longer caused him as much pain.

Then, with more effort than he had ever expended in his life, he forced himself first to his knees and then he finally stood and faced Jak. Jak still had his arms stretched towards Sam, desperately trying to regain control over him, but Sam was no longer overly troubled by it. He allowed his anger at Hadan's death to fill him like a fire. He limped forwards a step then flung an arm toward another portal. Again he drew on its power and it exploded. He stood a little straighter. Again and again he absorbed the power of the lines as the doorways smashed around him.

Fear was now etched into the part of Jak's face which was visible under his mask. Sam focused his presence and plucked a television screen from the ceiling and threw it hard. He felt Jak try to push it back when it was halfway between them but Sam gave it a flick and it smashed through Jak's defences, crashing into his head and causing him to stagger. Sam drew on more power. More doors evaporated into dust.

Jak gathered himself and directed one last enormous strike at Sam. Everything in the room was pushed before the blast. Broken furniture and lumps of concrete and glass flew at Sam enveloping him in a storm of dust and debris. When it had rushed past him and the billowing grey dust had drifted away. Sam stood. Untouched. Immobile.

'You killed my friend.' he said through gritted teeth.

'And I would again', said Jak. 'I'm the greatest assassin that ever lived.' But there was doubt in his high-pitched cackle.

'No,' said Sam, shaking his head. 'You're no more than one of those beasts you allowed here.' With that he extended a hand towards Jak and lifted him. He swung his hand and Jak flew screaming past Sam and down the long laboratory where he crashed into the nandi that towered over Kya and Weewalk threatening to crush them beneath its huge paws. The nandi recovered quickly, catching Jak in its teeth.

Sam turned then and saw the devastation behind him. Jak struggled against the teeth of the nandi. Sam raised his arms and a portal, as yet untouched, opened behind the beast and its struggling prey. Sam gave a nod to Kya, who quickly pulled Weewalk close, then he drew back his shoulders and pushed with every ounce of his power.

The last garoul and the nandi and Jak were pushed into the line and in a moment had vanished. The force of the blast carried debris on a wall of wind around the entire circular laboratory, bringing the lights on in a blaze of neon. A few moments later a rush of dust and grit blew past Sam from behind.

He looked to Kya and Weewalk. Kya had thrown a barrier of sorts around them and she sat on the floor, cradling the kobold between her legs, his bloody arm hanging limply, his hand resting on the floor before him. At last silence filled the room.

Sam turned his head to look at the pockmarked concrete ceiling.

'Weewalk,' he said, his voice wavering. 'Hadan is dead. I'm sorry. I couldn't save him.'

The kobold, his eyes shut tight, let out a wail which filled the space between them.

Sam walked the length of the circular laboratory and still found no conventional door. The only way in or out was through a line. No wonder the place had remained hidden and untouched since the last scientists had left. The room was a disaster area. Benches lay smashed into pieces; computer equipment fizzed and sparked over the bodies of the beasts that Jak had drawn here. A few lines remained in their archways. He tested them in turn. He now had some sort of sense where each led; maps began to form in his head. He came to the last doorway and sent his presence into it to sense where the line would lead to. He stopped in amazement, finding it difficult to believe what he had just discovered. Then with a shake of his head he walked around the room again, destroying each of the other doors in turn. He could not really say why he did this. He only wanted this place to be useless. It certainly felt useless to him. Each line popped away as he blew apart the archways. Power crackled on his fingertips. Men should never have tried to create their own lines. The project had been doomed from the start.

When the last door remained Sam walked to where Weewalk and Kya sat hunched and sniffing on the floor. Gently Sam encouraged them to their feet and guided them to the last line. He opened it and ushered them through. After one final look around the room he gathered their bags, picking up the lamp that Hadan had dropped when Jak attacked, and stepped through himself. That doorway would always remain open.

As with the other man-made lines this one bucked and threw them but they landed gently enough in a dark underground room. Sam lit the lamp and led them up a short corridor to another room.

'We can rest here.'

They unrolled their blankets on the cold floor. Sam bid each of them to lie down and, as he had before, he sent his mind into their bodies curing the hurts he found there. Finally, he turned his mind inwards and cured his own pain, soothing away the stressed muscle and flesh until his body felt strangely numb because of the absence of it.

When he had finished Weewalk shuffled over. His face pale and concerned in the light of the fire.

'Sam, the stories of the destruction of Montauk. It was you. You were the one. You are the one.' Weewalk shook his head 'Where do we go from here?'

'We continue.' said Sam simply. 'I won't let Hadan's death be in vain. Some good must come from this whole thing.'

'But we're back where we started.' said Kya, 'We're no closer to Mu than we ever were.'

'Actually, we're very close. There is another line nearby.' said Sam, 'A natural one which will take us away from here, to Tongue's Scar. I know where we need to go.'

'Where?' Weewalk asked confused. 'Sam, you seem different somehow.'

'I am different. I can feel presence everywhere.' Sam looked around at the dark featureless room around him. 'Do you remember what you once told me, my friend? Those with power must have spent time near lines in order to have amplified their powers. Well, Weewalk, I'm going home. Back to my grandfather's house. That's where the door has been all along. Our path must take us back to the start, back to the beginning. Out path has taken us full circle. The line is a circle.'

And so, on a cold winter's evening Sam led them from the tunnels in the woods near his house. The place where Weewalk had first taken him along a line. He soon found himself standing before the rubble of his former home.

This was where it had all begun for Samuel Hain. He stood with his back to the darkening woods behind him. The air was clear and the moon was shining brightly above. With a nod to himself Sam walked towards what had once been his home.

The building had all but collapsed. A few blackened walls remained standing but the house was essentially a pile of brick and charred wood. What few possessions might have remained seemed to have been removed. Sam was surprised by how small it looked when one could only see the foundations of what it had been. Living inside, it had seemed pretty large, but as tumbled brick and mortar it was small and sad. He stopped for a moment, standing at what used to be the front door. He looked down and caught sight of the wooden plaque on which his grandfather had carved the name of the house. 'The End of the Line.' Sam smiled to himself as he nudged at it with his foot. Then he stepped over the threshold and followed an imaginary path through the hall and to where the door to the cellar would once have stood. After a quick look around to check that no-one but Kya and Weewalk were watching he sent his mind into the tumbled stone and blackened wood and pushed it all aside piece by piece until he had uncovered the stairs into the cellar. Once the path was clear he descended into the darkness.

Holding up Hadan's old lamp he could see that this room had escaped relatively unscathed from the storm that had raged above. A few things had fallen through but nothing had caught fire. Most of the damage seemed to have been caused by smoke and the white walls had been painted a sooty grey.

Turning to look around as Weewalk and Kya came down the steps Sam felt a funny tickle at the back of his neck and he remembered how he had felt in this house. Scared of ghosts. It seemed as though one were here now. His grandfather perhaps or Hadan. He almost laughed then. It seemed absurd that he had been scared of something as intangible and insubstantial as a ghost. He knew now that there were real monsters out there. The legends of werewolves were true. Men should be more fearful of tooth and claw than spectre and spook. The real danger was men like Ferus. That thought set his resolve and he turned towards the hole in the wall that he had grown up casting sideways glances at but had never really thought to question why it was there.

He hoisted himself up and climbed through the wall of the cellar of his childhood home. Hidden, just out of sight, he saw a ladder leading through a rough hole in the floor. He called to Kya and Weewalk to follow him as he descended, down into darkness as the hum and chime of the line below began to sing up at him, calling him towards its caress.

Tarak Everune wanted to pace his cell. He wanted to stand and walk, with his arms behind his back. It helped him think. But he didn't. He had to maintain the broken persona that he had so carefully crafted for Ferus over the last few years. He had to be a man without a presence. He had positioned all the pieces on the board as carefully as he could. Now there was just one more piece to deploy. The Polish man, Aleksy, whose mind he had been so quietly and subtly affecting. And he was almost in position. If Aleksy didn't distract the King at just the right time, so that Ferus was acting alone without the presence of the King, then all would be for naught. The rest? Well, Tarak told himself that he just had to wait and let the game play out in the hope that he had properly predicted where the checkmate would come. And so he just sat, aware that someone could be watching through some gap in the stone wall. Besides, his cell was extremely cold and he had been given only enough food to survive. He felt weak. His stomach ached. He thought about little else other than food. And so, he continued to sit, hunched over his knees. A broken man but perhaps only in appearance.

He had fresh hope though. He could feel that something may be happening. Ferus had been to see him twice in the last two days which was an unusual amount of interest from the tyrant. Both times he had come only to check that Tarak had not moved. Tarak had not looked up on either occasion, but he knew it was Ferus. The man had seemed agitated both times and the second time Tarak had had the sense that Ferus had opened his mouth to speak before changing his mind and turning away again. Perhaps something was up. Perhaps Ferus' plans were not going quite as he wanted them. Tarak allowed himself a small smile under his lank hair.

Sam stood in front of the line beneath the floor of the cellar. Kya and Weewalk came up behind him.

'He knew it was here all along, my granddad. I wonder if he ever knew what it was or where it went.'

Sam looked around the small space that had been carved out of the earth around the line. A table had been built here and a wooden chair too. It was like the burrow office of some man-mole. Mildewed paper and a few old pens sat on the small desk but the paper was blank apart from spots of mould. How often must his grandfather have sat here looking longingly at what lay just beyond his reach, perhaps never understanding that it was a doorway to another world?

'Well, here we go.' said Sam, facing the patch of darkness. He waved a hand and the line opened before him. 'It's time to go to Mu. It's cold there. We should put extra clothes on.'

'Tongue's Scar, here we come.' said Kya softly.

Once they had finished dressing they stepped through together.

They arrived in a world of deep snow and tall fir trees that looked like very much like any other pine trees from Sam's own world. The sky above was a deep clear blue. It was extremely cold but Sam noticed that his breath did not seem to fog much in front of his face. Instead it sparkled like he was blowing out glitter, as ice crystals formed in the air. Despite the cold air there was warmth in the sun.

The whole world shone and, for a moment, Sam wanted nothing more than to plant new footprints in the fresh unspoilt snow that surrounded them. The place was beautiful, the air crisp and clean.

Weewalk gave Sam a nudge and pointed up to a tree some distance away. A single ropen sat glaring at them. It hopped on the branch once, twice and then spread its wings and flew off with a caw like a crow.

'Well,' said Weewalk, 'if anyone is around they'll soon know we're here. Perhaps we should follow its lead.' And with that he began to kick through the deep snow which immediately threatened to engulf him.

Sam and Kya pushed on too and overtook the kobold, tramping down the snow in order to make his passage easier.

'We could presence-leap.' said Kya.

'Let's walk for now.' said Sam, looking back at where their trail started in a pure white drift as if they had appeared from nowhere.

'Is now perhaps a good time to discuss how we're going to do whatever it is that we're going to do?' asked Weewalk.

'You two try to get to Tarak' said Sam 'I'll try to keep whoever is waiting for us busy.'

It was not long before the trees began to thin and they could make out a building ahead.

'I think this is it.' said Kya excitedly. 'Yes, this is it. We've come right to it. This is Tongue's Scar.'

They stepped into a clearing surrounding a squat, grey, single-story block of a building. Although the sky above was clear now, away from the trees, Sam could see that a storm was coming. The wind picked up suddenly and towering dark clouds raced towards them. In a moment the sun was gone. A door in the building opened as they entered the space away from the trees. Out stepped a familiar figure.

'How nice of you to visit.' said Ferus with a mocking bow.

This was it then. Sam had come prepared for a fight, but not with the most powerful person he'd ever encountered. He tried to keep the alarm and fear out of his voice.

'We're here for Tarak Everune, Ferus. Let him go and we'll be on our way.'

'Ha, ha, pathetic. At least try to sound like you've got some balls, boy. Besides, what do you want him for? He's a craven coward and he's released all his secrets. The secret keepers are over. The only useful thing he's done is to bring you here.'

Sam felt movement next to him and was surprised to see Kya rush forward towards Ferus. A look of hatred on her face. But she had not taken more than a few steps before Ferus sent a huge blast of energy at the three of them. Even though Sam was prepared for it and threw up a shield he was knocked off his feet by the awesome power of it. It was like nothing else he had felt. The power that Ferus had just delivered so casually was far more than Sam was capable of.

Suddenly Sam realised he was wrong to have come here. It was a trap. He had nowhere near enough presence to beat Ferus. Besting Jak and his beasts might have even been part of the false trail. Now, he was doomed.

Ferus spoke again. 'We just can't have people going around opposing the King. People have already been talking, boy, about your time at the Mermaid. Some think you're pretty powerful, that you could be the new leader for the rebel cause. That the prophecy is about you.' He shook his head. 'It isn't. I'm afraid that it won't happen.'

He sent another blast at Sam who flew backwards, landing in a crumpled heap in the snow. He could see Kya and Weewalk now. They seemed to be pinned to the spot, lying prostrate on their backs. Evidently Ferus was holding them down while he toyed with Sam.

'The age of man is over. Your parents were easy to kill. I had hoped you might make a more worthy opponent.' said Ferus.

'Yeah, I've heard that before.' said Sam struggling out of the deep snow, gritting his teeth at the mention of his parents.

Sam saw something small and shiny fly from inside the folds of Ferus' cloak, a silvery object which moved in the air to near Ferus' hand. There was the unmistakable *'clink'* of a lighter flicking open and Sam dived to one side. A bolt of flame flew from Ferus' hand, sizzling in the snow. Ferus held the line of fire and began to snap and flick it like a whip. Laughing, he chased Sam around the clearing with the fire, flicking it at his heels. It was all Sam could do to push himself out of the way, bounding away from trees at the edge of the clearing and leaving round impacts in the snow where he pushed from the floor.

When Sam felt himself to be in the right place he threw himself with all of his might at Ferus, gathering all his strength and pushing against the trees behind him as well as pushing a massive force at Ferus. But he felt a terrible pressure in his shoulders and branches snapped and cracked on the tree behind him. Ferus remained immobile.

Sam darted away again, and felt the heat of flame at his back. He had to turn and fight. Ferus flashed another bolt of fire at him. Sam seized it with his presence and wrenched it away from Ferus, flicking it back so that it seared a line across Ferus' cloak.

'Huh.' said Ferus. 'So, you've learnt a few things I see.'

He raised his hands again with a bellow and threw a sustained burst of presence at Sam. Sam sent presence back and their opposing blasts crashed in mid air, ball lightning flickered and flashed in the air where their powers met. Sam pushed as hard as he could, but he could feel he was losing. Then Ferus gave an extra push and Sam's presence collapsed. He was suddenly grabbed mid air and thrown into the snow. Ferus walked over to him. Sam could not move and looked up at his foe and the stormy sky behind him. Lightning flashed above as Ferus crouched over him, speaking to him quietly.

'I'm going to kill you now. And when you're dead. I'm going to kill your two friends.'

Sam struggled but he could not move. He lay flat on his back, his arms outstretched. Ferus increased the pressure and Sam found he could do little to resist. He was utterly trapped.

'Do you know what it was all about?' said Ferus, his mouth now near Sam's ear. 'The greatest secret of our worlds? Tarak Everune's news? Have you ever wondered why some lines take you to another place in time in your world and other lines take you to another world entirely? It's a strange system isn't it? Time and space crumpled over each other. Still, we cannot understand the minds or wills of the gods who created the lines. Pyxidis made our world, complete with lines to yours, so who are we to question why he did what he did?

'But, our worlds are so similar aren't they?' Sam felt Ferus' breath hot on his ear, his voice was barely a whisper.

'It's because they're the same place. When you have

the full story it all just seems to fit. In the past of my world a terrible event caused the death of almost everyone who lived there. Ancient history tells us that almost the entire population was killed by our all powerful god in a blast from the heavens. Those few who were allowed to live were altered, affected in some way so that powers developed and new beasts began to form. That is my past. But it is your future.'

'Our worlds are one. There is no other place. Pyxidis was no mage. No wizard infusing the world with magic. We merely exist in different times. At some point in your future the world will almost end, and the Riven will be born.

'What did Tarak call it? Ah yes, a supernova, blasting away almost all life, causing radiation that would affect us all, that would turn some men into beasts and create rips in time that would forever cause us to loop back upon ourselves. The line is a circle.

This place. It's not Tongue's Scar, no. it is called Tunguska. In Russia.' He shook his head. 'Why the secret keepers kept that one to themselves I'll never know. Perhaps it was only recently discovered by Everune. Perhaps it was the magnitude of it all that drove him to drink.'

'Still,' he said 'there's no point in dwelling on the past.'

Ferus stood. Now that his mouth was not near Sam's ear the noise of the storm that was now in full force rushed to fill the gap and Ferus had to shout to make himself heard above the wind that roared between the trees, lifting the snow from the branches.

'Time to die, Sam Hain.'

Sam readied himself and saw Ferus tense for an attack. Sam realised he had but one chance. He concentrated his will on Kya and Weewalk. There was no way he was going to allow them to remain in danger. He had to get them out of here. He gave both a push sending them sliding through the snow and into the trees in opposite directions and out of sight. The move had surprised Ferus and broken his hold on them.

Ferus rolled his eyes. 'Urgh, one of those heroes. One of those 'I have to get my friends out of danger' types. Well, I'll track them down soon enough after I've dealt with you.'

Sam looked up. He had nothing left. The end was upon him.

In a cold, dim and silent hall Aleksy hurried towards where the Riven King sat on his throne. He could scarcely believe that he had made it in here. He would never have made it without Allende's help. Although no wind entered the room the King's black robes billowed silently and slowly around his immobile body, obscuring his head, carried aloft by some weird magic. A single bright shaft of light hit the floor before the King, in the centre of the room, a stark contrast to the blackness around it. There was only one sound in the room despite the presence of the few silent servants who, like Aleksy, were careful to keep to the shadows, keeping as close to the walls as they could. The sound was a low hum, the noise of a coin spinning in the air, but maddeningly elusive. The servants huddled into the corners trying to avoid the crystal shards that shifted slowly around the room before the throne, like a window breaking in a slow tornado. Aleksy had learnt from Allende that each of these was a weapon, wickedly sharp, taken from the mines below and with properties which ordinary men like Aleksy could not fathom. They span slowly around the room in arcs, a maelstrom seen in slow motion. They drifted through the shaft of light throwing bright patches onto the dark walls.

Frequently these white lights flashed patches of red as some shards were coated in dried blood where the Riven King had directed his anger at those who dared disturb him, pushing a shard through the body of the unfortunate by using the power of his mind. There were tens of thousands of pieces of crystal, every one of them held in the air by the King's presence. It was said that when they all turned red then the world would fall, but not many had seen them and lived to speak of it. No-one had ever seen a shard fall, never seen the King lose concentration for even a fraction of a second.

The Riven King was old. No one was sure just how old. He sat immobile on his magical throne, a relic, Allende had said, from experiments that men had carried out in a place called Montauk many millennia ago. The King was deep in concentration as he sensed the world around him. His eyes, just visible in the shadow of the dark cloak, were completely white, blank, like those of a blind man, yet they saw much. Aleksy crept towards him. He would kill the King. He would gain his freedom. He pulled a wicked looking shard of broken glass, bound with string for grip, from beneath his tunic and crept towards the throne. The King did not stir but then, suddenly, Aleksy felt the King's presence take hold of him. He was held, his mind stripped bare and he felt everything leak from his brain.

The Riven King stiffened. A single eye rolled in its socket and a black pupil and a brown iris snapped to the front to stare at Aleksy with a gaze that utterly terrified him. If he had not been held by the presence he would have been paralysed in abject fear. The Riven King's other eye remained blank. Then the hood fell back to reveal the face underneath. Unable to move Aleksy could only stare in horror. It was Allende.

An eyebrow twitched and then a laugh escaped the

King's mouth which caused everyone who heard it to fall to their knees in fear. But Aleksy could not move. He could not even shake with the terror that consumed him. He could not even ask why. But Allende, the Riven King, sensed his question.

'Men like you fascinate me, friend Aleksy. Men like you just won't quit. And there is no sweeter moment than watching men like you come to the very edge of success only to see it collapse around you.' Allende giggled hysterically. 'I enjoy watching men fight and fight, unaware of the complete futility of their actions. I enjoy watching such men die. I will never be beaten.'

Then the crystal shards began to fly quicker around the room in a terrible hurricane of ice. More than a few emerged from the shadows red, blood dripping from them as they ripped through the servants.

Aleksy felt the fire inside his chest flicker. No, it would not end like this. He gathered every ounce of emotion. From somewhere he found strength. His hatred of the man before him consumed him and he drove a leg forward, moved an arm. He slashed with the knife.

The King's laugh lost its pitch and became a bellow of pure rage that echoed out of the room and into the complex beyond. A tiny droplet of blood appeared on his cheek. Aleksy's lunge had barely scratched him. Aleksy was held immobile again and he knew then that he had lost. Then, the size of the crystal whirlwind narrowed and the blades ripped through him with terrible force. His tattered body fell to the floor, soft and bloody. He had failed. The roar of the King's voice continued to echo. The Riven King was awake and his anger was terrible to behold.

In a cell Tarak Everune felt the delicate hold that he had on Aleksy's mind stutter and wink out. Tarak hung his head in sorrow and closed his eyes.

Ferus gathered himself and sent what must have been every ounce of his power into the boy lying before him. This was the killing blow. Sam closed his eyes a spilt second before it hit and said a silent goodbye. His final thought was of Kya and what might have been.

BOOOOOOOOM.

A thousand miles away Piotr leapt from his chair as he felt the ground rumble. The glass window trembled and then burst, showering the floor with glass. He dashed to the machine on the desk by the window and looked in amazement at the wide scribble that the arm had produced as the graph paper scrolled through. He studied it for a moment, trying to get to grips with the size of the tremor shown on the seismograph. Then slowly he raised his head to the cold air that streamed in through the empty window frame. The building was set on a large hill. You could see for miles up here, out over the empty woods of snowy northern Russia. He stared out of the window, unsure what he was seeing. The woods looked different. Suddenly he realised why and he staggered in shock, grabbing the side of the desk to steady himself. The woods looked different because every single one of the trees he could see ahead of him now coated the floor of the valleys and hills like a box of dropped matches. Every single one of the thousands of trees he could see had been knocked down.

The impact was like a tsunami of sound. Snow and splintered wood flew from the point where Ferus had struck Sam. An avalanche spreading in every direction. Yet, it was Sam who opened his eyes. Coughing, he dug himself out from underneath a foot of snow that had gone straight up in the air when Ferus had thrown the full force of his power onto Sam's chest. Sam rubbed his face and spat snow and blood out next to him. Everything hurt as he sat up and looked around.

What he saw was unbelievable. Every tree of the immense forest that had stood around him had been torn down and flung away from him. He looked to the grey building but it was almost entirely gone, scoured away as though the giant fist of some god had punched into the earth at the very point where Sam was lying. Ferus was nowhere to be seen.

Sam suddenly thought of Kya and Weewalk and struggled to his feet, dizzily coughing out more blood as he shouted for them croakily. There was no answer.

Sam staggered towards the remains of the building unsure where else to go. His ears rang and he could not hear very well. He shouted again but his tongue was thick in his mouth. He reached what was left of a crumbled wall and again looked around wildly, holding on to the grey concrete as though he might collapse at any moment. Still he could see no-one. He closed his eyes. He tried not to imagine Kya pinned under a fallen tree unable to cry out in the cold snow, or Weewalk's small body blasted away like a pebble thrown across a lake.

Then he felt a hand grip his ankle and he shouted and fell sideways into the snow. He looked down to see Weewalk's face emerge from the whiteness at his feet.

'Wha?' he managed. Then he saw. As the kobold pushed away the snow Sam realised that there was a square hole in the floor and a flight of steps that went down, underneath what remained of the concrete building. Weewalk had been in the cellar. He pushed his way out of the hole, looking in amazement at the devastation around him. He was closely followed by a grinning Kya who supported a man who, Sam realised, must have been Tarak.

Sam stayed sitting in the deep snow in amazement as the three flopped down in the snow before him. Then Kya gently set Tarak with Weewalk, rose to her knees and flung herself into Sam's arms and he was enveloped in her warmth.

When Kya eventually released Sam from the embrace Weewalk shuffled over and slapped him on the shoulder. Then Tarak came to greet him. His hair was long and lank, greying at the temples. He had a straggly beard, full of knots and tangles and his clothes were little more than rags. But his face, flushed pink from the cold, was kind and happy. He wore a smile, just visible under his unkempt moustache.

'Sam,' he said, 'I am Tarak Everune. I owe my life to you and your friends. I am honoured to meet you at long last.'

'At last?' said Sam. 'How long have you known about me?'

'For several years and for several thousands of years. Time is a strange thing. But would you mind if we found somewhere else to discuss it all? I'm rather cold. There is another line within the building, if you would be so kind as to remove the rubble so that we can reach it.'

'Of course.' Sam said and pushed himself out of the snow. Kya and Weewalk lifted Tarak between them and they supported each other. Sam noticed, with an irrational burst of faint jealousy, that Kya held the old man particularly tenderly, looking at him with obvious fondness and affection.

Sam tensed and felt his body complain but he moved away the chunks of concrete to create a space where the building had stood before. When there was room he opened the line that Tarak had mentioned. Stepping through they arrived in an old timber-framed house on a fairly normal looking village street. There was soon a fire blazing in the grate and the four of them huddled round it, wrapped in blankets and sipping tea which Weewalk had produced from the bag that he still carried.

When he was judged to be well enough and warm enough to speak they let Tarak begin to talk.

'Well,' said the secret keeper, 'I am sure there are some things you wish to ask of me. Which question will be first?'

'What happened to Ferus?' asked Sam immediately. 'How did I survive?'

'Aha, now that is just about my last secret. It is the heart of the whole business. Perhaps I had better start at the beginning.'

'Although you probably know of me as the last in the order of the Secret Keepers, that is wrong. I am also the first of that order and, during my travels through the lines and through time, I have found others and gained their support. I did this because, whilst in another time, I became aware of some very important and incredible information. Part of it I think you already know for I admitted it to Ferus, as he needed to believe that I had divulged every last secret I had.

Yes. Mu is no more another world than last week in London is another world. It is merely another place in time, albeit a time a long way away from here. A time that exists after something terrible happened. This world, as you know it, is doomed. It seems that there is nothing we can do about it. Something out there, out in space, is about to pop. The event will not just damage the instant world but the effects will be felt through history and throughout the future. That cannot be changed. It will create the rips in space time that you know as lines. Our knowledge of the lines is still scant. We are still at the very beginning of discovering where they go and what the effect of our using them is.

'So, if Mu is simply the future, then it must be inhabited by those who survived. Sam, some, but by no means all, of the people of Mu are your ancestors.'

Sam looked startled.

'Of course, not just you. There will be many who live and repopulate the world but there was an ancestral line that I discovered which was of particular interest to me. That line was part of the history of one of the greatest tyrants for a thousand years. Ferus could never have known that he would not have been able to kill the reason he ever came to live. Have you ever heard of the grandfather paradox Sam?'

Sam shook his head.

'Well, imagine you invented a time machine and travelled back to a time before your parents were born. There you encountered your grandfather as a young man. Let's say that, for whatever reason, you tried to kill that man before he fathered one of your parents. What would happen? One of your parents would never be born and as a result, you would never be born.' He pointed a finger at Sam's forehead. 'But if you never existed, how did you come to kill your grandfather? It was this that was Ferus' downfall. He tried to kill a relative. Albeit a distant one.'

'What? Ferus is my family?' asked Sam unbelieving.

'Yes, and he was killed by a paradox' said Tarak with a laugh. 'One day, Sam, you will have children and they will have children and so on and so on, until, sadly, Ferus will be born. But, he will never be able to kill you for to do so would destroy his own existence and that is, I believe what happened. That blast was the result. I had decided that there were two possibilities, that things would always simply go wrong for Ferus in his attempts to kill you or that it would actually rebound if he used enough power. It seems both were true. His efforts to get to you never quite succeeded did they? But when he had a clear shot and put all of his power into you, it backfired. I just had to ensure that he was acting totally independently, without any borrowed power from the Riven King. It was lucky that my cell was underground and that these two came through to rescue me. I doubt we would have survived otherwise. In a battle against Ferus you, Sam, could be hurt but he could never kill you. You were invincible.'

Sam looked across to Kya who seemed as stunned as him.

'And here I have a confession and an apology to make. In predicting this, I allowed myself to be captured and I also allowed my secrets to be discovered by Ferus. It was a tremendous risk. He had to think that you were a real threat to him and the Riven King. That you fulfilled some prophecy. Ferus had reached a point where he was so powerful that the only thing which could destroy him was his own power. Get the fire hot enough and even iron melts. Sam, I'm sorry but it was my information that led Ferus to pursue you so relentlessly. I led him to believe that he needed to kill you. That you were special. The subject of a prophecy.'

Sam felt hollow. He had been a pawn in a game.

'You were not alone in the risk. I gambled with my own daughter in entrusting her to find you.' At this Kya moved to him and he put his arm around her.

Weewalk spoke then. 'Is the prophecy real? We thought Sam was the one!'

'Well, he may be important.' said Tarak 'There are many prophecies but whether Sam's absorption of the powers he has is relevant remains to be seen. It can be interpreted in a number of ways. I just needed Ferus to believe that it was about him to bring them together. But I have more secrets, and good news I hope. Speaking of grandfathers leads me on nicely to another relation of yours, Sam. I believe you knew him as Adam Hain.'

Sam looked up quickly.

'Did he leave you anything important when he died?'

'What? How do you know about my grandfather?'

'Please, humour me a moment. I have been looking forward to this. Did he leave you anything?'

'He left me a house but it burnt down. He didn't have anything else.'

'There must have been something else. A book perhaps?'

Sam thought then stopped in surprise. 'Wait, there was something.' He pulled his rucksack over from where it lay in a corner of the room.

'I put this in here on the day of the funeral and then forgot all about it. It was in a separate pocket inside so I never looked at it.'

He withdrew the package still wrapped in brown paper just as it had been when he had been given it by the solicitor in church, all that time ago. Nervously, Sam tore at the paper until it came away. He found his hands were shaking. The book inside had a soft brown leather cover. He held it for a moment. He still owned something of his grandfathers. He didn't care if it was nothing more than an empty book. It had come from the man who had protected him his entire life. With a deep breath he opened the book to the first page. Just three words were written on that page.

I am Hadan.

CHAPTER SIXTEEN

Sam sat outside the house, hugging his knees on a wooden bench, looking out into the garden. He heard someone approach and he turned to see Kya. She came and sat next to him, her legs dangling over the edge of the bench. She pressed her body close to him and swung her legs slightly but didn't say anything. After a minute she rested her head on Sam's shoulder and he felt his stomach flip.

'Kya, no.' he said moving away. 'I... I can't. Not after the way your father has treated everyone. Why didn't you tell me more about what you knew?'

'I honestly didn't know much.' she said 'My father told me that he would be captured, that only you could save him. That I had to take you to him. He said that if Ferus ever found him that I had to find you, and bring you here. That only you could save him. That only you could save us all.'

Sam tried to calm the anger that been burning inside him. He had been used. With effort he checked himself and took a deep breath.

'Your father doesn't care about who he uses to get what he wants, whatever that is. He's responsible for all of this, just so that he could use me as a weapon to get rid of Ferus. He didn't know for sure that it would even work. Kya, I hate him for what he's done.'

'He was tortured, Sam.'

'He allowed himself to be captured and tortured so that Ferus would think that there was some stupid prophecy about me! So that Ferus would try to kill me! My parents died because of it!'

'He was doing it for the greater good. He knew that Ferus had to be stopped. You know what Ferus did to him, to us? Do you? Do you know? He took my mother. Not long after I was born Ferus took my mother and he tortured her for a week before he killed her. He let everyone know he was doing it to lure my father out to him. To get him to reveal the secrets he held. But my father didn't go. He couldn't risk Ferus getting hold of the information he held. So, he left her there. But I don't blame him. It was Ferus who was responsible. Do you realise the risk he took in eventually letting himself get captured?'

'I didn't know about your mother. But it still doesn't make it right.' said Sam. He was quiet for a minute then he said softly 'I've read more of the book. Hadan left me what information he could, but it wasn't much. He didn't know a great deal when he was pushed through that line. It's a sad book. He tried to tell me to my face more than a couple of times, but he realised that it just made him sound mad and he was extremely worried about changing the order of events for the worse. Perhaps, perhaps if he'd known he was about to, you know, die and I'd been at his bedside when he went it would have been different. Instead he went suddenly in his sleep without ever pointing me to the clues that he had put in place.

'The journal was his way of telling me what I needed to know. The page which we came across in Professor Keel's laboratory is still there. At some point I guess I'll tear it out and it will end up in the Professor's postbox.'

'Will you leave anything else?' asked Kya.

'I don't think so. My grandfather, Hadan, made the decision that that was the right information to leave. It all works out. If we hadn't taken the line in the Deeps then I would never have gained the powers I did in Montauk and I would not have come to face Ferus in Tunguska. Hadan might still be here and alive now, and who knows what that would mean, but it would almost certainly mean that I would not exist.

'I will, at some point, find a line and I will leave that poem in the right place where my grandfather will find it in the library. I know he'll make the right decision. If I told my past self what was going to happen would I go through with it? Actually, Kya, I suddenly think that I need you to do this. Here.' Sam tore the page from the journal. 'Will you ensure that that page gets to Professor Keel in time for our arrival?'

'Can't we do it together? I'm coming with you!' said Kya.

'I think I need to go on ahead alone for now.' said Sam.

Kya was quiet for several minutes. Then said 'What happened in that lab?'

'Well, Jak was pushing Hadan to a line that would have killed him had he entered it. At the last moment I managed to knock Hadan sideways and he slid through another of those portals and ended up where he did. If I hadn't I would have ceased to exist. So would Ferus. Then Ferus wouldn't have sent Jak to follow us. It makes my head hurt to think about it.

Anyway, Hadan tried for a while to find a way back

but with no presence to open a line or any way to contact us he became stuck. I think in the end he became used to it. He settled down, married, had a child and eventually became a grandparent. It must have been the shock of a lifetime to realise that the grandchild was me. Perhaps he realised before. It probably made him pretty uncomfortable to be reunited with a life he had given up as lost. In some way it must just have been too painful for him to talk about. Looking back I can see that he tried to tell me but he could just never get it across. He rebuilt the house himself. It was abandoned and tumbled down when he found it. It must have been agony for him, to live so close to a line, to know it was there, but to never be able to find out what lay at the end.'

Sam picked up the book and turned it over in his hands.

'Did you realise Adam Hain is an anagram of I am Hadan? This journal even tells me about my own name. I've never seen my birth certificate. I always assumed that Sam was short for Samuel, but I'm just Sam. Sam Hain. Samhain is the name of an old festival celebrated on Halloween, the day I met Hadan. Samhain is about the end of the summer, and the start of the period of darkness. It's a time when the barrier between worlds was thought to thin, allowing ghosts to cross into our own realm. I think he used things like that to reassure himself that he was giving me information.'

Sam shook his head. It all seemed so incredible.

'Hadan had faith in me all along. He never knew how the story would end. As a young man he never knew or even suspected where he would end up. As an older man his experience of me ended in that laboratory in Montauk. But he had faith. He knew I would find the powers and make it that far. I wonder when he first realised about me. It must have been when my parents died, or when they named me perhaps. He chose my surname when he had to create a conventional identity that would allow him to live as part of normal society so maybe he even suspected then.'

Sam looked down at the scar running up his finger and along his forearm.

'He would never have known that Ferus was his descendent. Imagine if he'd known!'

Kya tried to snuggle in closer to him and Sam sighed sadly.

'Kya, I can't. I really like you but I can't. Not with the way that your father is using people. He just wants revenge! I just can't be around you. Besides, how can I ever get into a relationship knowing what my future will produce. Knowing that one day Ferus will be born because of me.'

Kya drew back, startled.

'I know what my father did was wrong and reckless but you have to see what he's trying to do. No-one has seen as much of the future as him. It's the greater good, Sam, always for the greater good. All for the future of men. And he hates that he has to do it.'

'It caused my parents death! How do you know he's even telling the truth now? What is the real prophecy anyway? I can't do it, Kya. I can't stay with you, or him. And I can't allow Ferus to exist.'

'I don't think you'll have much say Sam Hain.' she said crossly 'I think destiny will guide you more closely than you know. Besides you know Ferus' days are numbered.'

With that, she rose and walked away, leaving Sam alone.

Weewalk came then and sat next him. Tarak stood nearby but didn't venture close. He looked completely different. Gone was the straggly beard and baggy clothes.

His beard was closely trimmed and his hair, now more brown than grey, was neatly brushed. Colour had returned to his cheeks. He looked slim and handsome.

'So, you're heading off?' Weewalk said.

'Yes', said Sam, firing a look of disgust at Tarak. 'I, I need to get away.'

Weewalk clapped him on the shoulder.

'I understand', he said, and Sam saw tears in the creases around the kobold's eyes. Then his own vision blurred and he hugged the small figure.

Three days after the explosion which had almost killed him, but in another year entirely, Sam stood alone before a new portal. He had been able to sense it from far away. It led far into the future. He gathered his power and focused it where he knew the door would appear. The entrance materialised before him. He paused for a few moments feeling the familiar tingle of electricity as it entered his body. Warmth ran up his spine. Then, setting his jaw, he stepped through.

He arrived on a wide plain, a sea of yellow grass, devoid of trees. The sun seemed to be just rising above the horizon and a thin mist nestled in small valleys and folds in the landscape. Sam looked over the grassy plain and sighed. It was difficult to continue now that he knew the awful, almost incomprehensible truth. Mankind as he knew it was doomed. Many millions of lives snuffed out in an instant by the supernova that would strip the earth bare. Millions more would die afterwards of sickness, starvation and natural disaster. More deaths would follow as the radiation caused both man and beast to warp and change. There was nothing he could do except avoid it in another time. Could he save others, take them through a line perhaps? He didn't know. But here, in this future, man was beginning to find his feet again. They were starting to take a stand. He had never moved so far into his own future before, to a time after the supernova that had changed the world forever. In the far distance he could just make out the highest roofs of a distant city. Turning toward it, he began to walk.

A body lay, discarded and broken, at the edge of a pit in the depths of the Rivenrok Complex. Torn and bloody, it looked as though a thousand knives had ripped at the flesh. A single rat sniffed at it, unsure whether it was safe to begin to gnaw at the bones. As the rat scurried over the lifeless body it disturbed a piece of torn and bloodied cloth on the back of the head. As it did so a piece of crystal glittered, lodged deep within the skull of the hapless victim. The rat sniffed again, interested at the smell of blood, but suddenly wary. Then, just as the rat was about to begin its feast a finger twitched and the rat lifted into the air as though picked up by an invisible hand. It was thrown away with a squeak. Aleksy felt his presence envelop him and his anger burned more fiercely than ever.

APPENDIX

Extracts from the diary of Adam Hain relevant to the events of *The Circle Line*

Entry 3

On the assumption that you, Sam, will read this I must tell you what I know about the origin of your name. Of course, through meeting you in our adventures I became aware of the name Sam Hain and so when I was struggling to fit myself into normal society here, the surname Hain came naturally to me. It was the only one I knew! I tried a couple of first names but when I came across the story of Adam and Eve I felt that Adam would suit me well, being a man with no ancestors. I find that Adam Hain is an anagram of I am Hadan. When did I have that idea? I am not sure. But the genius of the name Sam Hain delights me even now and I enjoy the circularity of it all. Samhain means literally summer's end, which can be taken to mean the end of the period of light and the beginning of the period of darkness, the dark half of the year. The Oxford English Dictionary tells us that it is a festival celebrated by the ancient Celts, marking the beginning of winter and of the New Year according to their calendar.

According to Celtic lore, Samhain was a time when the boundaries between the world of the living and the world of the dead become thinner, allowing spirits and other supernatural entities to pass between the worlds to socialize with humans. Does that sound familiar? You may know this day as Halloween, the very day that we met.

I have also uncovered some reference to a festival called Sânziene. I mention it here because it is another time, at the summer solstice, when the barrier between worlds is said to thin, just as with Samhain. Strange things and magics are said to happen on Sânziene night and men are told not to walk alone. If there is a thinning of the barrier between worlds at certain times then that is good advice!

Entry 8

I came across more evidence of the Riven's incursion today. My time at the library leads me to countless myths, stories and events which cannot be explained by the people here. The past is littered with it all. If only I could find some sort of pattern, or a reference that would allow me to find my way home. But perhaps I have been here too long already. As much as I miss my old friend Weewalk my place is here, with Sam. I must keep him safe, and give him a happy childhood, before that which will come to pass begins. One day I will tell him all this, if it does not drive me mad first. I will record my findings in this journal in the hope that it will, some day, be of use to him...

Entry 15

I read today of a disappearance at a site called Stonehenge. Men cannot fathom how the stones came to be here. They cannot see the lines. Apparently, a group of people disappeared from the site during a strange storm. How many of these unexplained events and urban myths are true?

Entry 17

Telekinesis. A rudimentary form of presence. Some men can apparently do limited things such as bend spoons. They must be absorbing energy from lines without realising just as Weewalk suggested. It must be that you, Sam, will absorb some of that same energy whilst in this house. Strange but I do not feel that I am. It must be that some do and some don't.

Entry 19

Men call it hysterical strength. It is the moment when presence is awakened. The most frequent stories I can find are about people lifting cars into the air, following accidents, to rescue those trapped underneath. The flow of a body chemical called adrenaline seems to flood these people causing them to be able to do things which are superhuman. In 1982 a woman called Angela Cavallo lifted the full weight of a car high enough and long enough that others could drag her son out from beneath it. Sometimes it can manifest itself in another way – the beserker. When this happens rage combines with the presence and the man goes mad and cannot be subdued. The strength of the truly mad man with presence is something to fear.

Entry 23

There is a fascination with supposed mythical and undiscovered creatures. Men even have a name for the study of it – cryptozoology. There have been famous sightings of 'Bigfoot' as they call him and his cousins the 'Yeti'. Men have found footprints that seem impossibly large. It seems Squatch is leading them a merry dance and if I ever see him again I will tell him of the intrigue he has caused. If I thought I could track him myself I might be able to find one of the lines he uses but I fear I would never manage it. There is a well known if not widely believed film of Bigfoot taken in 1967.

Entry 31

Egyptians. Aztecs. Mayans. Where did these people find the advances that made their civilisations great? Who were the gods that the Egyptians so revered? Someone from a future Mu? It seems likely. There was an ancient group of peoples in the country of Peru, the Inca. They created stone buildings with an ability that men have not been able to replicate, fitting stones together with absolute precision so that massive temples were built with no mortar to seal the gaps between blocks. Presence must be involved in the setting of those stones.

Entry 35

Aha, success today. I found the origin of the ship, the

USS Cyclops. It was referenced in a history book. Sometime after 4 March 1918 it sailed into the area men know as the Bermuda Triangle and vanished without trace. 306 passengers and crew vanished with it. Those poor men must have thought they had steered into hell when they smashed through that dark cavern into a nest of wendigo. Interestingly, the sister ships of the Cyclops, the Proteus and the Nereus vanished in the North Atlantic during the Second World War.

There are plenty of newspaper headlines about the USS Cyclops.

"More Ships Hunt For Missing Cyclops", *New York Times*, 16 April 1918

"Fate Of Ship Baffles", *Washington Post*, 16 April 1918.

The same book tells of another disappearance. In 1915, during the First World War, 250 soldiers and 19 officers vanished from a battlefield in a place called Dardanelles. They were seen to enter a stand of trees when a strange cloud descended upon them. Shortly after the cloud lifted into the sky and the men were never seen again. I wonder which of the Riven caused that horror.

Entry 42

The rolling rocks of Death Valley are the subject of some mystery. Despite scientific analysis men have yet to discover how such enormous stones seem to move independently across the flat plain called 'Racetrack Playa'. Apparently two geologists called Jim McAllister and Allen Agnew were mapping the rock in the area in 1948 when they came across the tracks. The best theory I found relates to the forming of ice under the rocks which are then driven forward by strong winds! Vallalar would be amused to know that his training ground has caused such fascination!

Entry 46

The stories of werewolves are well known. Garoul, as we know them, have appeared again and again in human history. Interestingly, the folklore seems to point towards werewolves as men who can either change their shape at will, or to whom it happens involuntarily during the full moon. It's right that the garoul have always been more active during that phase of the moon but they cannot change back into men. Of course, there is a theory in Mu that they were men once but have, over generations, morphed into something beastlike.

Less well known are animals such as the Sitecah, Nandi and Ropen although I did find some references. It seems that a group of Sitecah giants were wiped out by Native Americans. Mummified skeletons were found in a cave in 1911. There is a theory that their name refers to their diet. Of course, it is a Murian word. As for Nandi, again there seems to be some blurring over the name. They are here called Nandi Bears and are thought to take their name from the Nandi people of Western Kenya. Information is even more scant about the Ropen which are said to be mythical flying beasts which perhaps live in Papua New Guinea.

Funnily enough, as I was searching for these 'mythical' creatures I found a reference to our friend Hödekin. It seems he has quite the following in Germany!

Entry 48

I decided to look at some children's books today and

what a surprise. There are endless examples here contained within what men amusingly call fairy stories. I found a dozen books about mermaids and, looking further, it seems that legends of such beings date back almost as long as man has known of the sea. Men seem to think there are two sorts of 'mermaid'. The beautiful benevolent woman and the dangerous menacing siren who lures men to their deaths. This is an interesting development. So far as I am aware the Nommo have always been peaceable. J?ran's wife was certainly both pretty and kind. Perhaps in my own future they will be the subject of some change which will lead them to hunt men. I discovered in one book that a tribe in an African country called Mali have spent more time with the Nommo than any other. It is claimed that, before a man called Galileo theorised that the planets revolve around the sun and that Saturn had rings, the Dogon tribe had gathered this information from the Nommo who apparently arrived in some kind of aircraft which created fire and thunder.

Entry 55

Vallalar, the old rogue. I have discovered a story about him. He is described as a saint who on 30th January 1874, after lecturing on the 'nature of the powers that lie beyond us and move us' disappeared forever from a locked room. I bet that impressed the audience! He must have had the entrance to a line within his chambers. Clever!

Entry 57

I think I have found the location of a line. There is so much to learn about this world that I feel it impossible to find a path through all the information, but I think I have found a line. I thought it existed in Mu, but it is here. The Island of the Pelicans (Isla de los Alcatraces in Spanish) off the coast of modern day San Francisco was long feared and believed to be cursed by the native Indians who lived in the area before white men arrived. They said that the island was the haunt of evil spirits and contained a portal to another dimension. The island is now known as Alcatraz and is the site of a notorious prison. I think this is a place that Weewalk and I visited in the past. It seems that the cell 14D might hold the line. A prisoner was apparently murdered within the locked cell by a figure with glowing red eyes. Jak perhaps? I will do more research on him.

Entry 64

Hmmm, Jak has been making a nuisance of himself it seems. He was spotted in Victorian England and had already fashioned himself the nickname of 'Spring-heeled Jack'. He was seen frequently in 1837 and occasionally in subsequent years all over England. But the trail goes cold in about 1904. Much is made of the great leaps he could make, his clawed hands and glowing red eyes. It was often said that he looked like the devil. I wonder how far back in time Jak has visited. Is he the devil himself? Here a quote

'This here is Satan, we might say the devil, but that ain't right, and gennelfolks don't like such words. He is now commonly called 'Spring-heeled Jack'

What to make of that? Either way there is a great amount of material written about him, much of it in well respected newspapers. *The Times* was one paper which reported one of his early attacks on a woman named Jane Alsop. The headline on 2 March 1838 was "The Late

Outrage At Old Ford". This may be as close as men have come to one of the Riven.

Entry 67

There was a story in the news today about a number of strange sinkholes appearing across the planet. They are almost perfectly spherical and the ground opens up without warning. This sounds like someone is carelessly opening lines underground. The newspaper said that a large one had appeared in China. I wonder whether it was near the entrance to Shambala. It seems that men in ancient Tibet came across a line and were able to enter it. Their ancient texts describe a 'hidden kingdom' which led to the legend of a lost valley called Shangri-La. It seems they even travelled as far as somewhere they called the Palace of Kalapa and very ancient illustrations show that they saw aircraft. The ancient Tibetans predicted that in time the inhabitants of Shambala would gain great powers such as telepathy and the ability to travel great distances at great speed. Is this presence or did they simply move forward in time to find miraculous technological innovations which men today find ordinary. One important thing to note is the date I found. The Tibetan texts predict the world will end in the year 2425.

Entry 72

The Great Fire of London. September 1666. I know with certainty how that came about. Indeed, I feel I must accept some responsibility for leading Ferus to that bakery on Pudding Lane. There is a great deal written about the event (including by a man called Samuel Pepys, I wonder whether this wasn't my Sam peeping?) but interestingly, not often reported, is that the men of the time believed the fire to be a great conspiracy by some foreign power. There were rumours and reports of suspicious men throwing 'fireballs' into homes.

Entry 75

I have found some evidence that Tarak means 'protector' and 'rune' means secret thus his full title would seem to be 'Protector of the Enduring Secret'. How apt. I wonder what the secret can be.

Entry 77

It seems that more people than I would have expected are sensitive to the location of lines. There are widespread stories of ghosts and people have monitored changes in temperature, the appearance of orbs, static electricity and magnetism, all phenomena caused by the friction generated where our two worlds rub together. Some have even heard the hum that lines create. It's been heard in Bristol in the 1970s and particularly in Taos, New Mexico.

Entry 81

I sometimes feel overwhelmed by the fiction literature out there. It's so full of references to the Riven that is has become clichéd. I cannot seem to find a fictional reference to a magician that does not wear a black cloak. This must surely be because of things that have actually happened in the past and it has become a stereotype. I wonder what Ferus would say if he knew he was the father of all these stories, that every fictional dark magician is a product of his actions!

Entry 84

At the Tavern Kya told us that a woman called
Eusapia had helped her to find us. I have found mention
of an Italian woman who displayed what men call
'telekinetic' powers. Her name was Eusapia Palladino.
She lived from 1854 to 1918. She said that a great store
of ancient and lost knowledge is held in India or Tibet,
passed down from people in a world called Atlantis or
Lemuria. I wonder what this can be?

I also found mention of another woman called Ninel
Kulagina, apparently a housewife who, during the Cold
War, was the subject of some study by Soviet scientists. It
is said that she could separate an egg yolk from the white
using her mind. Did Vallalar not teach Sam the same
thing?

Entry 88

Weewalk knew all about the Montauk project and
explained it to you, Sam, so I will not repeat it all here.
Even now the name of that place fills me with gloom.
There is plenty of material available. I'm afraid that you
must do your own research into the events there. But one
thing I will mention is the chair for I think that might be
important in some way. It is said that a chair was found or
created in which one could sit and receive new mental
abilities and prescience powers. A prototype duplicate
was apparently put in a facility on the River Thames. I
have heard that the Riven King sits upon a most unusual
throne. I wonder....

I will say something about the 'Montauk Monster' as
it was known. The body of this beast was washed ashore

in July 2008. From the photographs I cannot identify it but it must be from Mu. It was called the 'Hound of Bonacville' before the 'Montauk Monster' name became more widely adopted.

Entry 90

I read of a sad event today. I had wondered whether those green children had ever been found. Kya told us that she had arrived in Suun-t-Marten village just after their disappearance. It seems that they did arrive in the village of Woolpit in Suffolk, sometime in the 12th Century. The men there could not understand their language but eventually the children began to adjust to their new life and learn the same dialect. It seems it was not long before the young boy died. How sad. The girl was given the name Agnes and lived out her years there but was always a foreigner and was never really accepted by the villagers. Their images still appear on the village sign today. Their strange appearance also gave rise to a famous story of the Babes in the Wood. Some men have since put forward the theory that they came from another subterranean or extraterrestrial world. The children were able to explain that they came from somewhere that is recorded as St Martin's Land

Entry 93

Men seem to be aware only vaguely of Yonaguni and the pyramid that now lies beneath the waters of Japan. It was 'discovered' in 1987 but men have not been able to ascertain whether it is natural or manmade. For me it is simply another line I know of but will never get to use. The door to Atlantis.

Entry 94

Aha, I recognise this quote 'The forthcoming end of the world will be hastened by the construction of underground railways burrowing into infernal regions and thereby disturbing the Devil'. Reverend Dr. John Cumming in 1860. How right he was!

Entry 96

Certain people in North America and Canada seem to be aware of the Wendigo. There seems to be some dispute about whether they are humans affected by an all-consuming mental deficiency which drives them to cannibalism.

Entry 99

I am reminded of the cleverness of the men and creatures of Mu in going undetected. As soon as men on this world find something that cannot be explained they begin to attempt to uncover its truth. Those who use the lines seem then to whisper a 'plausible' explanation in the right ear. Thus it was today that I read of something that I had done as a young man and which had been unexplained for many years has since been 'solved' so that men believe the supernatural mystery is cracked. I wonder who covered up that particular event. And why?

Entry 103

It seems that there is a group of people, the Aymara of South America, who have a reversed concept of time so that the past is ahead and the future behind. Perhaps such an idea has come about through being able to influence and travel to the past. But the more I think about it, the more I realise we might be similarly confused. If one says 'The event on Wednesday has been moved forward by two days' does it now mean that the event will take place on Monday or Friday? Apparently, English speakers will be divided 50 /50.

Entry 107

There was, it appears, a mysterious explosion in a part of Russia called Tunguska on June 30, 1908. It was apparently a very large blast, toppling some 80 million trees over 2000 square kilometres. The most widely held theory is that some kind of meteorite or comet blew apart as it hit the earth's atmosphere. I faintly remember something about a place called Tongue's Scar. Could it be the same? My memory is so poor these days. If the Riven have developed a weapon that could generate that sort of power then we are all doomed. I wonder, could the Riven King be powerful enough to pull the very rocks out of the sky?

Entry 113

I am starting to think, but no, even now I hesitate to write this for it is almost inconceivable. No, I must write it down. Who knows who will eventually read this book and what part it might play? What if the lines that connect our two worlds throughout time actually connect one world in time? I wish I had someone to discuss this with. Only someone able to travel freely along lines would be able to rule this out and I expect it would take many years of searching to find the evidence, if it even exists. I often wonder what Tarak's last secret was, that Kya was so certain we needed to hear from him. Did my friends even ever manage to rescue Tarak? What does the future hold? I will never know.

Entry 124

I am finding that I'm increasingly forgetting things. My brain does not seem to function as well as it once did. It may be time to tell Sam, but I've delayed for so long. I don't want to scare him and I find myself confused. Did he know all this when I met him. I can't remember. Trying to keep the train of thought is maddening.

Entry 127

I began to tell him the other day. He looked at me with so much fear and pity that I could not continue. He knows my mind is failing. Have I left it all too late? How then do I convince him that what I have to say about Mu is true? It is true. I wrote it here as a younger man...

Entry 129

Today I felt such a pain in my chest that I could do nothing but sit for an hour. Whilst there I thought of something important that I must write in this book, but now I am here with my pen I realise I have forgotten it. I must make Sam see. I shall leave him this book so that he will have it when I pass on. I think that's right. He had it when I met him as Hadan didn't he?

ABOUT THE AUTHOR

Ben Yallop grew up in the 'haunted' house in the English county of Kent where the opening chapters of The Circle Line are set. After studying at the University of Leeds and then various stints of international backpacking he settled down into the occasionally bizarre but wonderful world of the UK Civil Service. Initially donning wig and gown as a clerk of the Crown Court he now works as something of an adviser to the senior judiciary in London.

He lives with his wife and two daughters in Farnham, Surrey and can often be found tapping away about giants and monsters on the commute to Waterloo. Ben has been writing for many years although this is his first chance to employ properly his degree in philosophy. And they said it would be useless!

Tamám Shud

Printed in Great Britain
by Amazon.co.uk, Ltd.,
Marston Gate.